WIND RIVER
OUTLAW

WIND RIVER
OUTLAW

WILL ERMINE

M. EVANS
Lanham • Boulder • New York • Toronto • Plymouth, UK

Published by M. Evans
An imprint of Rowman & Littlefield
4501 Forbes Boulevard, Suite 200, Lanham, Maryland 20706
www.rowman.com

10 Thornbury Road, Plymouth PL6 7PP, United Kingdom

Distributed by National Book Network

British Library Cataloguing in Publication Information Available

Library of Congress Cataloging-in-Publication Data

Library of Congress Control Number: 2014936919

ISBN: 978-1-59077-416-8 (pbk. : alk. paper)
ISBN: 978-1-59077-417-5 (electronic)

∞™ The paper used in this publication meets the minimum requirements of
American National Standard for Information Sciences—Permanence of
Paper for Printed Library Materials, ANSI/NISO Z39.48-1992.

Printed in the United States of America

CONTENTS

CONTENTS

Chapter I

SMILING REB SANTEE

THE early sun, flushing the tawny range world of southern Utah, found the M Bar summer beef-cut already well on its way toward Moab. It was a small bunch, the best Dan ˙Morgan had been able to do this season, but because of the broken country through which it must pass he had sent three men along.

They made a happy-go-lucky trio, hardened and rugged. The prospect of a night in town loosened their tongues and left them careless and competent in the saddle, hazing the bunch through the brush and pushing it along with shrill yips and snatches of song. Chaff flew back and forth.

"The boss is shore takin' a chance, puttin' yuh in charge here, Reb," Pony Clark called out derisively from his position at the drag. "Why he don't give these cow critters away an' be done with it, I dunno."

Reb Santee flashed a grin over a brawny shoulder at him. "Yo're jealous, Pony," he drawled provokingly.

"Why, no," Steve Cabanus put in from across the brindled, bobbing backs of the steers; "Pony ain't jealous, Reb. He's jest got a careful habit of mind. Which," he went on meaningfully, "may account fer him not bein' in the lead in that rustler chase last week, puttin' up a stiff runnin' fight an' gettin' shot at an' all—an' may or may not be the reason Dan didn't put him in charge today."

The jibe at a last-week's exploit of his own left Reb

unmoved. "You boys are green with envy," he declared. His smooth voice, honeyed with guile, held a joyous challenge. He took nothing seriously.

The man to whom Dan Morgan had entrusted the responsibility of delivery and collection in the tough little Mormon town of Moab was a stranger to the habitual hard caution which makes a good ranch foreman—a fact his companions well knew.

He was one of that big-boned, untidy breed in worn overalls and sweat-stained sombrero, unadorned by the usual gaudy trappings of his calling, common in that day and that place. But there was nothing common about him. Chunky and straight astride his wiry buckskin, he was in his early twenties, with an open countenance, a shock of unruly flaxen hair and an ingenious smile in his puckered, blazing blue eyes that few men could resist.

"Wal," Pony pursued, mopping his wind-burned face as the sun began to warm up, *"I* wouldn't want to be in our friend Reb's boots, if we was to run into Doc Lantry in town—after dustin' him with a six-gun a week back."

"But on the other hand, we ain't dead shore it was Lantry who was mixed up in that rustlin' business," Cabanus countered, more for the sake of argument than anything. "Dan's got an idee the rustlers are hittin' at him from the Roost."

This country around Moab was not far from the notorious Robbers' Roost, hidden where the red bluffs drop away to the vastness of the Colorado basin. Right or wrong, Dan Morgan's often-voiced suspicions of the frequenters of that outlaw retreat at least had some color of credibility.

"Yeh—an' Reb says he's got other idees," Pony agreed shrewdly. "He ain't tradin' lead with a man at close range without some notion who his man is." He turned his attention to Santee. "How 'bout it, Reb. Was it Lantry or not?"

The freckled rider smilingly held his peace while his companions put words in his mouth. Lightly as they spoke, they did not come so far from the truth. Personally Reb was convinced that Doc Lantry, a well-known figure in that country, was responsible for the recent raids on M Bar stock. But it was not easy to pin these things on a man without getting him dead to rights, and this had not been accomplished so far. Reb was in consequence not saying all that he thought.

"Yuh notice whoever it was, the rustlin's stopped almighty short since we sweated 'em out into the open," he contented himself with saying now in quiet pride.

"Sho'! Bowlaigs, I do believe the man's braggin'," Clark murmured to his horse. "Tsk, tsk!"

For his part, Steve Cabanus shot a quick glance at Reb's face. He knew the other's indifference to the possibility of running into Doc Lantry in Moab was not a pose. Reb was one of those direct souls who live for the hour as it passes. What had gone before meant nothing to him, and what the future held but little more. Coupled with this insouciance he had the courage of a cougar. He had long since proved that he could ride the meanest horse that ever traded ends in the air; that he would fight for the fun of fighting; that nothing overawed him and he was ice in a pinch. He had already put a lot of living behind him for one so young.

Dan Morgan, owner of the M Bar outfit, was also aware of the potentialities of his man. The present trust, despite Santee's well-known recklessness, was in the nature of an experiment—and by way of reward for his recent activities.

All this passed the rough-and-tumble cowboy by, however. Honest to the bone, he trusted himself implicitly. Let other men look out for themselves and he would do the same.

Pony Clark broke off a lugubrious croon to return to his ribbing.

"But then, Lantry, he ain't the only man Reb's got to watch out fer in town, either," he let drop with studied casualness.

Reb flicked him a cheerful look of inquiry, but it was Steve whose curiosity finally got the best of him. "What yuh drivin' at now?" he grunted.

"Why, his friends are the ones who'll lead him astray," Pony supplied knowingly, "comin' up on the soft side of him with a chunk of money in his jeans. Not us, o' course," he added hastily, flashing a grin; "we sympathize with Dan's troubles, knowin' Reb's pore, weak nature an' all. But some other careless fellers—"

"*Unh-uh,*" Reb denied, with a vigorous shake of the head. "Not me, brother. I ain't even goin' into a saloon —maybe."

Pony and Steve laughed at him for the prudent reservation. He took the grin off their faces with his next speech.

"I was thinkin' some of hittin' back for the spread the minute I dispose of this stuff," he said with an air of rectitude. "Dan'll be worryin' till we git home."

"Like hell yuh will!" Steve burst out, staring at him, his jaw dropped. "I know yuh!" But he was uncertain.

It was Reb's turn to laugh and he took full advantage of it, rolling out an infectious bellow that more than anything else told his friends he did not mean what he had said.

The M Bar steers clattered into Moab's single street in late afternoon. Across the open valley of the Grand, the Orange Cliffs stood out to the southwest, a long, serrated bluff purpled with shadows where the land fell away to the Colorado gorge.

Moab was a weatherbeaten collection of unpainted pine structures, its denizens as craggy as the setting. Santee knew all but the wild horse hunters who drifted in from the nameless wilderness to the west. He was not long in locating Luke Dent, the grizzled beef-buyer with whom Morgan was wont to deal.

"Wal, Reb!" Dent exclaimed gruffly, pretending surprise at finding him in charge. "Gittin' up in the world, ain't yuh? Dan laid up or somethin'?"

"He was able to git around when we left," Reb grinned, giving Luke the benefit of a glance that bored straight into him.

The cattle buyer, an old friend of Santee's employer, covered his curiosity smoothly. He said no more then, turning to business. The M Bar steers were run in his corrals. The money, amounting to something above four hundred dollars, was handed over on the spot.

"I'd keep an elbow over the pocket yuh carry that in, Reb," said Dent, before he turned away. "Dan ain't rightly fixed to lose that amount jest at present."

"He won't," Reb assured him. He saw no offense in the remark.

Dent nodded and went on about his affairs, with no intention of saying more. But it had been enough. Glancing after him, Santee knew what he was driving at. It was Luke's way of telling him to take it easy. Morgan himself had revealed his awareness of the chance he took, for almost his last words to Reb that morning had been a warning to stay clear of the usual temptations of a cow-town for a man with money in his pants. Reb had agreed cheerfully, finding no occasion to take exception to even so bluntly expressed a doubt of his staunchness. Dan was the boss; and maybe Luke Dent was right, too. Reb *had* slipped a time or two in the past. He didn't intend to this time.

"Git a move on, Reb," Steve called from where he sat his saddle, waiting. The work with the steers, insofar as it touched them, was done and the puncher's tone was impatient. His eyes yearned toward the inviting bar up the street. Pony Clark had already started for it.

"You go ahead," Reb told him, "an' git yore drink. I'll hunt yuh up later." He fumbled the straps of his cinch, held back by a strange reluctance.

Steve didn't make it easy for him. "There's a lot of sense in that, ain't there!" he exclaimed sarcastically. "Whut do yuh figger to do in this town besides drinkin'? . . . Come on, don't keep me waitin'!"

Reb had no idea offhand how to deal with the situation. The easiest way seemed to pretend acquiescence and keep a watch of himself, but still he hesitated, hoping Steve would go on ahead and give him time to roll a smoke and think it over. Steve did not. To make matters worse a small band of punchers rode down the street and drew in near at hand with a scattering of dust and gravel. There were four of them, all from the V Cross T, with Gif Inch in the lead.

"Ole Reb hisself! . . . This is gonna be swell!" Inch burst out, good cheer shining in his face. "Don't say yuh wasn't lookin' fer us to show up, yuh doggone hoss-thief!"

Santee turned a nonplussed look on him, his instinctive grin concealing his thoughts. He had had many a hilarious frolic in Moab with the V Cross T bunch in the past. They looked on him as a sort of leader in deviltry. It had pleased him before, but now it left him troubled. He covered his uncertainty, chaffing with them lightly.

Inch swung down from the saddle. "Whew! Mighty hot, ridin' in from our layout. Mebbe we could all do with a drink," he suggested.

Reb debated briefly. The promise of a few hours with Inch and the boys was enticing. After all, he had a month's pay on him. He had a perfect right to spend that as he chose, he told himself.

"I'll jest go yuh on that," he said, with little apparent hesitancy. "The first round is on me."

They trouped into the Only Chance and lined up at the bar. While the bottle clinked they were quiet with expectancy, but after the first drink was downed, joviality made them all brothers. Under cover of the movement this occasioned, Pony Clark edged into the group and nudged Reb with his elbow.

Something in Reb had loosened up. He was his old self again, careless and ready for fun. It was moments before Pony got his attention. At last he turned and gave heed. Without words, Pony jerked his chin around over his shoulder in a guarded manner.

Reb got his drift. It was his way to turn around and seek boldly the thing to which Pony directed his notice. At a poker table in a corner of the room he saw an engrossed foursome over their game. Reb passed them by, a furrow between his eyes. Then, sitting alone at a table a little removed, leaning back in his chair with his chin dropped on his chest, Reb spotted Doc Lantry.

Lantry was skinny, gangling and on the wrong side of forty. To Santee, with his strong, sharp-carved swarthy face and burning eyes he seemed already old. He was a quiet, almost morose man who ran a small outfit up in the breaks ten miles to the north—when he was there to run it. Mostly he hung around town and had the name of being a rash gambler when he was in funds, which was comparatively often.

At the moment Reb's glance alighted on him, Lantry's level, inscrutable gaze was fixed on the puncher. He never moved; never so much as opened his thin, iron lips. For a little interval the two locked eyes without a sign and then Reb turned back to his companions carelessly.

He had no fear of Lantry or of what he would do, but as time passed and the bunch at the bar grew noisier he found the man sticking in his thoughts. Even when someone suggested a round of poker and Reb sat in as a matter of course, he felt Doc's dark eyes on his face.

The game ran on until dusk. One by one the V Cross T boys dropped out and drifted away to eat. Still Reb stuck. He had lost nearly all his month's pay and was bent on getting some of it back before he got up. Soon he was the only puncher left at the table. He was playing his cards close to his vest now. Pony Clark paused at his side. He noted the smallness of Reb's stack of chips.

"Cash 'em in, Reb, an' we'll go get us a bait," he offered.

"Wait'll I finish this hand," Santee responded; "I got good cards here."

It was as if the others at the table had not heard. But a moment later Reb lost, and he hung on for one more chance to recoup. His luck was no better. When Pony left half-an-hour later, he was still playing. But now he was gambling on borrowed money, and as the cards stubbornly refused to better he found more and more reason to stay in.

Doc Lantry had not moved from his solitary seat several tables away. Although a hanging lamp had been lit, his face was in shadow. His eyes glinted. He watched the game in brooding silence. Reb no longer lifted an occasional glance in his direction. He had something more important to think about.

Late in the evening Steve Cabanus made another attempt to draw Reb away from the game. His tone was sharp, for he suspected what was afoot. "When the hell are yuh hittin' back fer the spread?" he growled. "Next week?"

Santee grinned uncertainly and concentrated on the play. His eyes sharpened to pin-points as he studied the pips on the cards. It was as if the devil himself dealt the hands of his opponents. They continued to get into him with a steadiness that was rapidly becoming serious.

It was a streak of luck destined not to break. At ten o'clock Reb stumbled up from the table penniless, having lost not only his own pay but every cent of the beef money as well. Dazed by this blow, he turned toward the bar to seek solace with an obliging friend, when a heavy footfall at the door brought him around. Some instinct keener than thought told him what to expect. He was not disappointed.

Dan Morgan, a tall, broad-shouldered, heavy-faced man in his fifties, having ridden to town with a belated sense of caution, stepped into the Only Chance and came forward with his sharp, raking gaze fixed on Reb Santee's face. Reb stared back at him, blinking. His smile was gone now.

Chapter II

AN EXCHANGE OF FAVORS

W ELL, Reb." There was a gruffness in Dan Morgan's tone that only partially masked his uneasiness. "Pony told me I'd find you sittin' in at a poker game. I'll admit I'm some relieved to find you ain't. I had you figured to stop short of that."

He was reassuring himself, but when he paused Reb only continued to meet his gaze blankly, finding nothing to say. Morgan misread his expression. He went on more easily: "I'll ask you to step outside with me. I want to talk with you for a minute." He did not intend to waste any more time claiming the money for the steers. Reb knew what he was getting at. He found his tongue at last, shaking his head as he spoke. "There ain't a bit of use in goin' outside, Dan." Genuine regret showed in his whole manner. It told only too plainly how matters stood.

Morgan's eyes blazed up. "What do you mean?" he barked, his voice rising angrily. "Are you tellin' me you have lost my money? Good gravy, man—!"

Reb tried to grin, but it was a sickly effort. He was feeling acutely uncomfortable. "I reckon that's about what happened, Dan," he confessed reluctantly.

If the remaining men at the card table were listening, they gave no outward sign. But they held themselves silent and alert. Steve Cabanus leaned with his elbows on the bar, attentive; behind it, the bartender listened, with open mouth. Men in chairs along the wall or at the rail smiled to themselves at the fix Reb was in. Even Doc Lantry, slouched over in the shadows, lent ear as Morgan cussed out his puncher in a gust of burning resentment.

"Yo're no damned good fer anything!" Dan wound up bitterly. "You can't be trusted out of a man's sight, you saddle bum! All you want to do is hell around and shoot and fight booze and let the work go to blazes!"

Reb honestly thought that was the way any sensible man looked at it in his secret heart, but there was no fun left in his eyes now. He did not need to be told that he had lost his job. Morgan told him all the same, and a good deal more with it. It began to get under Reb's skin. "If you'll hold on while I—" he began.

"Hold on, hell!" Morgan exploded. "Nothin' you can tell me will mend matters!"

Hank Albee, the Mormon deputy sheriff, had been listening at the door for some minutes. He strode forward now, having got the drift of things. There was a ruthless expectancy in his beady, close-set eyes.

"Reckon yuh got use fer me, Morgan," he said unctuously. He was no friend of Reb's, never having made an acquaintance he considered unlikely to advance him politically. "Jest say the word, an' I'll take this feller in custody."

Dan Morgan waved a scornful hand at him, his ire gushing over anyone who chanced to come under his notice. "A fine lot of good that would do, wouldn't it?" he snapped with disdain. "No, I don't aim to have Santee arrested, Albee. That won't help me any. Firin' him is about all I can see my way to do right now." There was a sturdy practicality in the rancher, despite his smoldering glare, and it was to this that Reb was indebted for the lenience of his present course.

He was not insensible to it. "That's white of yuh, Dan," he put in; "an' I won't forget it. I'll see that yuh get yore money back."

Morgan had no faith in the promise. "Mebbe you can tell me how a forty-dollar-a-month puncher can turn that trick!" he retorted contemptuously.

"Well, I—" Reb was crestfallen, for this was something he had not thought of; but he did not avert his direct gaze. "I can try," he finished lamely.

Morgan snorted his abysmal skepticism. Turning on his heel, his big frame stiff with antagonism, he left the saloon. Reb looked after him helplessly for a moment. Then shrugging, he moved to the bar. "It's yore treat, Steve," he declared. Cabanus accommodated.

"Man, yuh took a tongue-lashin' if I ever heard one," he averred, as Reb bent over his glass. "Once, there, I thought yuh was goin' to bust Dan one on the nose."

Santee shook his head briefly. "Why should I?" he rejoined. "I had it comin' to me, no two ways about it."

If he was passing through one of the worst hours in his carefree life, he refused to admit it by word or sign. Nor would he accept the consolations of Steve or the V Cross T boys who had drifted in, on hearing the news, to commiserate with him. Dan Morgan's abuse, and even his discharge, he stolidly maintained to be justified.

"What'll yuh do now, Reb?" Gif Inch demanded.

"I dunno." Reb wasn't worrying about it. "Plenty time enough to take care of that when I git to it," he said. His blue eyes were already beginning to lose their smoky look, the indomitable snap once more brightening them. He did not bother to glance toward Doc

Lantry, who had taken in the whole proceeding, and who still watched him with eyes as inscrutable as ever.

There was more talk, to which Reb listened with half-an-ear while he downed a drink bought by one of the others. He was facing the bar, and as he threw his head back his eyes dwelt on the big mirror. Something he saw there narrowed his gaze and snapped him to attention.

Clearly reflected in the glass was a corner of the gambling table. Under it, even as he looked, the knee of one of the players sagged to one side with a card lying on it, out of sight of the players across the table. From the lap of the next man a stealthy hand reached out to take the card. A similar maneuver was enacted from the other side as the trade was completed.

It told Reb plenty. He knew in a flash why he had lost so steadily. At the knowledge, hot blood surged through him with a rush. As always, he acted before he thought. A long stride took him to the card table; a darting grip nailed the clandestine hand to the knee under it, imprisoning the passed card.

"Gents," he said softly, grinning into their startled faces, "I crave discussion of some things you've jest made clear to me."

"Get the hell away from here!" snarled one of them, jerking at his hand so violently that the table rocked. The other tried to struggle up, and Santee's fingers fastened on his shoulder.

"Don't git previous," the puncher warned them both with a wolfish pleasure. "All I want is an understandin'. You boys just hand me back my money, an' we'll consider the matter closed." His tone said that he hoped they would take exception to his proposal.

For the moment an ugly tension held the room. A good share of the loungers here were friends of the challenged men. One of them stepped out with a belligerent mien. "Stand away, cow-poke!" he ripped out, authority ringing in his insolent words. On the instant he went for his gun. Others made a similar move.

Someone else was ahead of them. Before even the surprised punchers at the bar could make a move, Doc Lantry sprang to his feet, and his gun barrels were shining circles of menace, covering the group.

"Don't anyone be foolish," he purred, his eyes glinting a flinty defiance under the worn brim of the Stetson. "It's plain enough Reb was trimmed, an' he wants his money back."

A greater expectancy than before held the room. What could be the meaning of this? Not a man in Moab needed to be told that Santee and Doc Lantry had nothing in common. Yet here was Doc apparently springing to the other's aid. What was his hidden object? One and all, they waited for Reb's reaction.

That Santee was surprised by the unexpectedness of Lantry's intervention was evident only in his momentary stare. He recovered speedily, turning a pugnacious regard on the two gamblers. It had been these two who had relieved him of his money. "Come on," he rasped without preamble; "shell out!"

If they were inclined to argue the matter, they repressed the impulse. First one and then the other, they counted out Reb's money and handed it over. Santee coolly made sure of the total, and thrust it in his pocket. His chest was out again now, the old mocking smile on his lips.

"Too bad yuh couldn't see yore way to argue the

point," he told the gamblers, fight in every line of his whip-hard body. And to Lantry he nodded briefly, "Much obliged."

Every eye in the room watched the play of glances here. Lantry appeared to ask nothing in return; yet not a man but felt that Reb would one day pay his price, and a high one. Reb himself appeared indifferent to it all, turning to leave the bar.

But a few minutes later, walking up the dusky street in search of Dan Morgan, a question turned and screwed in his mind that would not let him alone. Why had Doc Lantry horned in the affair on his behalf? His knowledge of Lantry's undercover occupations gave him his answer. Doc had an idea he could use a good man. There could be no better explanation.

Reb nodded, his indomitable smile unseen in the dark. "Once in a great while, there is use fer his kind of a gent in the world," he mused speciously.

He found Dan Morgan in Basher's store. The rancher turned on him in choleric disgust, his face darkening; but he trusted himself to no words, breathing noisily.

"I told yuh I'd pay yuh back, Dan," Reb said easily. He could not resist the impulse of ostentation that impelled him to pull out his money and pay Morgan in the presence of Basher and one or two others.

Morgan looked at the money suspiciously as Reb counted it out. He listened, still without speech, as Reb told how it had been recovered. When it was reposing safely in his own pocket at last, he cleared his throat harshly. "I s'pose you understand yo're still out of a job, money or no money," he said severely, with no sign of relenting.

Reb grinned a ready response. "I didn't expect yuh to look at it any different, Dan," he replied. "But I told yuh you'd git yore steer money back, an' you've got it . . . I can git another job."

Morgan grunted. He was pacified to an extent, but his judgment was no less inflexible than before. "Mebbe you can," he said grudgingly as he turned away.

With the better part of his month's pay once more in his pocket, Reb was indifferent to the rancher's implied prediction that he would have trouble finding work. The next day found him still in Moab, and the next. He spent his time at the Only Chance saloon until his money ran low. In a poker game he won enough to eke out his period of idleness a little longer, and it was ten days before he was faced with the necessity of hunting a job.

During that time he got acquainted with Doc Lantry in a casual way. Lantry was a cool hand who appeared to take nothing more seriously than Reb himself. In this, at least, Santee saw a quality that he could admire. Then he began to ride out to the ranches, and he saw no more of Doc for a while.

For some reason a job did not come his way. Friendly as everyone was, he found a barrier raised against him. For a week he rode the grubline, hoping the next ranch he called at would hire him on. The time stretched over another week, and another, and Reb began to entertain moody thoughts behind his smiling exterior. Everyone was glad to see him come, sorry to have him leave; but nobody did anything about it. Finally, urged on by a curiosity to see how far this thing would go, he tackled old Ike Borden.

Borden was a slave-driver; the grub in his bunkhouse was poor and far from plentiful; the two or three men in his outfit were usually the scrapings of the range. A job with him was in the nature of a last resort. But even he found no opening for Reb Santee.

"Why not?" Reb demanded, stung to bluntness, although the cheerful crinkles still persisted in the corners of his eyes.

Ike Borden was as dry and outspoken as he was parsimonious. "If yuh wanto know," he growled, "I can tell yuh. Santee, men're sayin' yuh can't be trusted."

Reb was astonished, but his pride was touched too. He gave up after that, riding back to Moab. Discouragement was not in him, however. Some of his friends among the M Bar or V Cross T hands could be depended on to lend him a few dollars to tide him over until he made up his mind what he would do next.

But it was Doc Lantry who met him in Moab—Doc who greeted him as though nothing had happened, and lent him money. Reb told the man his troubles in a joking way.

"What are yuh figurin' to do now?" Lantry asked casually.

"I'll pull out for another range, I reckon," Reb replied carelessly.

The days slipped by, however, and Santee remained. He spent more and more time with Doc, borrowing an ever-increasing sum from the other. He knew he didn't have the man wrong in the rustling scrape he had helped to break up, but despite this uncomfortable knowledge he had come to like Doc.

It was easy to put off the necessity for a decision

in regard to his new friend even when the rustling stories started up again. Sam Heffron, out at Cottonwood Wash, lost a dozen head of prime horses, and Hank Albee, the deputy sheriff, went through the motions of doing something about it. There was little enough anyone could do. This country of pine forests and sage flats and rocky barriers was vast, its rugged acres thinly settled. The intricacies of its trails made it no hard task for rustlers to strike and fade into nothingness with bewildering speed.

Other stories of stock losses drifted to town. As the total piled up, the murmurs grew louder—became an angry protest. Doc Lantry evinced a mild interest in these things, but nothing more. He and Reb went on their casual way.

"Look here, Reb," said Steve Cabanus one day when he rode in for supplies, "I know yo're in a spot an' all, without no job—but yo're travellin' in the wrong comp'ny, if yuh hope to pull out of it right soon."

Reb waved a hand, his glance vague for once. "Lantry, you mean? I ain't ridin' with him, Steve."

"Yo're drinkin' with him," said Cabanus bluntly. "Ridin' comes next." But nothing he could say would move Reb.

"I'll take care of myself," was all he would say.

It began to look as if that was more than Doc Lantry could do—without assistance—for the next morning Reb received a tip from Pony Clark to the effect that the ranchmen around Moab were tired of lawlessness and were going to take matters into their own hands. Dan Morgan was one of them. It was their intention to raid Lantry's place that night and string Doc up.

"String him up!" Reb exclaimed, jarred. "Kind of sudden, ain't it?" There was no more proof of Lantry's guilt than there had been before.

Pony flashed a smile. "You know whether it is or not," he countered. "Are yuh ridin' with us?"

"I'd be liable to ride with these cowmen around here, after the way they've been breakin' their necks for me, wouldn't I?"

Clark was sorry he had said anything. "Whatever yuh do, keep it to yoreself," he warned.

Reb grunted noncommittally. But as soon as Pony was out of sight, he swung into the saddle himself, rode out of town toward the south, made a wide circle to the east and headed north at a brisk pace for Doc Lantry's place.

Doc was there to meet him. His brows were shaggy as he stood waiting in the door of his shack, for Reb had never ridden out before. "What's up?" he demanded.

"Doc, can yuh think of some place a long ways off yuh ought to git to in a hurry?" Lantry made no comment and Reb went on: "A bunch of ranchers are plannin' to visit yuh tonight. They don't aim to take yuh back to town with 'em."

Doc understood him completely. "Thanks, Reb." He hesitated, his eyes sharper than before. "I take it yuh know where I stand in this?"

"Yeah, I know. But I ain't forgot what yuh did for me—"

"Yuh never tried to reform me," Lantry went on, with something almost gentle in his voice. "Mebbe you'll lend me a hand."

He was suggesting something which Reb could not immediately see. "Name it," he said, grinning.

Doc put his cards on the table. He had about eighty head of horses back in the canyons and he made no bones about admitting that he needed help to get them out of the country in a hurry.

"Hosses yuh couldn't do much with around here, I expect?"

"Yeah," said Doc evenly.

Reb knew then that they were stolen. He thought over Lantry's proposal for a minute, and couldn't see much in it. He didn't want to get mixed up with that kind of business. Even as he was shaking his head, Doc put in mildly:

" 'Tain't as if I was askin' yuh to go any further'n yuh want, Reb. But it'll help me out a lot—an' there ain't nothin' around her fer yuh. Yuh might's well ride north as any other way."

He didn't mention Reb's money obligation to him, and Reb was conscious of this. He reconsidered.

"I got one man out with the stock now," Doc continued. "If it was anyone else, I might git along by myself. But Gloomy's kind of hard to stand. I dunno's I could do it fer three-four hundred miles."

A mention of such a distance appealed to Reb at once. Going along with Doc would solve every one of his immediate problems, he told himself, whatever else it led to.

"If we was to start right away, an' keep goin'—" he began on a new note.

Lantry took his hands off his hips, his eyes flashing. He knew that he had won. "Bring up them pack an'-mals in the corral," he said. "I'll throw a bait together an' we'll clear out of here."

Chapter III

THE OUTLAW TRAIL

GLOOMY JEPSON, a dull-witted, long-faced fellow in ragged riding apparel, met Lantry and Santee at the mouth of the canyon in which Doc's horses were hidden. He had a rifle across his saddle-bow.

"Who's this feller?" he queried, disinclined to give ground until he had satisfied himself. He wore a faded walrus mustache which added nothing to the brightness of his appearance.

"Meet Reb Santee, Gloomy," said Doc. "He's ridin' with us."

Gloomy's opaque scrutiny wandered over Reb and came to rest on the laden pack horses. "Whut you aimin' to do with them?" he grunted.

"They're going along too," Lantry grinned. "We're leavin' these parts immediate, an' ridin' a long trail." He did not explain why he found this necessary, nor did Jepson press him for a reason.

The three rode up the canyon until they came to Lantry's hidden brush corral. It was a large one. A sizeable and spirited bunch of range horses moved around in it, milling, only a portion of them broken saddle stock. Plainly they were as wild as elk.

"I'll open the gate," said Doc. "You boys keep 'em bunched as they start off."

"Which way you takin' 'em?" Gloomy demanded.

"North."

Jepson stared. "North! There ain't a thing that way fer a hundred miles, Doc!"

"Fine," said Doc; but it did not satisfy Gloomy. "Nothin' fer a hundred miles—an' then the bad ones," he croaked, shaking his head, his face longer than ever. "Trouble. That's whut'll be waitin' fer us."

Lantry wasted no time on him. "That's what'll be follerin' us, too," he flashed. "You do as yo're told, an' do it fast."

He opened the corral gate and the horses streaked out, heading up the canyon. The men had hard work keeping them in hand. A few miles up, the canyon gave upon broken land. Then it was no easy task to keep the bunch headed in the chosen direction.

Some fleeting question of whether he was doing the right thing had lingered in Reb's mind after his decision to throw in with Lantry, but now he found no time for self-argument. As for Doc, he did not refer to the subject again, employing his spare time in keeping a strict watch to the rear.

The afternoon waned. By dusk they had put a good twenty miles behind them. It was at Reb's suggestion that they pulled up in a wooded hollow for a rest and a bite to eat. Even then Lantry insisted on sending Gloomy a half-mile down the back trail to stand guard. Jepson grumbled, but he went, talking to himself.

He was back before the last light had faded out of the sky, tearing into the hollow as if the devil were after him, and stirring up the horse herd. Lantry sprang up from the fire, his lean features darkening.

"Whut in hell—" he began.

"They've cut our trail, Doc!" Gloomy blurted. It proved that he had all the while had a pretty accurate idea of what they could expect from behind. "There must be a dozen of 'em, not five miles away!" He added further details.

"Shut up an' git busy!" Doc snapped. "We're pullin' out of here pronto!"

Reb's face was sober as he hastily made ready to push on. He wished now that he hadn't got into this, but he wasn't quitting. To go through with it was the only course he could see.

They hazed the horses on into the thickening night. It hadn't taken them long to get started, and there was at least the hope that the posse of ranchers might lose their trail in the dark and be held up until morning, by which time they would be well out of the Moab country.

They struck east until they were over the Colorado line, where Lantry said the going was easier. Then north again, straight as the crow flies. Santee knew what that meant. Brown's Park! He had heard stories of the outlaw rendezvous, almost as well known as the Robbers' Roost. There could be little doubt that Doc Lantry was heading for it as fast as he could cover the ground.

They saw nothing of their pursuers during the night, although they found it prudent to rein in from time to time to breathe the horses. A forced camp was broken up in mid-morning, however, by Lantry's warning yell. Once more they threw themselves in the saddle and galloped away just in time to avert disaster. All that day there were signs of the wrath of the Moab men, dogging their rear.

Santee began to get a grim picture of the life of any man who rode outside the law. To keep better than eighty head of horses moving ahead of a determined pursuit, without loss, was no light undertaking. It was impossible to avoid leaving a broad trail. Had there been less than the three of them, the thing could not have been done. But the outcome was never really in doubt, in Reb's mind, as far as their personal safety went. They could always throw saddle on an unjaded mount and make off by themselves.

It proved not to be necessary. Late the second day, the last of the pursuers were shaken off. Unwilling to take any chances, Lantry insisted that they push on until long after dark, when they pulled up for a much needed rest. The following morning they moved on at a moderated pace, and three days later reached their immediate objective.

Brown's Park was situated in the extreme northwest corner of Colorado. It was a wild and lonely region, miles from the nearest ranch or mining claim of the Mormons, down the gloomy canyon of the Green River. To the west, lay the Uintah Indian reservation, and to the north the stark and blazing Red Desert. It was a country of deer and bear and lion, and of men scarcely less wild and lawless.

In one corner of a spacious wooded basin stood a group of tumbledown log cabins. Reb Santee knew that every man he found here had a price on his head, just as they supposed him to have. It had little outward effect on him. They reached the spot shortly before sundown of the last day and allowed the horses to spread out and graze, and when Lantry introduced Reb to men who were to figure in his life later on, the blue-eyed one was his same old careless self, free with his jests and full of irrepressible spirits.

"Yo're shore a happy feller, Santee," commented the Sundance Kid, a thin-faced, black-haired man of thirty with a reputation for unbridled savagery. "A few years of this life'll take that out of you."

Reb shrugged, his grin stealing up his likeable face again. "Mebbe so," he returned with an air of indifference. But inwardly he was not so thoroughly at ease. He knew that the border between these hunted men and such as himself was of the narrowest. He had no desire to slip over to their side, a step so easy and so irrevocable. The more he studied these men, the more sure he was of this.

Besides the Sundance Kid there were hard-eyed, soft-voiced New Mexicans, a man from the Indian Territory, fugitives from justice in Arizona and even a rustler from Idaho. Over them all hovered the shadow of honest men's enmity. They took it jauntily enough. Their talk that night around the fire was both free and illuminating. Taking it all in with a bland assurance he did not feel, Reb learned that outlawry in its every branch was becoming organized; that from Montana to the southern deserts the long riders had a series of hide-outs where they could always get grub, fresh mounts, information and a helping hand. The chain included such places as the Hole in the Wall, the Lost Cabin Country, up in Wyoming, Brown's Park and the Roost.

As for Doc Lantry's favorite branch of his trade, horses that were stolen in Utah or Arizona were easily hazed along over the Outlaw Trail into Montana, where they could be sold safely. Northern horses were disposed of in Utah with equal ease.

It was a shrewd and daring conception, and on the surface at least, Santee applauded it with enthusiasm. But his uneasiness grew, for he saw a net spreading around him which it would be difficult to escape. Could he hope to put the acquaintance of these men behind him? He knew he should make the attempt, and that before long. But there was something about the long rides they talked of, their rugged and adventurous life, that made its appeal.

It was not Reb's way to hurdle down timber before he came to it, and he put off his worries when he rolled up in his blanket for the night. Even the knowledge that someone had gone through his personal belongings while he was occupied elsewhere could not keep him awake. Doc roused him out with the dawn.

"Stir yoreself, Reb," he said. "We got to be on our way."

There was relief in the look Santee turned on him, and curiosity as well.

"Where are we headin' for, Doc?" he asked, voicing the question that had plagued the Sundance Kid and his brother Lonny the evening before, but which they had refrained from putting.

"Wind River Basin," Lantry supplied. "I got a small ranch leased up there, waitin' fer us."

"Us?" Reb thought; but he said nothing, struggling into his boots. He had to admit that there was something between Lantry and himself, now that they had weathered danger together, that had not been there before. He determined to wait at least until the Wind River Basin was reached before he mapped out his future course.

They started away from Brown's Park without delay. The Sundance Kid, his brother and two other men helped to round up the horses and start them off; they sealed their pledge of future meetings in a bottle of whisky. "Yo're a likely feller, Santee, if you don't get careless," remarked the Kid. A minute later he and his companions turned back up the park. Despite their good will, Reb saw the last of them without regret.

The next few days were hard on man and beast. The Red Desert, a vast barren tract before them to the north, blazing with alkali and hot as hell, could not be avoided. They took it in their stride, making long gruelling stages between water. Gloomy Jepson was more lugubrious than usual, predicting disaster in hopeless tones. Reb on the other hand was ever cheerful, even with the sweat streaming down his face and his throat parched. As a result of his good humor, he saw not only gratitude in Doc Lantry's looks, but admiration as well.

They passed Green River, swung east to round the barrier of the Wind River range, jutting down out of the north, and the next day crossed the alkali sinks and found themselves in Wind River valley. A rough trail through the eastern foothills of the range took them wide of Lander and the ranches around Fort Washakie. A last long leg carried them to the end of their journey, high in the sparsely settled Basin, a good seventy miles north of Lander and the railroad.

The small ranch Lantry had leased was unpretentious. Unoccupied for months, it consisted of a sod dugout, a tumbledown barn and some pole corrals in need of repair, standing on a flat on the edge of Ghost Creek. Available forage stretched away undisputed in every direction. And it was excellent range, Reb saw with approval; he couldn't remember ever to have seen better.

"Place will stand a lot uh fixin' up," Gloomy observed without enthusiasm as they surveyed their surroundings.

"A little elbow grease'll take care of that," Lantry returned. "Mebbe some work will help you git yore appetite back, Gloomy." Jepson had been complaining of the rigors of travel for days back, although he had been eating like a horse.

As if he had not heard Doc, Gloomy ticked off the tasks facing them. "Roof uh that dugout's gotta be patched; corrals're 'bout busted down; new dam'll have to be slung acrost the crick—an' I bet there ain't a inch uh fencin' in miles," he growled.

He was wrong on the last count. At some time considerable fencing had been strung up somewhere nearby, and then pulled down again. Barb-wire in big rolls, rusted but serviceable, lay tumbled against the rear of the dugout.

"We'll use that to throw up a pasture along the creek," Doc decided. "One of us can be doin' it while the other two makes a stab at sellin' hosses."

"Hell, I'd ruther knit than string bob-wire," Gloomy began querulously, as he saw the job coming his way.

"I'll do my share of it," Reb relieved him by saying, with his ready grin. He had been on the lookout for time to spend by himself, and it pleased him to have Lantry think of his remaining on the ranch occasionally as an accommodation.

True to his word, a few days later Reb snaked the wire out to the creek and got busy. Doc and Gloomy were away, visiting the far-flung spreads of the upper

Basin in their turn, in an attempt to dispose of some of the horses. Lantry felt safe here. All three of them had shown themselves at different points in the Basin, more than one cruising rider had stopped by to pass a word at the ranch, but as yet no one had questioned them. No trouble threatened.

Reb responded to the changed atmosphere in characteristic style. His unfailing grin became genuine once more. He forgot the worries of the Outlaw Trail. Moreover, he had found a new interest, and one that took his thoughts far afield as he pushed his work ahead with a zest.

This country had hit him pretty hard. All of the Basin range that he had seen, deep in last year's grass and rich with the new, was excellent. It was far and away superior to southern rangeland. The Wind River peaks, hanging against the western sky, were pretty as a picture. This was high country, the air like wine. It made him feel like a king and brought a sparkle to his eyes that had not been there for days.

Doc Lantry took the Basin as he took everything else—without saying much. He was not a garrulous man. His plans were vague, for Reb had refrained from asking what they were; but it was unlikely they included a change from his usual ways. As for his own, Reb was secretly determined to play it straight and settle down here for good.

Only now that the danger seemed over did he perceive the narrowness of his escape. For long days he had followed the trail of the hard-eyed gentry, and it was not to his liking.

"A little more of this an' I'll be over my head," he

told himself soberly. "I'm in over my hocks now. Doc won't make the move to turn me back, that's a cinch."

He was deep in these speculations, a light-hearted song belying his seriousness as he strung the wire along Ghost Creek, when a clatter from up the slope caused him to jerk to attention. A team and a light spring wagon came dashing down the grade toward him. In the instant in which Reb's glance took in the white-faced girl bouncing around on the seat, he saw that which brought him erect with a frown slashing his forehead.

The girl had lost all control of the run-away horses. She sawed ineffectually on the lines as the team made for the creek on a dead run. Whoever she was, she was headed for disaster, if not death, unless something was done about it and in a hurry.

Chapter IV

ACES UP

THERE were no useless injunctions on Reb Santee's lips as he read the girl's danger. One comprehensive look and he sprang for his pony, standing in the shade of the willows with hanging reins. The clatter of the wagon was louder as he hit the saddle. He sank in the spurs; the blue roan, having swung him up with his first bound, put on a burst of speed.

He realized it would be impossible to turn the thundering team before they hit the creek; that he could never reach their head in time. He raced across a long angle and swerved in beside the wagon. He saw that he was not going to be able to gain on it. The wheels rasped and bounced at his side; fear-ridden snorts and a rumble of flying hoofs rolled back.

Reb's decision was lightning swift. He pulled the grullo over, found himself behind the wagon. The pony raced madly, its head drawing up over the tail-gate. Without taking thought of his own peril, Santee loosened his feet in the stirrups and, watching his chance, plunged forward to grasp the wagon.

The grullo dragged from under him. His legs came down on the uneven, flying ground with a thump that threatened to tear loose his grip, if it did not tear his arms out of their sockets. Then by main strength he dragged himself up, got one knee over the gate, and after a writhing moment of struggle gained a footing on the swaying wagon-bed. The brush-lined creek drew near with rushing speed as he flashed a look. He flung himself toward the seat.

The girl had seen the start of his wild race to come to her assistance. Not by the slightest outcry did she indicate what her feelings were in that moment. She had no time to follow each step of his fight; but flinging a wild glance over her shoulder, she saw him make the leap to the wagon. Reb was conscious of a wind-whipped banner of black hair and a white face washed clean of expression turned toward him as he made a grab for the lines. She surrendered them with a limp relaxing of tired arms. He had time to get a grip on them and hurl his weight back, and then the team and the wagon struck the brush-choked dip to the creek.

There was a loud thrashing, a sickening lurch; one of the bays floundered, caught himself as Reb yanked his line; the wagon's careening speed slowed a shade. But the horses were still thoroughly terrified. It was plain they had no intention of stopping when they struck the open, shallow creek and started across. Silvery sheets of water splashed up, wetting man and girl.

Reb's expression in this moment was one of grim pleasure in the fight. His blunt jaw was thrust forward and his eyes flashed. The girl, gripping the jolting seat with bloodless knuckles, did not miss it. There was a touch of wonder in her look as it clung to his face.

He knew what he was doing. He did not battle with the ribbons, satisfying himself with holding up the heads of the bays as he swung them imperceptibly toward a long, brush-cluttered slope. They flung out of the far edge of the creek and struck the brush, still running furiously. It hampered their stride, dragged back on the wagon bottom and the wheels, and a dozen yards from the top brought the team to a trembling halt.

"Whoa, boys," Reb soothed. He sprang from the seat and approached cautiously. The bays stamped and snorted, rolling wicked eyes, but gradually reconciling themselves to his touch.

"You have certainly given me something to thank you for," the girl called herself to Reb's attention from the wagon. He looked up to find himself meeting a pair of gray eyes startling in their directness. She seemed aware that in turning his attention to the horses he had given her time to collect herself. "If it hadn't been for your timely appearance I don't know what would have happened."

"Shucks, that's all right, ma'am." He grinned at her, for there seemed no other way to dissemble the effect on him of her strong and charming personality. Her face was a small, firm oval, with a delicacy which did not detract from the decision of her chin or the royal bearing of her head. He could see with half-an-eye that she had breeding, and of the best. Her wide-set eyes were possessed of a candidness that grew on him with the moments. She was dressed in a fresh-laundered woolen shirt which set off the skin of her neck and throat to decided advantage by its roughness, and a skirt of some heavy, dark material. Her boots were trim and stout. Her body was small and straight and fine; there was, he realized bewilderingly, nothing whatever about her that was not only fine, but immeasurably finer than anything her sex had ever revealed to him before.

"I am Ronda Cameron, of the C 8, over on the Shoshone Meadows," she was saying in even, unhurried tones. "I don't remember ever having seen you before—"

"Reb Santee, Miss Ronda," he introduced himself. "I'm with Doc Lantry, who's leased the old Farr spread, down the creek." Never one to miss a bold stroke, he felt safe in addressing her thus. She appeared several years younger than himself—perhaps eighteen. Moreover, there was something boylike in the directness of her speech and the way she handled herself as she swung down and proceeded to examine the wagon. It was undamaged.

They talked over the runaway. When Ronda called attention to the shrewdness with which he had dealt with it, the stern pleasure he seemed to take in the contest, Reb flushed. The faint, quizzical smile on her lips as she noted this only added to the impact of her feminine appeal. It got to Reb from a side he did not know how to guard.

He got her mind away from himself by the jocular narration of runaways he had experienced or witnessed in the past. Soon he had her laughing merrily, joining in with his own bubbling bass tones. There was nothing forward in his manner, however, a circumstance she was quick to appreciate; for in this lonely land, rich in men and almost barren of women, she had been called on to deal with all manner of advances. It had given her a self-reliance of her own.

The ice broken, Reb drew from her the information that she was on her way to the store at Washakie Point. A sudden-flushing quail, flying almost in their faces, had been the cause of the bays' terror, just over the east ridge.

"I expect I look a sight to go anywhere now," she

remarked with unconscious candor, reaching up to deal with her disheveled hair.

"No, no. You look fine," Reb declared. From his vehemence it was easy to tell that he meant it. The luxuriance of her tumbled hair, the roses slowly blooming in her cheeks as the blood came back, gave her a freshness that would have made her welcome anywhere, and rendered her doubly beautiful to him. He choked off an uprush of guileless compliments, and for the first time in his life began to fear lest he should overplay his hand.

He did not attempt to deceive himself. He found a stake in this girl such as he had never played for. He hesitated to commit himself, for some instinct told him that to play and lose would bring to his days a darkness no man could bear for long; but already he felt an interest in her that it seemed impossible to keep out of every word and gesture.

The bays had by now been restored to calm under Reb's expert hands. He led them and the wagon through the brush to the top of the slope, straightened out the reins and handed them up as Ronda Cameron resumed her place on the seat.

"I must thank you again for your help," she said earnestly, looking down at him; "but I hope I am not forced to allow the matter to drop there. Won't you ride over to the C 8 sometime? I should like you to meet Father."

"I sure will, ma'am," Reb promised, grateful to her for having gracefully bridged over the problem of when he was going to see her again. "There's a lot of things about the Basin I'm beginnin' to like, an' it looks like I'd stay awhile. I won't lose no time makin' the acquaintance of my neighbors. An' yore dad'll be one of the first . . . I'd favor that off hoss a mite, if I was you," he added, as she made ready to drive on. "He's barked up some. I couldn't help it. He'll likely be sore."

After a few more words, which Reb scarcely heard in his pre-occupation with her soft face, they parted. Standing on the top of the slope, with Ghost Creek behind him, he watched until the spring wagon was only a small dot far out on the rolling surface of the Basin. Then heaving an unconscious sigh, he turned back to his work, his mind a jumble of disturbing visions. He did not know what to think.

For her part, Ronda Cameron was thinking with clarity and vigor as she rolled away in the wagon. She had heard of the new outfit on the Farr place, said to be horse buyers. Her experience at the creek was her first meeting with any of them. She felt that if the others were anything like Reb Santee, they would be a distinct addition to the Basin range. It would have been impossible not to like this laughing, homely fellow, even apart from the brave thing he had done in her behalf. But as she remembered the boldness of his act, the sheer virility of his whole bearing, she felt admiration as well.

Ronda put the bays to a brisk pace. An hour later she drew near to Washakie Point. It was not a pretentious place, even for this country, consisting simply of the old Farragoh ranch house and its corrals and ramshackle sheds.

Five years ago this had been a prosperous spread, with longhorns dotting the range in every direction.

Then, on a wild night of storm that was the climax of a terrific blizzard, Cleve Farragoh had died, leaving his wife and their young son to carry on. They had done so to the best of their ability. But dark days came. Another winter, and storms blew down out of the north which all but wiped out the brand. Mrs. Farragoh let the hands go and gave up ranching then, to open the store, for which the Basin showed its appreciation by christening it Washakie Point. It was the only store this side of Lander, but no town grew up around it and it remained a solitary place, ten miles off the freighting trail which crossed the Basin to the southwest.

As Ronda drew up before the store porch a young man appeared in the door. He was only a year or so older than herself, tall and slim, with hair as dark as her own and brown eyes that lighted up the instant he saw her.

"Hello, Ronda," he greeted, coming down the steps, with a warm smile that rendered him uncommonly handsome. "I was hoping you'd drive over today. Let me put up your team and you can stay to dinner. Ma's been busy with it for an hour."

"Billy," Ronda queried as she got down, "have you something to put on Charlie's legs? He got scratched up on the way over." She rested a hand lightly on Billy Farragoh's arm with the same pleasure she had always taken in this clean-limbed, upstanding boy. They had known each other for a long time.

"Sure have," he returned, more than ready to do anything for her. "You go in and talk to Ma while I take care of it."

After a word or two, which brightened the faces of

both, Billy led the bays away, calling back over his shoulder. With a lighthearted rejoinder from the porch, Ronda stepped inside.

The store was simply the main building of the ranch house, transformed by some shelving and a counter Billy had knocked together with loose boards. It was given a mercantile look by the stacks of air-tights and yellow plug tobacco signs, and the blankets and bridles hanging from the rafters, the barrels of flour and other commodities standing in the corners.

Mrs. Farragoh stuck her head through the kitchen door. "There you are, dearie," she called in her peculiar gruff voice. "Come out here an' let me look at you." When Ronda came forward, she brushed the graying hair back from her perspiring brow and kissed the girl, a hearty, vigorous smack.

Cleve Farragoh's widow was big and muscular and brusque. Her eyes were much like Billy's, but capable of a certain fierceness too. Her face was bony, square, commanding. As long as Ronda had know her she had been a salty, unsentimental personality, as blunt and resourceful as a man. There was a wisdom in her which did not come from the refinements of womanhood; but although she could, when occasion demanded, cope with the roughest customer, she was a motherly sort at heart. From the beginning she had made a special friend of Ronda.

"Well, I declare," she said now, looking the girl up and down. "Purty as a picture—after bein' out in that hot sun, too."

"No, I'm not," the girl laughed. "I'm mussed and freckled and what-not. It's just your opinion of me, Mother Farragoh."

Mrs. Farragoh abused her genially. "Slick yoreself up, Ronda, an' set yoreself," she said. "I'll have dinner ready in a little." The steam arose about her in clouds as she worked at the stove. "I declare, I cook more with one boy to feed than I used to when I come out of Texas in a wagon, with seven men lickin' the pot!" she rambled on.

Billy ducked in the back door, a grin on his face. He found a chair for Ronda.

"I'll slack off of eating when I've got my growth," he said in reference to his mother's remark.

She snorted, hearing it. "Yo're most six foot now; it ain't to make you bigger I'm feedin' you up," she retorted. She turned to Ronda. "I got to nourish his brains as well as his body," she went on, "as long as I got hopes of makin' him the best lawyer in Wyomin'. I ain't entirely discouraged yet, but—" She shrugged expressively.

Billy flung a laughing gibe at her. They ragged each other without stint, these two, and their love was deep. Ronda was familiar with the older woman's ambition to be able to give Billy a legal education.

"Hurry up, Ma," said Billy. "Ronda's hungry, she says. I'll get the table set, soon as I wash my hands."

"I?" Ronda caught him up. "What nonsense, Billy! Is it necessary to hide behind skirts at your age?" she disparaged lightly. She had never used a gentle hand with him, for they had grown through their long-legged years together, ridden to the school on Sage Creek side by side, and their companionship had been boisterous. It had grown into a romantic attachment, at least on Billy's part, during the last year or so. Ronda was aware of it, but she did not choose to reveal her knowledge of it to him by any change of manner.

They sat down to the table a few minutes later. It was an excellent meal, and Mrs. Farragoh did it full justice, as did Ronda and Billy, despite her deprecation of her own cooking.

"Your Charlie certainly got himself in a fine condition," Billy said to the girl at an interval in the animated range gossip, supplied mainly by his mother. "He'll be all right now; but however did he get in that shape?"

Ronda told them about the runaway. Billy put down his fork and stared as she described the danger she had run. But it was Mrs. Farragoh who broke in, when Ronda came to the man who had ridden to her aid.

"Hold on. Was he a yella-haired feller, youngish, with blue eyes, an' laughin'—all the time?"

"That sounds very like him," Ronda admitted. "He certainly was irrepressible." She attempted to give them some idea of the joy Reb Santee had found in pitting his brain and his muscle against the unreasoning terror of the bays.

"Ain't he ridin' for that new feller over at Farr's old place?" Mrs. Farragoh persisted. At Ronda's assent, she went on: "We've been hearin' about him. His name's Sandy—Sandy—" She groped.

"Santee. Reb Santee," Ronda supplied.

"That's it," Billy's mother beamed.— "But tell us the rest of it, dearie."

Ronda completed her narrative. When it ended, the talk turned to Reb Santee once more.

"I hear he's a top hand wrangler," Billy said. "Al Brett was here yesterday, telling about Santee riding that big wicked dun of his brother's, out at the Lazy B. You know they'd about given up that horse as an outlaw. Santee topped him and wouldn't accept a cent for it. He offered to break it for them right."

Ronda told more of what she had learned of Reb during their brief meeting. Both Billy and his mother listened with attention, plainly impressed.

"He sounds like one accommodatin' feller," said Mrs. Farragoh with an enthusiasm uncommon in her. "Al Brett's say ain't the first we've heard of him, an' none of it's been bad. I hope he rides over before long. I want to git a look at him."

"He will," Ronda felt she could safely assure her. "He said that he liked the Basin and probably would stay. He's going to visit Father soon. I've no doubt he will come over here as well."

"That's fine," said Mrs. Farragoh; and despite Ronda's obvious approval of the newcomer, Billy added generous agreement.

Chapter V

A CALL BLUFF

L ATE one afternoon Doc Lantry returned to the ranch on Ghost Creek after an extended trip around the Basin. He had sold a number of the horses at a good price, and was in excellent spirits.

"The dang fools around here take me fer a hoss-trader," he told Santee. "Blamed if they ain't been tryin' to git me to buy some o' their scrub stuff!"

"Didn't you take a few head?" Reb asked.

"Why sh'd I do that?"

"For the looks of it, for one thing," Reb caught him up. "Doc, I'd play the game straight if you don't want to pick up an' run again in a month or so." The warning was plain; only his tone was mild.

"I been studyin' my hand. It looks purty good to me," Lantry retorted levelly. "There'd be a lot of sense in me buyin' stock I could have fer the trouble of runnin' it off, wouldn't there." He went on to describe some easy hauls that he thought could be made in the Basin.

Reb was not interested. While he couldn't see his way to tell Doc that rustling and horse stealing held no appeal for him, he listened with an inattention that left Lantry testy.

"What's got into you?" he growled. "Is yore conscience botherin' yuh at this late last? Or mebbe yo're gittin' keen on this C 8 gal yuh saved from tippin' out of the wagon," he changed his front with a touch of ridicule, probing to learn where Santee's scruples lay.

49

He had heard the story of the girl's rescue, given a wide currency by the good offices of Mrs. Farragoh.

The easy smile went out of Reb's eyes. Their blue became the chill hue of sun on an ice pack. "We won't discuss the girl," he bit off, an edge to his tone.

It should have warned Lantry to ease off. But it did not. "Why won't we? . . . By God, you *are* sweet on 'er!" he cried in disgust.

Reb caught his arm in a vise-like grip, "I said we'd leave her out of it," he jerked out. "Don't go too far with me, Doc!" There was no mistaking his hard intent now.

Lantry met his boring gaze for a moment, breathing heavily. Then he jerked free. "What're yuh goin' lame on me for, then?" he backed down, not without animosity. "My hell, Reb! Here we got a lay in a thousand, an' you have to go gittin' religion." He was expostulating, a hand held out in appeal.

"All the religion I got is common sense," Reb told him bluntly. "A little of the same won't hurt you none."

Doc snorted angrily. He could find no adequate rejoinder, turning away with a face like a thundercloud. He had no more to say to Santee that day. Something told him that his arguments would have no effect. Reb was forced to listen to the pessimistic complaints of Gloomy Jepson. During supper and throughout the evening he was conscious of Lantry's brooding eye on him, asking a question the man would insist on having answered some time. Reb was indifferent to it.

In the morning Doc was as taciturn as ever. He rode out and set Gloomy to work on the pasture fence. Then he left for the day, without having made any suggestion to Reb as to how he might put in his time. Reb

loafed around the dugout for an hour and then saddling
the grullo, cantered out to join Jepson.

If Gloomy was surprised at the unexpected company
he was careful not to reveal it.

"I dunno whut Doc wants this blasted bob-wire
strung up fer, anyway," he grumbled. "He'll see to it
that we pull out of here 'fore long, leave it to him—an'
there goes all this work fer nothin'."

Reb had himself wondered over Lantry's order to
fence the pasture. He at first attributed it to Doc's
desire to keep up appearances, for at the rate he was
disposing of the horses it was apparent the enclosure
would not be needed for them; but from Doc's course
in other matters he had drawn different conclusions.
The outlaw cared little for the good opinion of the
range, so long as he was left to himself; of that Reb
was now convinced. He voiced none of his mystification
to Gloomy. "Where's Doc headin' for today?" he
queried casually, as they worked at the fencing.

"Said he was studyin' 'bout the trails out," Gloomy
answered. "He'll ride around the hills fer a day or two.
Doc don't never feel to home till he knows where to
find the back door. It won't do him no good. Some
day he'll slip, an' it'll be too bad."

Reb knew then that Lantry had no intention of
giving up outlawry, even for the time, unless something
occurred to shunt him off on another tack. Not that
Doc needed the money; he had plenty for the present;
it was the habit of years that drove him on to his ne-
farious activities.

When he arrived at this conclusion, Reb felt easier
in his thinking. For some reason he had no desire to
turn his back on the whole business and ride out of the

Basin. He told himself he had met with something here that had never come his way before, even in prospect. If bringing a little pressure to bear would keep Doc in the traces for a while, it was worth trying.

Lantry appeared to have experienced a change of heart when he rode in that evening. He had been doing some thinking of his own. He talked easily and seemed to have forgotten what had passed between them. Reb was cool to him, for Doc deliberately lied about where he had been that day. Moreover, Reb had not forgotten the other's contemptuous reference to Ronda Cameron. Doc chose to overlook his aloofness and was almost affable. It secretly pleased Santee, for he knew he had the man coming his way.

But cool as he was in a pinch, Lantry was not noted for patience. Having tried his best to regain Reb's full confidence, and failing, the next morning he rose in a surly temper. The shorter he grew, the broader Reb's tantalizing smile became.

"Damn him anyway!" Doc fumed under his breath. "He c'n shore git under the skin with that infernal grin of his!" He flung out of the dugout with a thundering scowl.

There could be no question they were at odds; and when Doc rode away alone once more to be gone for the day, Reb felt that he did so to avoid an open breach.

"Lantry wants me," he told himself. "He thinks he needs me. It's the only hold I have got on him." He had no illusions about what would happen the moment Doc made up his mind he no longer needed him.

But Lantry couldn't make up his mind. It stayed with him that with his likeable nature, Reb was an ideal confederate for his business, and one no man not unnaturally suspicious would be likely to doubt. Hadn't he already made an easy conquest of the Basin? Too easy, Lantry growled to himself. Santee did these things and went on his way, unaware of his own capacity. Doc wavered between the hope of awakening the puncher to his potentialities and the fear that Reb was playing a shrewd game of his own and would never come around to seeing things his way. And Reb read all this and more in his baffled demeanor, and laughed at him.

The situation was not improved when, several weeks later, two men dropped in at the ranch at a time when Doc and Reb and Gloomy were about to sit down to a meal. It was Lantry who went to the door and invited them down.

"Ike Lucas an' Stony Tapper, boys," he introduced, as the men shambled in. "They got a little place up in the Owl Creek Mount'ns." He gave out that he had met the pair on his horse-selling trip.

Tapper and Lucas were blunt-faced and close-lipped. Both were around Doc Lantry's age, but bigger, and wore an unprepossessing stubble of beard. Red didn't take to their shifty eyes or their way of sizing him up. Neither struck him as being self-respecting enough to make good punchers, let alone ranchmen. Their boots were run over and their clothes threadbare. Everything about them was cheap.

"Sit up an' help yoreselves, boys," Lantry told them, sliding out extra plates and rattling the tin forks.

Reb wasn't done eating yet, but he got away from the little table to make room. He seemed to find it worth while to roll a smoke and keep his mouth shut, as cagy as the newcomers.

Lucas and Tapper shoved up without much ceremony. They ate fast, wolfing their food down; and it was noticeable that neither would sit with his back to Santee or to the door. He made occasion to get a look at their horses. They hadn't ridden either very far or very fast, he noted. Exactly what they were was not apparent, though there might be some indication in the fact that a running iron was thrust under the guard of each saddle together with a rifle, and a different brand had been vented on the flank of each mount.

Doc was talking to the pair at the table as if they were old friends. They opened up to him grudgingly. They seemed to want to appear not so much suspicious as just unaccustomed to talking a lot, for they paid Reb little or no direct attention. Their eyes rested on him briefly, heavily, when Doc referred to him in a casual way, and then were gone again.

The things they knew about the range, however— the movements of different outfits and the like—finally gave them away. From an occasional unguarded remark they dropped, Reb wasn't long in deciding that their particular business was running an iron on other men's stock.

What they had come to see Lantry about, if anything, did not develop. Reb was sure it was not alone for the sake of a meal. They left after a while, as noncommittally as they had arrived. As soon as they had ridden out of ear-shot he took Doc to task in his easy, telling way.

"I wouldn't say they was the best comp'ny," he pointed out, gazing after the departing riders. His inflection was brusque.

Lantry whirled on him. "I didn't ask fer no opinion

on 'em," he rasped. "Far's that goes, you don't always make the best there is either."

Santee was looking at him with a half-smile, not at all ruffled—an expression that goaded Doc at a time like this more than harsh words would have done.

"Look here, Doc," he said, and his tone was lazy. "Nobody needs to tell me those gents ride with a wide loop. An' not only that, but they're small fry. I got no use for 'em—an' if yo're wise, you won't have either. If you an' me have got to turn to rustlin' fer a livin', we'll do it with bigger men."

It made sense. And it was entirely unexpected. Reb could see the struggle going on behind Doc's visage. The man's gaze was hard and glinting. He fronted Reb squarely, and his next words were in the tone of an ultimatum: "Do you mean that, Santee?"

The lines in the corners of Reb's eyes crinkled deeper. His white teeth showed.

"Would I be fool 'nough not to?" he countered, without any change in his bearing.

Lantry's chest swelled with a long breath. "By God, that relieves me aplenty!" he burst out. "I ain't knowed what to make of you fer days. If the wind sets in that quarter—"

"Mebbe we've differed a bit on these picayune deals," Reb bluffed without batting a lash; "but that's all, Doc. Why, hell's fire! What's the sense of me sayin' anything if you can't see it? We don't want to git ourselves in bad here because we're too lazy to ride out a ways. If Lucas an' Tapper git in a jam they'll be on the long ride again; an' if we're thick with 'em, or even known to be seen with 'em, we'll be asked some mighty embarrassin' questions. It ain't worth it."

Doc was ready to agree, persuaded as he was by his desire to have Reb on his side.

"An' that ain't all," he took him up now. "Reb, you'll find I've been doin' some prime figurin' on my own hook. Look here." His manner had undergone a remarkable change in the past few minutes. Gone were his suspicions and doubts. Tapping the palm of one hand with a finger of the other, and lowering his voice, he revealed his plan to make the little ranch on Ghost Creek an over-night hideout for the big-time outlaws who were running stolen stock down from Montana to Brown's Park and the Robbers' Roost, as well as those who were working the other way.

"There's always a break fer a little spread like ours here," he explained his scheme. "The big fellers are most of 'em so well known they don't dast try to dispose of their stuff. Somebody's got to do it. That's where we come in."

Doc's face was lit up now with something like lust; there was little Reb could not have got out of him for the trying; but by the same token there was little he wanted to learn that Lantry was holding back. He contented himself with a shrewd expression as he listened, nodding his head or offering suggestions.

"Now it sounds like you was playin' a real bet," he said at the end; "an' that's all the more reason for not bein' fast an' loose about it. It's up to us to put up an eighteen-karat front here in the Basin, an' we'll do it." Lantry reluctantly agreed, and Reb had to let it go at that for the time; but inwardly he was conscious of chagrin to think that he had committed himself, at least in Doc's mind, to a full share in this proposed wholesale outlawry.

Chapter VI

MAN TO MAN

IT was only a few nights later that the occupants
of Ghost Greek ranch were roused out of their
bunks at midnight by the sodden thump of hoofs
outside and a guarded call. A rumble of thunder was
murmuring in the west. There had been a fall storm
earlier in the evening; there would be another before
morning, unless it blew around.

Doc Lantry was the first to stamp into his boots.
Reb followed suit. Gloomy blinked owlishly in the light
of the lantern he lit.

"Git a fire goin', Gloomy, an' put on coffee," Doc
told him. He turned to the door and went out.

Reb didn't have to remind himself that it probably
was not just a bunch of range men out there. He
looked after Doc, hesitated, and then remained where
he was. There were times when it didn't pay to stumble around in the dark. He'd find out soon enough
what was afoot.

If there was any lingering doubt in his mind as to
its nature, there was none in Gloomy Jepson's. "Hell
of a time of night to git up!" he grumbled, the lines
of his face drawn down. "Hell of a business to be in.
Dang it all, I'm goin' back to punchin' cows, see if I
don't." This was the burden of his perpetual complaint. According to him outlawry was a fool's para-
dise, a snare and a delusion. He was forever on the
verge of forsaking it. The only insult he recognized
was to be told that he never would; but he never did.

Santee paid small attention to his ramblings, intent on the murmur of voices outside, indistinguishable above the prolonged roll of the thunder. But a moment later, corral bars rattled and boots sloshed toward the dugout.

A blurred face showed momentarily at the door. Then: "Hullo, boys!" The Sundance Kid stepped in, followed by Doc Lantry and three other men. One of them was the Kid's brother, Lonny Logan. Reb did not know the others. All except Doc dumped wet saddles in a corner.

"Santee, you didn't meet these boys down at the Park," the Kid said now. "Bob Leigh an' Flat Nose George," he introduced them.

There was some reserve in the chorus of acknowledgments, despite the Kid's assurance that Reb was all right. But Logan himself was not so reticent, his black eyes glinting in the lantern light, a lock of raven hair drooping over his sallow forehead.

"Not a bad place you got here, Doc," he averred; "an' damn handy fer us too. We would've had a wet, mis'able night of it." He shook his head.

"You must've been pushin' them mustangs pretty hard," Lantry suggested. "How far'd you come today?"

"Dern nigh from the Bitter Root country," Lonny Logan put in with a grin. "An' if that sounds like three days to yuh, don't blame us. It still seems like t'day to me."

Lantry whistled. "Chased yuh, eh?"

The Kid looked at him humorously. "Hot an' close," he said. He glanced toward the stove. "How do we stand on the coffee, Jepson? Man, I could drink a hogshead of it an' sleep a week." The lines in his haggard face showed this to be only a mild exaggeration.

"It'll be ready fer yuh, if yuh can drink coffee in the dead o' night like this," Gloomy responded lugubriously. "I can't." He was already rattling the tin cups about.

The Kid didn't hear him, telling Lantry about the pursuit. They thought they had shaken it off now, but were not sure. "We got to snatch some shut-eye, if the whole state of Montana is on our necks," said Logan easily. "We'll pull out before dawn. This rain should wipe out our tracks fer a ways back." Plainly he was not overly worried, nor were the others. Reb did a lot of listening.

"How yuh pullin' out of here?" Doc queried.

"We'll foller the Basin east an' keep to the fastest ground till the weather changes."

Lantry nodded. "That's the best way. The pass'll be slow an' hard in the mornin'."

The coffee was passed around. The outlaws drank it in noisy sips, smoking hot, and asked for more. The Kid was questioning Doc about his activities now. He remarked that the Basin was fertile ground, and broke off to ask Santee what he thought of it.

Reb was aware the man's familiarity was largely a pose, and that Logan was still studying him. Conscious also of the effect his words would have on the listening Lantry, he answered with an evasive quip: "A basin's a handy thing to wash in," he said lazily. "I never yet tried to hide in one, if I thought anybody around near wanted to look me up."

Logan's companions laughed, and he was not himself displeased. In a way it loosened the stiffness, and in a few minutes Reb had them all in a good humor. It was easy to see they were ready to take to him.

"Sensible feller, Santee," the Kid observed to Doc Lantry, under cover of the jests that accompanied the removal of boots, damp vests and the like. The men were not inclined to put off their rest much longer.

Doc said nothing.

It was only a short time before they were settled for the duration of the night. Sufficient bunks had been built in the dugout originally to accommodate nearly a dozen punchers, and there was room for all.

Thinking over the newcomers, Reb did not allow their presence to cut into his sleep. He realized that he had not the same argument against them that he had used with Lantry against Lucas and Tapper. The Sundance Kid and his men were distinctly not small fry. Wild and reckless as their stories told him they were, there was a shine of virility, of manhood, in their eyes that set them above the scavengers of the range. He sensed that they were slated for still bolder activities than those they already related without boast; they would go far, and some would come to a violent death; but there was something about their wild freedom that had its effect on Reb despite his knowledge that it was all wrong.

Thunder rumbled throughout the early morning hours, one of the last electric storms of the season; daylight was delayed. Long before it broke, the Logans and Leigh and Flat Nose George Curry were astir. Gloomy made them more coffee, fried bacon and warmed up the beans, muttering under his breath. Half-an-hour later, as the first diluted light streaked the east, the outlaws were in the saddle. They had around fifty head of stolen horses with them, which had been put in the large corral.

"Better foller the creek south four- five miles an' then swing east toward the gap," Lantry told the Kid. "That way you'll miss any C 8 hands that might be moochin' around over back. That's all yuh got to worry 'bout."

Logan nodded, leaning down to yank straight his saddle-skirts. "Looks like 'nother shower comin' at us," he observed, scanning the leaden sky. "That'll drown our tracks fer a ways farther. . . . Well, boys, take care o' yoreselves." He lifted a hand to Doc and Reb and Gloomy, and turned his pony.

A few minutes later the horse-herd faded into the gloom down the bank of the creek.

The Kid's prediction proved correct. He and his men had scarcely got well out of sight before the rain began again. A sprinkle grew to a drizzle and then to a steady downpour which promised to endure.

"That puts 'em in the clear," Doc said with satisfaction. "It ought to wipe out any marks they left gittin' here too." He chuckled. "But they're jest crazy 'nough to crab because they got to ride in the wet."

"All but the Kid," Reb rejoined reflectively. "He knows when to stay out in the rain."

Doc glanced at him sharply. "You been doin' a little sizin' up on yore own hook, ain't yuh?" he grunted.

If it meant that Lantry had been narrowly watching the effect Reb had on the Sundance Kid's outfit, he gave no sign that he was aware of it.

"It's a habit I got," was all he said.

Not three hours later, Gloomy, who had started disgustedly down to the creek for water, stamped in with an even longer face, if that were possible. "Couple more o' yore playmates ridin' up," he announced.

Lantry took his boots down off the table and threw his cigarette away. This was something he had been vaguely expecting. Reb was behind him as he reached the door. They stood just out of the drip from the roof and watched two slickered horsemen advance through the mists.

"The old one's Jim Ward," Doc muttered, as they drew close enough for identification. His gaze was narrow. "That's Bob Calverly with 'im. Ward's sheriff of Freemont County, an' Bob's his chief deputy. Don't let on you know it . . . I'll do the talkin'." He raised his voice, simulating cheer. "Light an' come in, boys. It's shore plenty wet. Better pull off yore saddles."

The sheriff drew up with a long straight look out of wise, thoughtful eyes. His brows were gray and bushy under the dripping broadbrim. His mustache drooped.

"Thanks," he said. He stepped down, but made no move to unsaddle his horse, coming in the door with Calverly behind him as Lantry and Reb made room. Once in he stopped, and stood blocky and immovable. "I'm Ward," he said. "Sheriff of Freemont."

Lantry pretended surprise. "Sheriff, eh? Kinda off the beaten track, ain't you?" He did not overdo it.

Having tested Doc's response, Ward pierced Santee with a glance and took in Gloomy. Calverly, a stalwart, leather-faced man, was equally alert, his eye riding around the dugout.

The sheriff paid no attention to Doc's query. He put

one of his own: "Hear any men ridin' by durin' the night?" The words were abrupt and clipped.

"Which way was they headin'—?" Lantry began. He would have denied all knowledge of the outlaws, but Reb cut him off easily.

"Yes, we seen 'em, Sheriff," he said frankly. "They was here 'bout midnight."

"How many of 'em?" Ward barked.

"Four."

Calverly nodded, but the sheriff pressed on: "Tell us about it."

"Not much to tell. They made us feed them and then pulled out." Lantry made an attempt to break in and Ward ignored him. Reb was the acknowledged spokesman now. He was careful not to meet Doc's eye as he gave a straightforward, circumstantial account of the visit of Logan and his men, avoiding their names, however, until an interpolation by Calverly told him the fugitives were known. According to him the outlaws held them in the dugout while they wolfed down a meal, and departed immediately afterward.

"Which way did they go?" Ward bored in.

"Well, they warned us to keep our heads down till they was long gone. We stayed in till we was sure we was in the clear." Reb was speaking freely now, his whole manner artless. He was well aware that Lantry was in a killing temper, and that he would have to answer to him for his outspokenness as soon as the law rode on. But he gave no sign. "From the sound of it, I'd say they pulled away south and a little west," he said. He seemed anxious to make this clear, telling just how it had struck him.

Calverly unconsciously came to his aid again. "Hittin' fer Crazy Woman Pass, they was," he gave his opinion. "They figured *we'd* figure they'd go out that way, an' not expect 'em to fer that reason."

Even the sheriff gave a dry assent. He made ready to leave, pulling up the collar of his coat inside his slicker. "They got away around one o'clock, eh? . . . That puts 'em a full eight hours ahead of us. We ain't seen a real track since dark last night. Mebbe we c'n pick up a trail of some sort here."

Reb hoped they could. He said so anyway. Really he knew they wouldn't, for he had made sure of that. "If you don't, you'll probably pick up sign as you ride along toward the Crazy Woman," he went on. "This rain won't wipe out everything." It was true, and it was all the more reason he was ready to steer the officers off on the wrong track altogether.

Ward and Calverly left a few moments later. Doc Lantry waited until they were well away and then wheeled on Reb fiercely.

"Now suppose you explain to me why yuh pulled that damn fool trick—if yuh can!" he bit out. His face was dark with blood, his eyes flashing a steely challenge.

"What trick?" Reb met him coolly. Gloomy gaped, moving apart.

Doc was ready to erupt, more angry than they had ever seen him. There was murder in his red glare. He fought it back with difficulty.

"You know, damn yuh! Was it necessary to say the boys was anywheres near here?"

Reb was brusque. "Dammit, Doc, get hold of yore-self," he retorted. "They was here, wasn't they? Where in hell would we've been if you said no an' the sheriff found out yuh was lyin'?"

"How was he goin' to find out!" Lantry yelped.

"Easy enough. As soon as his eyes lit on these bunks he knew they stopped without askin'. Every one of 'em is damp yet. An' there's them dishes Gloomy's been in such a sweat to git washed, if that ain't enough." Reb was scornful now. "The first thing you thought of was to act ignorant—an' the fat would've been in the fire for sure in another two minutes, if I hadn't spoke up. I don't want no more to do with yuh, if yo're goin' to be so careless."

Doc sputtered, an impotent rage shaking him. Reb watched him for a moment and then went on:

"Don't forget, Lantry, we got ourselves to look out for as well as others. In this case, a straight story— or what sounded like one—was our best out. Now Ward'll ride on an' think no more 'bout us; but if he'd caught us in the smallest kind of lie, this place would be marked for good. You can see that, can't yuh?"

Doc had to see it, but he did so with reluctance and a bad grace.

"That may all be so; but I don't cotton to the way you take matters in yore own hands, Santee," he growled. "I told yuh I'd do the talkin'."

Reb faced him with short patience. "You do the talkin' after this. But you see to it you do a blame sight better job of it than yuh would've done this time, or I'll take it away from yuh again, I'm tellin' yuh." There was no defiance in his tone; only a chill, persuasive warning that made Lantry writhe.

In itself no small matter, Reb's ultimatum was only an example of the gradual change that had worked in him. He had started out much as a hand Doc had hired. But since that time he had asserted himself in a hundred ways until he no longer looked for or took orders. Of the two, it was clearly apparent that he was the strong man. Doc sensed it. Little good though it did him, he fought against it with all the power of his will. Both knew a time would come when they would face each other in a showdown.

Chapter VII

BAD BLOOD

THE next day it turned off clear. There was a tang of fall in the air that made the blood course through a man's veins. Reb was up and about with the sparkling dawn. Lantry and Gloomy Jepson soon followed him.

"I'm makin' another trip today," said Doc after breakfast. "If we don't sell these horses before round-up's over we won't git rid of 'em at all. Gloomy'll go with me."

The pasture had been completed. Lantry's mustangs high-tailed around in it with the same excess of spirits that Santee felt. Doc and Gloomy cut out a bunch, not without trouble. As the sun flashed over the range they hazed them away toward the south.

Reb watched them leave, his mind busy with his own thoughts. A week had passed since he had made the acquaintance of Ronda Cameron. He had not seen her again in that time, for all the tug exerted on him by the remembered impact of her presence.

It cost him no little effort to hold off, giving his attention to the game he played with Doc Lantry. Doc had accused him of being sweet on the girl. But he knew what the man was really driving at. Lantry was charging him with weakness: for him, inseparable from treachery.

Reb laughed at the idea that Doc should be able to keep him away from Ronda Cameron. He told himself he was biding his time.

The supplies they had packed in were running low. It fell to him to ride to Washakie Point for a few things.

After making a list of the needed items and saddling his pony and a pack horse he rode away from Ghost Creek. With plenty of time at his disposal, he amused himself by trying to pick up and follow the old tracks of the spring wagon Ronda had driven. It was near noon when he approached the store.

Nobody was around outside. But two saddled horses stood in front of the old Farragoh ranch house. Reb's brows knit as he read the brands on them. He had seen those ponies before. He was busy remembering when that was, when the sound of loud voices drifted out through the open door, to be followed by an angry exclamation.

Santee slipped off the blue roan and went up the porch steps almost eagerly. There was a harsh cry now; the sound of a tussle. Even before he made the door he knew who he would see. He was not mistaken. Ike Lucas looked over his shoulder, snarling as Reb's shadow fell across the floor. The heavy-set man struggling with the young fellow at the corner of the counter was Stony Tapper.

"What you lookin' fer?" Lucas flung out belligerently, noting the expression on Reb's face. He tried to cover what was going on behind him.

Reb had nothing to answer, no questions to ask; nor did he stop grinning. A fight was a fight with him. He had been right about this pair, the two of them ganging up on a boy. That was enough.

Lucas clawed with one hand for his gun, guarding himself with the other arm as Reb closed with him.

Belatedly he changed his mind and started a blow with his gun hand. Reb blocked it and sent one of his own slashing in. Lucas rocked back on his heels, bellowing like a bull calf.

The young fellow was having a hard time of it with Tapper. Santee didn't stop the rush that had given weight to his blow; it carried him on and he laid a rough grasp on Tapper's shoulder and yanked him sidewise and then over backward. The crash shook the floor, the shelves.

Lucas wasn't out of it, however. Even as Tapper rolled over and snatched at Reb's leg, Ike took two running steps, jumped, and with his arms open, landed on Santee like a rock-slide, trying to overwhelm him.

Quick as a flash, Reb turned his back just as Lucas leaped. With the fellow on his shoulders he bent down violently. Ike's weight carried him irresistibly over; his heels described a circle in the air and crashed on a shelf. Canned goods rained on the floor. Lucas's body landed across Tapper's legs with a thump that knocked the wind out of him and fetched a yell from Stony.

He jumped up, tumbling his partner aside. His brutish face was a mask of rage; there was a blind determination of the killer in the bitter set of his lips. But now the tables were turned. It did not discourage him.

Young Farragoh wanted to fly into him, mad clear through. He had spunk. Santee wouldn't let him, waving him back, away from Tapper's treacherous crouch.

"Snag the other one, if you want somethin' to do," Reb bit out. Lucas was beginning to come to, squirming; but Reb didn't take his eyes off Stony. The latter's gun had bounded across the floor at his fall. He knew from the lightness of his belt that it was gone. He did not look for it, making ready to spring. At Santee's jerked out direction to Billy Farragoh, he emitted a strangled ejaculation of wrath and snapped into action.

Reb was ready for him. At the moment they came together he laughed aloud. His flailing fist caught Tapper flush on his outthrust jaw. It knocked Tapper out, turning him completely over in the air and slamming him up against the home-made counter. Then he was on the floor, stretching out with a tired sigh and lying still.

Reb whirled. Lucas had gained his knees and was grappling with young Farragoh, one of his great hands ruthlessly seeking the boy's face. They swayed back and forth, their breath coming heavily. Santee took one long step; his fingers closed on the collar of Ike's shirt and he tore the man away with a jerk. An attempt to shake him like a terrier failed; Lucas's hard frame was too heavy. He lunged around, bawling—and thrust his face straight into Santee's upcoming knuckles.

The blow wrenched a grunt from Ike. An expression of incredulity overspread his swarthy features. He was gasping for breath, with the curious sensation of sinking in deep water; and when he succeeded in fighting loose, it was toward the door that he stumbled, leaving his companion to the mercy of this flaxen-haired laughing devil of a puncher. He had had enough.

Reb wiped the blood off his chin and found the young fellow staring at him with sober earnestness. It was as if he could not believe what he had seen, for his eyes were big and dark.

Reb said: "You're young Farragoh, ain't you?"

"Yes. And you're Reb Santee. I've heard of you—"
He expelled a long breath, then matched Reb's grin
with one as warm, if not quite so broad.

"Well—" Reb looked about—"I reckon the place
could stand a little straightenin' up. There's some rub-
bish to throw out." He turned toward Tapper.

Billy would have helped him, but he wouldn't have
it. "I'll make this my job, an' no mistake about it," he
said. Taking Tapper by the heels he dragged him to
the door. Lucas stumbled away from the steps, where
he had been sitting. He turned a face of sullen fear and
hatred to Reb. But Santee paid him no heed. He
dropped Tapper on the porch and said to Billy
Farragoh:

"Now, if you'll scare up a pail of water—"

Billy went to get it, and waiting, Reb met Lucas's
glower with composed silence. Something passed between the two which Santee had no trouble in recog-
nizing. Without saying a word, Ike Lucas was serving
notice in his vindictive way. Having once seen Reb
with Doc Lantry, he had his own opinion of what he
was; now he thought that Reb was elbowing his way
in, playing a lay of his own. Ike's eyes said he would
see about that.

Billy came with the water. Santee took it and sent it
over Stony Tapper in one drenching splash. Stony
gasped, struggling back to consciousness. He sat up.

Reb measured him contemptuously. "Get yoreself
out of this," he said shortly.

Tapper only blinked stupidly; but when Reb took
a step forward, he hastily rolled to the edge of the
porch and dropped off. He had little of Lucas's yellow
streak—the only thing that could make Ike really bad

—but he knew when he was well off. He and Lucas faced the porch, unable to fathom Santee's mocking grin and stung to impotent rage by it.

"Throw us our guns," Lucas growled. He had a rifle on his saddle, but he made no move toward it.

"I'll do that," Reb came back at him, after a moment, "jest to prove to yuh it don't bother me how many guns yuh got."

It was Billy who stepped inside for the six-guns. When he came back he had one thrust in his own trouser-band. Without punching out the cartridges, he pitched the two guns at the feet of their owners.

Lucas and Tapper picked them up in the midst of a dead silence. They straightened swiftly, sending long, wicked glances. There was care in the way they holstered the weapons.

Reb's smile widened. "You don't think you'll try it, eh?" he said lightly. "Mebbe some other time." His tone hardened. "But get me right, you two. If anything like this happens again, I won't wait. An' when I come after yuh, I'll come a-shootin'! Is that clear?"

If curses were answer enough, Reb had it. The pair swung into their saddles and savagely heeled the ponies away. They did not look back.

"Gosh—thanks," Billy Farragoh said as though he meant it. "You sure made short work of those two."

"Forget it," Reb turned him off with a shrug. "It was fun while it was goin' on. Mind tellin' me how it started?"

They turned back into the store and straightened up as they talked. Billy explained that Tapper and Lucas were in debt to his mother. She had ridden out to West Creek this morning—Mrs. Blanchard was sick—and before she left, she advised Billy to extend no more credit to the pair. They asked for it, as usual; and when he said no they jumped him.

Reb nodded at the end. "My guess is that they won't bother you no more." He said it with conviction, for he had no inkling then that he had gained two enemies who were destined to make him trouble. More important to him—though he was unaware of this either— was the fact that this meeting with Billy Farragoh was the beginning of a friendship that was to mold his life.

Billy was easy to talk to. He asked no questions, yet was as friendly as he could be. "I wish Ma was here. We've talked about you," he confessed shyly. "She wanted to know what you were like."

Reb laughed off the implied compliment. "She'll be tired of me before I leave the Basin," he said.

Billy filled his order, and he followed along when Reb carried the stuff out, stowed some of it and tied the rest on his cantle. They joked on, and it was afternoon before Santee pulled away. It hadn't taken him that long to find out that although there was no great difference in their ages, young Billy rendered him a whole-hearted admiration.

"He's a nice boy," Reb mused as he jogged home. "I like him."

Doc Lantry and Gloomy arrived at the ranch in the evening, with less than half of the horses they had started out with. They found Santee breaking a couple of wild ones in the big corral.

"What yuh doin' that fer?" Doc demanded.

"Somethin' to do," Reb told him, wiping the dust

from his perspiring face. "Makes it easier to sell 'em, Doc, if they got the rough edges knocked off."

Lantry grunted. "Better come along with me tomorrow, if yuh feel that way. I can't say Gloomy loves anything that looks like work."

"I'll do that," Reb took him up.

They were late getting a start in the morning. Before they got away, three men rode up. Two were punchers. The third, obviously a rancher, looked like someone Santee had seen before.

He said: "I'm Jube Cameron. The C 8, over back here, is my spread. Which one of you is Reb Santee?"

Lantry jerked a thumb at Reb.

Getting down, Cameron shook hands. "Howdy, Santee. I want to thank you fer helpin' my daughter." He was a bluff, full-blooded man, six feet tall if he was an inch, and with shoulders as wide as a door. A number of his characteristics Reb had first noted in his daughter's face. "I hear you've got some hosses to sell," he went on.

A glance at Lantry to see how he was taking this showed him keenly suspicious, inclined to take offense. It was Reb's turn to indicate him, as the owner of the horses. Doc instinctively melted as the rancher turned to him.

"You c'n have anything in sight, Cameron," he said, "except our private strings. We'll go down to the pasture."

"What're these here in the corral?" Ronda's father queried. "Somethin' yo're breakin' fer yoreself?"

"Why, no." Lantry hesitated. "Santee started toppin' 'em, but they're jest part of the bunch."

They rode around the pasture. Cameron picked

half-a-dozen likely animals and they were cut out; but when they returned to the dugout he asked that the price of the pair in the corral be added to his bill. "They look good to me; an' I figure they been worked over a little," he remarked. Doc said nothing; but when the rancher and his men were gone, Reb could not forbear to twit him a little.

"Yuh thought I was foolish last night, didn't yuh?" he said.

Doc's manner was to the effect that he hadn't changed his mind, but he passed the matter off with a dry laugh.

The next day after dinner the two of them started for the C 8. Cameron had invited them over. "We may be able to sell him a few more head," Doc remarked.

The Cameron ranch was a large and comfortable looking place on the bank of Rebel Creek. The pine that went to make up the sprawling ranch house had been hauled down from the heights of the Wind River range. Flowers grew in the shade of the lofty cottonwoods. A collection of barns and out-buildings littered the flat behind the house.

They were breaking some broncs in the dusty corrals. Ronda Cameron sat on the bars to windward, and Billy Farragoh was there.

"I'm glad to see you," Ronda told Reb, "even though it took two invitations to bring you." She was dressed in blue Levis and riding boots, with a man's shirt open at her throat, but the appeal of her was even stronger than he had remembered it. He couldn't keep his eyes away from her. They chatted easily. Jube

Cameron lit a cigar with Doc Lantry, discussing the horses.

Billy Farragoh had his turn with the wild ones and, tired out, come to join Ronda and Reb. Even to the girl he did not hesitate to show his strong liking for Santee. It embarrassed Reb. He strolled away, smiling, to take a whirl at a bronc which had thrown its rider twice in succession.

In the saddle, he could not resist the temptation to show off a bit. The bronc—a big, glass-eyed buckskin —had no luck with him. He wore it down with ease, and in a short time was ready for another, still grinning his pleasure in the combat.

Billy Farragoh waved his hat, and Ronda's eyes were shining, as Reb stepped up on his second bronc. It possessed no tricks that he could not master. Jube Cameron took his cigar out of his mouth and said to Lantry: "That boy's got a way with horses."

Doc's face was inscrutable; but before he and Reb rode away late in the afternoon, he had taken advantage of the opportunity to extract the rancher's promise of the purchase of another half-dozen horses. He knew, if Reb did not, that Cameron needed none of the broncs he had bought; it was his way of expressing his appreciation for what Doc's laughing, freckled, likeable companion had done for his daughter; but Lantry had no scruples about taking advantage of the situation.

Chapter VIII

TROUBLE IN THE SADDLE

THE hours of daylight shortened and the nights grew colder over Wind River Basin. The aspens were a blaze of gold on the high slopes. The hair of the ponies began to fluff out, bare hands stiffened on ropes. Winter was not far off. On the day the first white caps appeared on the Wind River peaks, a Cameron rider dropped in at the little ranch on Ghost Creek with news.

Next week the women of the Basin, with the exception of Mrs. Farragoh, were going out to Lander for the winter. On Monday, as was the custom, a big get-together was being held, something in the nature of a farewell party for them. Jube Cameron was giving it this year. Everyone was invited.

"Sure, we'll go to that," said Santee, scenting fun from afar. The fall work was almost over. It would be the biggest affair of the year.

"Mebbe we will," said Lantry grudgingly, as soon as the rider was gone.

Reb looked at him in surprise. His first thought, on hearing the news, was that Ronda Cameron would be gone. Doc must have followed him that far. For some reason Doc had taken an unreasoning dislike to the girl. He would have been glad to see the last of her. But Reb had given up trying to read the man's surly impulses. He said nothing. But he certainly intended to see Ronda before she left.

In the morning the three started out with the last

of Lantry's horses. Before noon Santee rode away to a branding, and was seen no more that day. He had got acquainted with most of the men in the Basin, and everywhere received a cordial welcome. For more than a month he had thoroughly enjoyed himself, lending a helping hand wherever the opportunity arose, spending hours in the saddle or at the store with Billy Farragoh, and even seeing a good deal of Ronda Cameron. Moreover, he had grown to have little liking for Lantry's morose silences and escaped them whenever he could.

Doc met him at the ranch that night with poorly suppressed resentment. "Where'd you disappear to?" he growled.

"Jest ridin' around."

"Look here," Doc took him to task, in a voice Santee was coming to recognize; "It's all right to put yoreself in solid if yuh want to, doin' other men's work fer nothin'; but business is business. We got to turn a dollar, an' don't you fergit it."

Santee had him there. "I've sold more hosses, head fer head, than you've been able to git rid of," he pointed out good-humoredly.

"Hosses ain't what I'm thinkin' about. They're small p'tatoes 'longside of what's layin' under our noses, an' you know it." Lantry reminded the other of the beef cuts invitingly near at hand, plainly unable to get out of his mind the opportunities for easy profit they were passing up.

It brought home to Reb their real reason for being there, something he had almost forgotten, so pleasantly had he been spending his time.

"Lay off, Doc," he warned, thinking fast. "No use

fightin' yore head. There's nothin' here fer us before spring."

"How so?"

"Look at it yoreself. We can't do nothin' before that party; folks'd be shore to notice if we didn't turn up there. An' snaggin' a beef herd now'd mean a long, hard drive, with the chance of gittin' caught in a storm."

"That sounds a hell of a lot like you!" Doc snapped impatiently.

"You think it over," Reb urged. "If yuh expect to make use of this layout, yuh gotta keep up appearances. A few more months an' the Basin'll git used to us. Then we'll have a freer hand. I'm tellin' yuh, Doc."

Lantry jerked away, openly disgruntled.

There were several days of this kind of arguing. By degrees Santee won his point. It was not because he wanted to that Doc gave in; his capitulation drove another wedge in the widening breach between them, which, however, he concealed as well as he could. For his part, Reb knew that the agreed-on delay was only putting off a decision he would sooner or later be called on to make, but he was content to let it stand that way.

The day picked for Cameron's fiesta for the women arrived. The party was to be held in the evening. Reb spent the afternoon getting ready, humming snatches of song to himself. Gloomy Jepson surveyed his preparations with distrust.

"I sh'd think the men'd wait an' have their bust after the women're gone," he gave his opinion sourly.

"You don't sound like yuh was aimin' to go, Gloomy," Reb grinned at him.

"Who—me? Go over there an' git tangled up in a bunch uh calico, sweat my head off, an' like as not ketch rheumatiz ridin' home in the dead o' night?" Gloomy snorted. "I reckon not!" But as dusk drew on, Reb saw him surreptitiously slicking his tangled hair down with grease and making ineffectual dabs at his boots with a gunny sack.

"How 'bout it, Doc?" Reb accosted Lantry after supper. "Yuh goin' along?"

"Naw." Doc was almost huffy. "Why should I? None of them women want t' say goodby t' me."

Reb's smile was deliberately provoking. "The men folks 'll be there," he said. "It won't hurt none to mix with 'em."

"You go on an' do yore mixin'," Doc told him brusquely.

Reb made sure that his shave was close, gave a last yank to his kerchief, and said, "C'mon, Gloomy. Time to pull out."

"I tole yuh I wasn't figgerin' to go," Jepson began testily, stealing a glance at Doc.

Reb disappointed him by refusing to argue. "Oka-a-y. I'll be seein' yuh," he sang out, pulling on his coat as he left.

Gloomy followed him to the door. "Shore yuh don't need nobody t' look after yuh, now?" he called uncertainly.

"Well, I might—" Santee grinned.

"I better go 'long, then," was Gloomy's decision.

They rode away to leave Lantry alone in the dugout. Reb wondered how long it would take him to make up his mind to come too.

The Cameron ranch was a blaze of lights as they

drew near. Laughter and talk drifted out over the range; evidently a good many people had already arrived. Wagons stood in the yard, saddle horses lined the corrals, the fences. The music—supplied by two fiddlers, all the talent the Basin could muster—had commenced. Gloomy held back, lingering with a bunch of punchers who had just come, but Reb headed straight for the house.

Ronda and some of the other young people pounced on him at the door. "'Lo, Reb!" "Howdy, Santee," the greetings sounded on every hand. He found himself in a whirl of pleasurable sensations, not the least of which were accounted for by the fact that Ronda was dressed in a dazzling fashion. It left him breathless to look at her.

"The time passed and I was afraid you were not coming," she told him frankly.

"Did you think anything would've kept me away?" he countered. The warmth he put into the words was an answer to his own question.

She gave him her sweetest smile. "I should have been greatly disappointed if anything had," she confided. "It will be some time before I'll have the pleasure of seeing you again, you know."

Reb was only too well aware of the fact. "When're you fixin' to leave?" he inquired, wondering if he could contrive another meeting before then.

"Tomorrow or the next day," she dashed his hopes.

He soon found that he was not to have her as much to himself as he would have liked. One after another the punchers claimed her favor. She was generous with them all. It made Reb writhe, for he was hopelessly in love with her now.

Billy Farragoh was much in evidence. Reb noticed that Ronda gave Billy more dances than anyone else but himself. His consolation was that, liking the boy as he did, he would rather have her dance with him than with another. His own feelings blinded him to the fact that Ronda was falling in love with Billy.

The store at Washakie Point had been closed, and Mrs. Farragoh was present. Neither quick to laugh nor light on her feet, she knew how to be gay on occasion. She and Reb whirled through a square dance to the delight of everyone. After a few minutes she gave up, breathless, but Reb had no thought of stopping. From then on he was the bright star of the party, cracking quips and clowning in his inimitable manner.

Doc Lantry had changed his mind about coming. An hour after Reb arrived, he walked in alone. Finding a place among the older men, he lit one of the cigars Jube Cameron was handing around, drank what was offered him, and made no pretense of joviality.

The party ran on through the evening. It was midnight before Reb was aware of it. When Gloomy asked him what time he was starting for home he made an evasive answer, but the fleeting time brought him to himself. He determined to make an attempt at some kind of a talk with Ronda. It would not be easy; but if he could get in a word that would tell her where he stood it would help a lot.

He was working his way toward where Ronda stood surrounded by punchers, with that view in mind, when a shot from outside the house laid a hush on them all. Women stared toward the windows questioningly. Several men, Ronda's father among them, made hastily for the door.

Santee was one of the first to reach the open. He was not long in discovering whence the signal shot had come. In the ranch yard stood a motionless horse, and in its saddle, darkly silhouetted against the stars, swayed a rider. The men crowded forward.

"It's one o' yore boys, Jube," a man declared. And addressing the mounted man: "What's wrong, Shorty? Why don't yuh speak up?"

The puncher lifted a hand in which dangled his six-shooter. The movement overbalanced him. He plunged toward the ground like a man with the starch completely gone out of him. Those near at hand caught and lowered him.

"He's been shot!" exclaimed one of them. "There's blood all over 'im. . . . Git a light, somebody!"

An ominous silence held while a lantern was quickly brought. By its rays they saw the gaping wound in the throat of the victim. Jube Cameron confirmed the identification of the man as Shorty Ducro, one of his riders from Upper Shoshone Meadows, where the Cameron beef cut was being held.

A whisky bottle had been brought with the lantern. A little of the liquor was poured into Ducro's mouth. He choked, shuddering, and his eyelids fluttered.

"Quiet, now!" Cameron warned, bending over the man. "He's tryin' to say somethin'."

"Big—fight—herd's gone—I—I can't—" Ducro managed, and then, a stricture closing his throat, he strained forward and relaxed, limp.

"He's gone," said Jube Cameron bleakly, after a brief examination.

"It's a dang shame! . . . But you got some idee where yuh stand, Jube," a grizzled veteran spoke up from the edge of the assemblage. "From the looks of things, it means rustlers."

The words struck a momentary silence of their own over these men. The news of Ducro's arrival, wounded, having found its way into the house, had put an end to the festivities. Everybody except the women joined the group in the yard. They all had a word to say.

"Wal! Might's well git organized an' start fer Jackson's Hole," suggested a big man, obviously a friend of Cameron's. "Mebbe we c'n head off the skunks that done this."

Others dissented. "We don't have t' look that fur away from home. How 'bout Lucas an' Tapper—them fellers up in the Owl Creeks?" one of them pointed out. "They didn't show up here t'night. I'll bet they know somethin' about this!" Several agreed with him.

A couple of the boys carried Shorty Ducro's body to the bunk house, but the rest remained where they were. Reb Santee had nothing to say, listening keenly. He was glad he and Lantry and Gloomy had come to the gathering. It lifted them above the slightest suspicion. There was even a look of gratification on Doc's thin features as he edged nearer the discussion; but he too held his peace.

"There ain't nothin' to be picked up here, that's shore," Jube Cameron put in now. "I aim to git out to the bed grounds in a hurry." Gathering those of his men who had come in for the party, he made ready to ride.

The affair at the ranch was breaking up fast now. The wagons were pulling away, some with only the wives of the ranchers to drive them. Many had volunteered to ride with Cameron against the common enemy of the range. They got away hurriedly in a well-armed body.

Reb found time for only the briefest of farewells with Ronda. She was deeply affected by Shorty's tragic death, and she listened to Reb's words as if her mind was far away. Reb's own thoughts were uneasy as he made ready to ride back to Ghost Creek with Doc Lantry.

Chapter IX

A MAN'S GAME

D OC, yuh might as well come clean," Reb told
Lantry soberly. "What do yuh know about
this business?"

The lights and the activity of the Cameron ranch
were far behind. They were riding over the dark range
in the crisp, star-lit night.

"I don't know anything about it!" Doc flared up.
"Yuh seen where I was all evenin'." He sounded
injured, and at the same time argumentative.

Santee beheld Lantry's belated appearance at the
party in a new light, or he thought he did. He had
long since learned that hardly a move the man made
was as innocent as it appeared. Doc's protestations
now didn't even make him hesitate. They rasped and
exasperated him. But Doc headed off his questions,
denying all knowledge of what had taken place at the
C 8 bed grounds. His attitude was that somebody else
had beaten them to a good thing.

"Yuh sound mighty interested, now it's all over," he
sneered, unable to resist the opportunity for so telling
a thrust.

Reb ignored it. He didn't see fit to explain that of
all the chances for rustling in the Basin, the beef herd
belonging to Ronda Cameron's father would have been
his last choice.

"It don't matter who done this," he declared bluntly.
"They was damn careless to go killin' a man."

Doc reserved his opinion, turning Reb off with a growl.

Ghost Creek was reached in a silence fraught with antagonism. Reb wasn't done yet. He proved it by making his own investigations. In the ranch yard he found fresh droppings and sign enough to tell him that riders had been there recently, four or five in number.

"So this is why yuh turned up at Cameron's party—an hour late! Damn yuh, Lantry, yuh lied to me, an' now I know it." In the light of the lantern, Reb's grin was conspicuous by its absence. "Who was they?" he broke off.

Doc glowered. Reb had him cornered and he knew it. "The Logans," he muttered.

"The Sundance Kid an' his crowd?" Santee had not expected that answer. He was surprised, and disgusted too. "Yuh knew they was doin' it, an' yuh covered 'em. . . . Come on; tell the rest of it!" he grated.

Sullenly Lantry admitted the truth. The Logans, Bob Leigh, Flat Nose George Curry and Harry Lonabaugh had pulled in a few minutes after Reb left, with plans to run off the Cameron steers. They were driving them into the Lost Cabin wilderness. It would be daylight before Cameron could hope to pick up the trail, Doc pointed out. That would give the Kid and his friends all the time they needed.

Doc's attitude, as he explained all this, was one of angry indignation. Reb's cool domination of the affair rankled in him, a cankering worm burrowing deeper and deeper. "What the hell's eatin' yuh?" he snapped, as he concluded. "If somebody else makes a haul, an' folks know our hands are clean, that'll make it easier fer us later on!"

Reb was not satisfied with any such superficial reading of the situation. The openly voiced suspicions against Ike Lucas and Stony Tapper had told him that Cameron and his men would ride to their place and question them. He said so.

"Yuh was free with them two, an' now they got a line on us," he charged. "How do yuh know they won't steer that posse over here to save their own hides?"

Doc scoffed the suggestion away, or tried to. But Reb knew that Tapper and Lucas hated him; they would do anything in their power to strike back. He was disinclined to take any chances.

"I'm goin' to ride to their place right now an' have it out with 'em," he decided with characteristic promptness.

"Lot uh sense in that, ain't there?" Lantry blasted him sarcastically. "Yuh ought to git there jest in time to meet Jube Cameron." His tone said there was little doubt what would happen in that event.

Reb had already taken that possibility into consideration. He knew he would have to reach the little spread in the Owl Creek Mountains before the cattlemen arrived there, and get away, too. If Cameron took his men to the bed grounds at Upper Shoshone Meadows before he did anything else, there was a chance.

"When Jube gits up there, he won't find anything but the leavin's of Lucas an' Tapper," he said with grim assurance.

Lantry's thin lips curled in a scornful smile. He offered no further deterrent, nor would Santee have listened to any. He was already busy with hasty preparations for getting a start.

A few minutes later he pulled away from Ghost

Creek on a fresh horse. The early morning hours held a steely edge of frost. Reb let the pony warm up and then struck out at a distance-eating pace. He knew where Tapper and Lucas's place was. It had been pointed out to him by Lantry himself.

Following a ridge up the flank of the Owl Creeks, he kept a sharp lookout. There was every likelihood that Cameron had dispatched a handful of men up here direct. Reb had no intention of showing himself to anyone but the men he had come to see.

Dawn light streaked the sky as he drew out at the head of a gulch and entered the fringes of pine and aspen. The shack occupied by Lucas and Tapper was not far ahead now. He approached it cautiously, making sure that no one had been before him. The way seemed clear.

The pair had not gotten up yet. No smoke curled from the rusted tin pipe jutting above the roof of the weathered shack. The door was propped shut from the inside. Reb battered it with the barrel of his six-gun.

A groaning yawn sounded from within. After a moment, "Who's there?" came in a gruff voice. Reb had no desire to be greeted with a gun barrel stuck through a crack. He banged again. Feet thumped; someone muttered curses; a stick clattered. The door creaked back.

There was a momentary silence. Then: "Whut in hell're you doin' here?"

Stony Tapper stood in the opening in his stocking feet, his hair tousled, the clothes he had not bothered to remove all awry on him. In that first instant of recognition his eyes had blazed up, then were as swiftly veiled. His tone was hostile.

Santee wasted no time in explanations. "Get ready to pull out of here, both of yuh," he directed curtly.

Tapper's swarthy face gradually set in lines of opposition. Behind him Ike Lucas burst into invective, venting a savage morning temper. He had taken in the import of that brief, distinct order, as had his partner; recognized the voice that delivered it.

Reb pushed into the shack to have them both under his eye. Tapper showed resistance. It only earned him a thrust that sent him reeling back. He caught himself and crouched, his lips working, his thought darting frantically to his gun, hanging on a broken chair ten feet away.

"Do we have this all over again?" said Reb. He was grinning now, eyes a-dance; but there was something wolfish about him that counseled caution.

The two heeded it. Ike Lucas had not made a move, arrested on the edge of his bunk, shivering slightly at the rawness of the air.

He said: "Where d'you git off, tellin' us what t' do?"

Reb surveyed them both alertly.

"Are yuh goin', or not?" His soft words made them jump; but after a moment's recovery, Tapper jerked out intolerantly:

"No!" He glared an inarticulate hatred, and added: "Did Lantry send yuh to us, or was it yore own brainstorm?"

Reb read instantly the set of the wind. The pair were convinced that Doc Lantry and himself wanted the Basin all to themselves. Their first impulse was to resist eviction for any such reason.

"If it'll help yuh any to know, Jube Cameron's beef

herd was run off last night, an' a man killed," he told them.

"An' so yuh want us to ride away with the blame, eh?"

It was Tapper who spoke; or rather, snarled. Reb turned his blue eyes on him, and his smile broadened. "Yuh can ride away with it, or yuh can take it here. Tapper, no less than five of the boys at Cameron's party voiced suspicions of you two. They're on the peck now. Prove to 'em yuh know nothin' about last night's work, an' there's still a few activities you've got left to explain away. You know better'n I do whether yuh can or not. They'll be here before yuh have time to agree on a story, if yuh don't make it fast."

Ike Lucas sputtered into noisy vituperation, but Stony Tapper was the dominant one of the two. A look of shrewdness crept into his hard features as he made decisive rejoinder:

"It don't go over, Santee. We're wise to yore game— all of it. Yo're tryin' to put us away, an' I will give it to yuh, yuh come flat out with it. But I reckon we've got 'nough on you an' Lantry to return the favor." He had become defiant. "Why, dammit, it's no news to me that yo're hooked up with the Sundance Kid's crowd! Mebbe Jube Cameron'll be interested to know that, an' a few other things, like where them hosses come from he was buyin' off of yuh."

Reb began to sweat. Would these men prove too obstinate? If they remained now to meet Cameron's men, the course they would take was certain. He saw with real annoyance that in Stony Tapper he had a certain shrewd intelligence to cope with. He made an effort to be equal to it. His laugh was jarring.

"I should've thought yuh had Harve Logan's part in this figured out the first time I told yuh where to get off," he responded coolly. "Shore I belong to his crowd." He felt safe in making the statement, for it was pretty widely known among the night-riding gentry that a yeast of rapid growth had begun to work through the Wild Bunch, as the gang headed by the Logans and their friends was called. In careless words, Reb elaborated on his connection with them. "Since yo're so wise about other things," he wound up, his voice thin with the barely-veiled threat, "mebbe buckin' me won't learn yuh much till it's too late." He affected an indifference to the outcome that was telling in its boldness.

Lucas and Tapper stared at him intently. Reb had put another face on the situation in a hurry. They had no desire to be marked for extermination by the Wild Bunch. Although nothing of the kind had been put into words, they were keenly alive to its possibility.

Lucas floundered up from his bunk, haste in his actions. He pulled his boots on without a word, and Tapper followed suit. It was the latter who stole a glance out of the window. He had not forgotten Santee's warning—disbelieved at the time it was given—that Cameron's riders would soon arrive. He suddenly did not want anything to do with them, bereft as he was of the story he would have told.

Reb, for his part, was ready to withdraw without further parley. He could only hope that the seed he had sown would bear fruit. The stubbornness of these two had already consumed more time than he could well spare.

"Yuh can make up yore own minds what you'll do,"

he said, turning toward the door. "I'm goin'." He stepped out.

He was back in an instant. "An' I wouldn't waste no time, either, if I was you," he flung at them. "They're comin' at yuh right now."

Still without anything to say, Tapper and Lucas hustled through the door for a look. Santee didn't have to point out the distant horsemen for them. Nor did the fact that these riders were converging on the place from both the south and west leave any doubt as to the nature of their errand.

"We better be leavin'," Lucas exclaimed nervously, shooting a look at Tapper. Stony made answer by starting for the tumbledown corral. Stepping up on his own mount, Reb watched them saddle their horses. They were soon ready.

"Which way yuh ridin', Santee?" Tapper snapped out as he swung aboard.

"With you," Reb responded tersely. "D'yuh think I want to explain to them fellers why I got here first?"

There was no more to be said. Without delay they turned into a canyon and followed its winding course upward. Cameron's men were several miles to the rear, but they had seen the hasty departure from the shack. There would be no time lost while they closed in and came on.

Reb prudently kept Tapper and Lucas ahead of him. He found himself in a position of double jeopardy. The last thing he could afford now would be to have the pursuing riders overhaul him. At the same time he was not entirely safe in the company of these two small-time rustlers. Ike Lucas, if not Tapper, would have no compunctions about shooting him out of the saddle. It was up to him to give the man no shadow of a chance.

For miles they were hard pressed. The posse had drawn up with surprising speed. The determination that drove this pursuit was not pleasant to contemplate. Lucas, at least, showed signs of cracking under the gruelling strain. "Gawd!" he burst out once. "Why'd we take it on the run? Mebbe we could've talked our way out. Blast you, Santee; yo're to blame fer this!" He spat blistering oaths and screwed around in his saddle repeatedly, hampering his horse.

"Shut up an' ride!" Reb told him, brutally brief.

Tapper unexpectedly seconded him in this. "There ain't nothin' to be gained by bellyachin'," he averred.

The trail became rougher and rougher as they penetrated deep into the untracked wilds of the Owl Creek Mountains. Though it was not far behind, the pursuit had been lost to sight for several hours by the time Santee judged he could afford to pull away from the others.

He chose his opportunity with care. Ike Lucas presented no difficulties; prodded by fears, he pushed on with no regard for the saving of his horse. Tapper was more cautious, keeping reasonably close to Santee and a little ahead. Nevertheless he was unaware of what had taken place until Reb had been gone a good five minutes, swinging sharply aside on ground that was unlikely to show tracks, and striking away at right angles. Santee spent an anxious hour before he was sure he had flanked Cameron's posse safely. Then he set his course in a wide curve back toward the Basin, taking his time now, but not relaxing his vigilance until there could be no question he was in the clear.

The sun swung low in the west when he rode up to the ranch on Ghost Creek. Doc Lantry met him, hawk-faced.

"Lord, yuh shore had me guessin' when yuh didn't come back," he ejaculated his relief. "What happened up there?"

"Lucas and Tapper are ridin'," Reb informed him easily. "They was pushed purty hard. I had to go with 'em a ways."

Lantry stared, his face reddening. "They took out, when yuh told 'em to?" he demanded incredulously. "The damn fools! . . . How'd yuh manage it, Reb?"

"I know how to manage in a pinch," was Reb's cool response. "It's dog eat dog, in this game. A man's got no place in it if he can't take care of himself."

Chapter X

RIDING BLIND

O N the third day after the rustling of the C 8 beef cut, half-a-dozen trail-gaunted men rode up to Lantry's ranch a little after noon, their horses jaded. Jube Cameron was at their head. Once back in the Basin, the posse had split up, to make its way home; these men were on their way to the Cameron spread.

Doc and Reb stepped out of the dugout to meet them. It was the former who put the question burning on his tongue.

"Wal, boys! Yuh made a real ride of it. How'd yuh make out?"

"We did our work the best way we knew how," Cameron replied. His grim expression did not relax as he explained that they had gone to Lucas and Tapper's place in the hills, that the pair had fled and they had clung to the trail without let-up. On the morning of the second day they had caught up; Stony Tapper, game to the last, had been slain in the gun-fight which ensued. Ike Lucas made good his escape.

"Did yuh find the steers?" Lantry put in. Watching him, it was easy for Reb to read Doc's thoughts. He was wondering about the Sundance Kid, asking himself whether the latter had gotten clear without difficulty.

"Not a trace of 'em," Cameron admitted. But there was no doubt in him, or in his companions, that they had gone after the right men. Innocent men did not run, he pointed out. It was plain that confederates of Lucas and Tapper had gotten the steers out of the country. "There was three of 'em when they pulled away from the shack up in the Owl Creeks," Jube went on, in corroboration of this. "That's enough to tell me there was more of 'em . . . My foreman says there must've been half-a-dozen that shot it out at the bed grounds."

"Who was the extra man, up in the hills?" Lantry queried. "Did yuh git a flash at him?" Santee awaited the answer, a cold chill visiting his spine.

"No," Cameron's response relieved him. "He made a clean getaway, whoever he was. We couldn't even cut his trail. But I reckon he savvies how healthy it'll be fer him an' his kind around here from now on."

There was more about the affair, and then Cameron and his men rode on, anxious to get home. They left a silence behind them in which both Reb and Lantry were busy with their own thoughts.

Doc was far from pleased. What he had just learned made him realize that there was no nonsense about these Wind River men when they went after a rustler. When he spoke, it was to touch nearly the thing which preoccupied Santee:

"Wal, how do yuh explain gittin' Tapper killed fer a crime he didn't commit, to yoreself?" he growled.

Reb met him with a level regard. "Never mind, Lantry. He had it comin', an' you know it. They would've caught up with him sooner or later. Yuh don't seem to get that I was coverin' you as well as myself."

"That's dealin' yoreself out of it, all right," Doc retorted. He had more to say, but Reb let him think it left him untouched. He did not need to be told that

Lantry cared nothing for Lucas and Tapper, or what happened to them. All his attention was concentrated on the vengeance the Logans and their companions had so narrowly escaped. To himself Red said that Tapper would not have been killed if he had gone when he had first told him to pull out.

The rustling and the activities of the posse had made a change in the plans of a number of the women. Ronda Cameron and her mother, at least, had not left yet for Lander by the time Jube returned from the chase. Santee learned this on the day he rode over to see if there was anything he could do in the absence of the men.

He didn't try to conceal his pleasure. Little of the work got itself done that he had come to do. He had a whole, happy unexpected afternoon with Ronda during which the problems and perplexities of the recent past rolled off his back as if they had never been. They did a dozen things they had planned to do together, and somehow missed doing before; even the addition of Billy Farragoh to the little party could not dull the edge of Reb's large contentment.

No girl in his experience had ever had the effect on him that this one exerted. Her sweetness and simplicity he could only contemplate with wonder. That she was so frank and natural with him did little to prosper his suit. Her candid gray eyes, the demure curve of humor at the corners of her soft lips, left him tongue-tied. The wayward tendrils of jet hair at the nape of her neck, the round smoothness of her arms—a dozen and one things about her warm, strong face and happy nature—only served to augment the inexplicable trouble that was with him whenever he thought about her.

Once more he lost his chance to speak. Ronda, who thought of him as the most joyous and gay-hearted of irresponsible companions; who admired his manliness and feared for his recklessness, had no inkling of the thing that was in his mind.

On the day after Cameron's return, Reb rode over to the C 8 ranch again. It was well he did so. The women were making ready to depart at last; they had little time to lose. Each day now the sun shone less, the sky wore a steely look that threatened snow. They faced the prospect of a rigorous trip if they did not get away before the winter storms closed down.

Several other women were starting with the Cameron party. Husbands and brothers were present. Much to his disgruntlement, Reb found time for no more than a brief exchange with Ronda, and that after he thought he had lost all chance for any. She and her mother were busy with last-minute preparations when he arrived. He joined the men, warming their reddened hands at the stove in the kitchen.

"Well, Reb," said a rancher from over west, "you'll see a real winter this year." Santee had talked much in a casual way of his life in the rimrocks of southern Utah, where the winters were more moderate. "There's no foolin' around about it here in the Basin," the man went on.

"We ought to 'nitiate him on the winter round-up," another suggested.

Reb was only half listening, his mind centered on Ronda, moving about in another part of the house in her preoccupation with feminine concerns, the clear tones of her voice coming through the door occasionally. But when the man who had last spoken jabbed him playfully in the ribs, he swung back with a jar.

"Shore, I'll take a whirl at it," he grinned.

He had heard before of the winter round-up, which was no real round-up, but an organized effort by the Wind River stockmen to keep their cattle from drifting out of the Basin when the snows buried the grass deep under the drifts and freezing winds blew down out of the north. Never one to shrink before the rigors of his calling, Reb had no fears of riding the line in the worst weather.

The talk went on, punctuated with easy silences—the deliberate discussion of shrewd men with time to think. At last the women were ready. They crowded themselves and their luggage into a democrat wagon. The men gathered around to assist, calling farewells, cracking jokes about the men of Lander.

Ronda turned to Reb before she climbed up. There was a ready smile on his lips as she put her small hand in his big one.

"Good-bye, Reb," she said simply. "I haven't forgotten what you did for me. I never shall. I will look forward to seeing you when we return in the spring." There was a wistfulness in her tone that said she meant every word of it.

Reb felt a warm glow steal over him. He found his tongue after a fashion.

"It won't give you no more pleasure than it does me, Ronda," he said fervently. "I'll be lookin' ahead real keen." He little realized, then, that the day was not far off when the arrival of spring would mean to him something vastly different from this, and that he was to wish for its delay with all the strength of his being.

She responded with a ravishing smile, and talked on for a moment; but with that smile something reached out from her delightfully to confuse him and entrap his senses. He could only stammer out a thoughtless reply to her unheard remarks. A moment later, she had climbed to her seat; the driver picked up the reins; there was a chorus of exchanges as the vehicle moved off—and she was gone.

Winter settled down without much delay. There was a knife-like edge to the ceaseless blasts of Boreas; for days the gust-driven clouds spat flakes, and the massive, gleaming shoulders of the Wind River peaks were obscured from sight. Although Lantry bothered himself little, Reb and Gloomy busied themselves making the dugout snug for the months to come. Not long after the task was completed, the first real snow whitened the range and made the ground crunch in the crisp mornings under the hasty step of boots.

Three days later, the Sundance Kid and his friends arrived at the ranch, on their way south to Colorado. Heavily clothed, they were seeking a milder climate, their breath hanging on the air in white plumes. They tramped into the dugout stamping their feet to warm them.

"Wal, Kid, yuh drew it purty fine when yuh left here last, whether yuh know it or not," Doc greeted.

Logan was unimpressed. "We traded lead with a few cowpokes," he responded indifferently. "After that it was jest work." An old and seasoned campaigner, there was a casualness in his manner that always made him seem inattentive. Yet he was alert to everything about him. He read without difficulty in the way Lantry told of the misplaced retribution which had overtaken

Tapper and Lucas, that Doc had something to tell him which he hesitated to voice.

"What's on yore mind?" he braced Doc later, in a corner of the dugout. Reb had stepped out to break up a little wood.

"Logan, it's young Santee," Lantry began, with an assumption of frankness. "He ain't really with us, an' it bothers me. I told yuh what he done to Ike an' Stony. He's been makin' friends all over the Basin—doin' their work fer 'em—he's gone on Cameron's girl—an' now, damned if he ain't fixin' to take part in this here winter ridin'." Doc shook his head soberly. "I can't make up my mind about him. He's got too much on us to pass over."

They talked it over in lowered tones. With characteristic bluntness, once he had got the situation straight in his mind, the Sundance Kid carried Doc's grievances straight to Reb himself.

"Santee," he said, "I hear yuh expressed the opinion we was damn fools to plug that Cameron puncher. How 'bout it?" Still amiable, almost negligent, his tone carried a challenge it would have been fatal to take lightly.

Reb found himself in a tight spot. He had more than half expected Lantry to make the attempt to turn Logan and the others against him, but he had not looked for it so soon. Long ago he had satisfied himself of the lethal potentialities of the Kid, and knew that in this moment his own test had come. He thought swiftly.

"Why shore, Kid," he responded, with a nice shade of gravity; "I don't mind sayin' I'm some disgusted with yuh. I know Doc can't see it," he added, with a meaning glance at that individual; "but the way I look at it, it's stupid to run these chances so close to yore hideouts."

The boldness of his opinion served to catch the attention of them all. They gathered around to follow what they believed was coming. Even Lantry began to feel that it would result in nothing less than annihilation for Reb.

"Suppose you explain that," the Kid told him, a trifle more dryly.

Reb proceeded to do so, first telling his own version of the part he had played in establishing the false scent the stockmen's posse had followed, resulting in death for Stony Tapper. He repeated the estimate of the pair he had once expressed to Doc. "They didn't use no sense at all," he declared and proved it by relating their crudeness at the store at Washakie Point. "But Doc played up to 'em, an' they both knowed what our game was. A little pinchin', an' they would shore's hell've spilled it all to Cameron's crowd. We would've had to clear out, an' you boys wouldn't've had this place to come to no more."

Logan nodded understandingly, his misleading liquid eyes slitted as he glanced at Lantry. Doc scowled. "Go on, Reb," said the Kid; and Reb continued with renewed energy, a trace of authority creeping into his tone as his inventive inspiration carried him away. It was too late now to think of where his ready tongue and nimble brain were taking him.

The gist of his suggestions was that if they were smart they would organize their activities on an even greater scale, banding all the frequenters of the Outlaw Trail with a common interest; establishing an even closer-knit chain of hideouts, after the fashion of the Underground Railway of the South; and carrying on their depredations at a safer distance and regulating them to a system, instead of by the sporadic and haphazard method they were using now.

"That way yuh could levy on the railroads an' banks an' mines—nab the big money, from those who can afford it—an' after a job, the boys'd simply fade from the scene without leavin' a trace." Reb jerked his chin downward decisively, as if he had thought all this out carefully, and couldn't see a loophole or a flaw in it.

"By God, he's got somethin' there, boys!" Flat Nose George exclaimed admiringly. Others nodded. Even the Kid caught fire at the idea. He had many questions to ask.

Reb emerged from the discussion which followed with a different status. No longer could the insinuations of Doc injure his standing with these men. He had painted a picture of easy spoils that left them amazed at his cleverness. Very definitely it made him their real leader, in brains, at least. They deferred to his judgment on a hundred points, while Lantry, frowning and none too well satisfied, kept his own counsel. He alone, of them all, suspected the truth—that Reb had talked his way out of another jam with his usual adeptness.

The Wild Bunch stayed over a day, perfecting plans. There was much to talk about. Excited by his prominence, Reb kept them all laughing over his jokes. Then, the next night, they were gone.

"Dammit, Santee, you won't go through with this!" Doc Lantry snarled, the minute they were alone. Suppressed indignation twanged in his tone; his lips were set in the vise of his distrust.

"Do yuh mean that—or are yuh hopin' I won't?" Reb countered, grinning. There was a blank opacity in his blue eyes which baffled Lantry, left him impotent with wrath. But inwardly, Reb was asking himself the same question the other had posed.

Would he go through with this thing? He thought of Ronda Cameron, of his hopes of her and her faith in him, and told himself that of course he could not. It wasn't to be thought of. Yet neither had he any desire to leave the Basin, where, as long as he remained, the influence of the Wild Bunch could reach out at will to touch him. What was he going to do?

"My own imagination is doin' me dirt," he thought with an amusement tinctured with chagrin. "I'm gettin' into this deeper'n I had any thought of doin', jest tryin' to pull my foot out of the bog. Damn Doc an' his jealousy, anyway!"

Fortunately all his lightly voiced plans must wait on the arrival of spring. It gave him some months' grace of decision, of continued freedom of conscience, and—lightness of heart. It was the latter impulse that bade him put his fears away for the time being.

"I never got in a fix yet that I didn't get out of somehow," he consoled himself. He was willing to leave it up to the same Providence which had aided him in the past to see to it that his good fortune continued to hold.

Chapter XI

BOREAS' THREAT

WINTER on Wind River can be long and dreary. Reb Santee found it so. There was no more riding to the Cameron ranch to spend a careless afternoon in the delightful company of Ronda; no more touring the Basin for the first diversion that came to hand. Late in November a cold snap set in that kept the three men in the dugout for a week. The direst consequences of the coming spring could not make Reb grateful for this dragging isolation.

"Yo're worse'n a trapped cougar," Doc growled at him, nursing a villainous-smelling pipe by the fire. "Why don't yuh settle down, or else git out an' ride it off."

"I'll do that," Reb flashed at him, with a challenging grin. "I'll go over an' find out from Cameron when they start ridin' the line." Before the Wild Bunch left, he had said that his offer to participate in the winter round-up was a whim; he probably would not go through with it. Now he embraced the prospect with eagerness.

"Go 'head," Lantry flung back. "This place can't be no worse with you gone than it is with yuh in it." His lips essayed a sour smile as he said it, but his eyes were implacable.

Wrapping himself against the bitter weather, glad to get on the move at any cost, Reb rode away on a steaming pony. At the Cameron ranch he learned that the line camps to the south had been established, the riding already begun.

"We thought yuh decided to let it slide, or we would've let yuh know," said Jube.

Reb told him no, he was anxious for something to do. He'd ride out now, he thought, and join the boys. Cameron made it plain that it struck him as being a fine idea. He was just leaving himself.

"Plenty men out there now," he said; "but some of 'em have to git home occasional. They c'n shore use yuh, Santee."

In his company Reb rode south with the wind at his back, feeling better than he had felt for days. It was good to have to care for the cattle lurking in draws or pawing down through the snow for grass. He'd been away from all this for some time now; this was like coming home. It served to strengthen the sense of security he had built up, like a wall, between himself and the shadow that threatened him from the future.

At Wolf Flat the line riders welcomed him with grateful warmth. Not only were they glad for his sunny company, but it was clear that his willingness to help, although he had no investment in the Basin stock, meant something to them. No one drew extra pay for this work, though it did keep some of the punchers off the grub line. Reb would draw no time at all.

He was not the only one, however. He found Billy Farragoh taking his place among the others. They teamed up without ado, and the strenuous days which followed saw them much together on the frozen range and in camp.

But there was a lot more to it than pleasant companionship. The winter had begun in violence; it promised, and displayed, a further severity. There were days when one heavy snow after another swooped and whistled about the riders, when the mercury dropped into a bottomless well, and it was all they could do in the few hours they dared remain in the saddle at a time to keep the cattle from drifting south to scatter for miles along the lower Wind River valley.

Reb stood it with the stoicism of the seasoned veteran. Billy endured without complaint, his limbs numb and his skin turned blue. Once he frosted his face so dangerously it had to be rubbed with snow. Another time he disappeared, and Santee rode in search of him for more than an hour, fear gnawing at his heart, before he found young Farragoh afoot and leading a lamed horse, though he was not even sure where he was. It was a close call for Billy. Still he persisted. Reb could not withhold a growing admiration for the boy's qualities. The bond of friendship between them tightened; for Billy, by this time, accorded the other a whole-souled devotion it would have taken a harder man than Reb to resist.

December dragged out toward its end. Santee rode back to the ranch on Ghost Creek but once during that time, and then only to pick up some extra clothes he had left behind. Gloomy and Doc were hibernating like bears. The latter pounced on Reb as if he had brooded long, awaiting this chance.

"Yo're a fool, Santee!" he exploded. "Whut in hell do yuh expect to git out of this, anyhow?"

Reb overlooked the venom in his tone. "Trouble with you, Doc," he retorted deliberately, "yo're so used to somethin' for nothin', yuh think yo're gettin' gypped if yuh have to work at all."

Lantry snorted intolerantly. He went on arguing sourly until Reb was glad to escape from the dugout once more. "There he goes!" Doc raged, when the puncher had ridden away. "He can't wait to see the last of us. . . . More I see of him, the better I think o' you, Gloomy."

"It all boils down t' what kind o' fool a feller'd rather be," Jepson responded, with a long face. "This here's no place t' spend a winter. We'll regret it, one way or 'nother. Like as not they'll bring Reb home froze stiff as a poker, one o' these days."

"It'll simplify things fer me if they do," said Lantry with sudden fierceness.

Christmas, in the main camp to the south, was a disappointing affair, if there was anyone to care. One day a puncher rode in to declare that the holiday had slipped by them unnoticed. Another claimed it had not; that Christmas fell on the following day. All had an opinion. No one was sure. They celebrated anyway, with extra liquor, juicy, fried steaks—though these were no novelty—and beat biscuit; and the days slipped by. For Reb, even that was more pretentious than many a Christmas he had spent in the past.

There was no argument about New Year's, for something came up to banish it from their minds. One day a brace of the boys were taken down with heavy colds. Jube Cameron would not hear of their standing their trick in the saddle. The others doubled up and the day was got through cheerfully, if not easily.

"We'll make out," Reb said in answer to the sufferers' expressions of disgust at their condition.

The next day three more had colds, and the first two were worse. They lay in their bunks sick and wan-looking, burning with fever one minute, shivering the next.

"It's the grippe," Jube Cameron announced soberly. He looked out of the cabin window. Snow whipped past in a smother, the sky was heavy. A penetrating chill seeped through the chinks of the logs. "Be tough if we have to stand a siege of that out here. I'll ride to Washakie Point for medicine if they ain't no better by mornin'."

But the next day, Cameron himself was down, and two more with him. Billy Farragoh was one of them. Reb Santee was as yet untouched, but he began to see the situation in a serious light.

"I'll ride to the Point myself," he told Jube. "You better stay in—yuh can look after the others till I get back, anyway."

The storm had slacked off during the night. It was colder, with a bitter wind. Reb got an early start. It was all he could manage to make the blue roan buck the wind and the drifts. Because it was easier, he fol-lowed the ridges which led toward Ghost Creek. Once there, he stopped at the dugout.

"Now what?" Doc Lantry demanded, as he stepped in.

Reb described the situation at the line camp. "No-body's said a word, but we c'd shore use you an' Gloomy till we pull through, Doc," he concluded.

"No sir!" Lantry refused flatly, before Gloomy could speak. "An' what's more, Santee, if yo're carryin' them germs yuh can keep right on goin'!" He presented a front of unfeeling opposition that made it useless to argue.

Reb reached the store at Washakie Point shortly after noon. Mrs. Farragoh, bulwarked cozily within, was surprised to see him. In a few words he explained why he had come. Billy's mother gave him such simple remedies as she had on hand. Anxious as she was about her son, she made no special plea for his care.

"It's a shame it's so fur down there. I dunno's I c'd git the wagon through," she said thoughtfully. "But if yuh think I ought, I'll make the attempt an' take care of them boys."

"No, no," Reb protested. "I'll make out all right. Reckon yuh don't know I'm a doctor."

"You!" Mrs. Farragoh snorted derisively, her man's eyes raking him from under bushy brows. "You'll be down with the grippe yoreself, after this ride." But she was pleased with him, too.

Promising to return with news in a week's time, Reb rode away. At the camp he found Jube Cameron feverish in his bunk. The other cowmen complained of sore throats. Reb made them all as comfortable as he could and dosed them up. Only Cameron appeared to discern the gravity of their position.

"Yuh better stay 'way from us as much as yuh can, Santee," he croaked. "If you come down with it, we will be in a pickle."

Reb laughed at him. "The Injuns fed me onions when I was a kid," he declared. "I never catch a cold."

He did not, though he spent all the time he could spare astride a pony. It was useless for him to attempt single-handed to stem the southward drift of the cattle, but he did what he could. No one spoke Doc Lantry's name to him, nor did he ever mention the aid Doc had refused. Time dragged by, and the sick were no better. Regularly he made his trips to Washakie Point.

"Doctor Santee," he would announce himself to Mrs. Farragoh, "with a report on my patients. Yuh got any more medicine for me?"

It was at these times that he got really acquainted with Billy's mother, talking of a great many things while he warmed himself at the wood stove or put his legs under her amply-supplied table. The ingeniousness in his puckered blue eyes, the readiness of his humor, warmed her to him. She began to share something of the admiration her son and Ronda Cameron bore him.

"Shore, that boy of yores'll be on his feet before any one of the others," he reassured her more than once. "Billy's thin, but he's made of rawhide; he's got guts. I like him."

To make conversation, she often grumbled at the dearth of business in this season. Reb always listened with attention, agreeing that it was hard; Billy's legal education wasn't coming any closer this way. But what drew Mrs. Farragoh closer to him than anything else was what he did about it.

February turned off milder and less tempestuous; a few of the trails stayed open; and one day Reb showed up at the store when a dozen Shoshone Indians had dropped in to hang around. He looked them over, noting the tightness of their pockets and joshing with them a little. It was not until he transacted his business with Mrs. Farragoh, however, that he made his play.

Wandering about the store under the watchful eyes of the Shoshones, he picked up one of a pile of small round mirrors from the shelf. He examined it attentively. Before he did so he palmed a silver dollar, and to the astonished red men it looked as if in the midst of his investigations he rubbed the dollar off the back of the mirror. He pocketed the dollar and, his face a study, shook the mirror and rubbed another dollar from it.

"This is good," he said interestedly, looking up at the proprietor. "I'll take this. How much is it?"

Without cracking a smile, Mrs. Farragoh told him it was a dollar. He apparently rubbed another dollar off the mirror, and handed it over. "I'm ahead of the game already," he told her. "Much obliged." He turned away, intent on his purchase.

A few minutes later he made ready to leave, but not before he had seen the Indians eagerly digging up dollars to exchange for the miraculous mirrors.

"You scamp, you!" Mrs. Farragoh laughed at him, when he came in a week later. "I sold ten o' them mirrors, what with that foolishness of yores!" She gave him back his dollar. "Them bucks was inclined to kick when they found they couldn't rub off no silver from 'em, but they hesitated when I offered, real pleasant, to trade back; an' the upshot was, they hung on to 'em. . . . What'll you be doin' next?"

Reb grinned, passing it off as he usually did such things.

"Yeah, the boys seem to be pullin' out of it okay," he said, in answer to her questions concerning the influenza sufferers. "All but Jube Cameron, anyway. It's settled on his chest, an' I'm afraid he's bad. . . . Billy'll be gettin' ready to ride in a few days," he added.

Thus reassured, Mrs. Farragoh stuck to the matter in hand. "What about Jube?" she demanded. "Somethin'll have to be done fer him. . . . I better git out there, after all. A little hot goose grease—"

"I been thinkin' of drivin' him in to Lander," Reb confessed. "Reckon I could get through now." His tone said that he was not quite so sure, but it was no part of his plan to think overlong about it.

Mrs. Farragoh looked at him seriously. "Bad as that, is he?" She immediately made her plans to allow him the use of her own wagon, a flat-bed with extra stout wheels.

Reb drove south that afternoon behind a pair of mules. "You'll find 'em tougher," Mrs. Farragoh had said of them. "They'll stand a longer haul. Yuh can't take no chances with Jube, no matter how yuh look at it yoreself."

Arriving at camp, he went at once to the cabin. "How is he now?" he asked in a lowered voice.

Billy Farragoh was around once more. He shook his head. "Not so good, Reb. He was out of his head for a while today."

Santee turned to the rancher's bunk. "What do yuh say, Cameron? I'll drive yuh to Lander to a doctor if you'll take the chance. I got a flatbed wagon out here, an' we'll wrap yuh up good." There was real solicitude in his manner; gratitude in the faces of the other men in the cabin, coughing and weakened as they were. They were well aware it might mean Cameron's life. Reb was the only one among them fit to go.

"Mebbe yuh ought to," whispered Jube hoarsely. "I don't git no better here . . ."

Reb soon had the wagon ready, piled with blankets.

There were a couple of shovels stowed under the seat, and extra harness. He carried Cameron out, bundled heavily, and deposited him in the back. They started off at once. Once settled, Jube said nothing, flushed and breathing stertorously; but his eyes sought the northern horizon even oftener than Reb's did.

It was getting along toward evening. The temperature had risen during the day; the air was muggy, with a hint of fog in the draws. Behind them, the sky darkened to the north, instead of in the east as was its usual wont. The fading light over the whitened range was lowering and sullen. The circumstances carried every promise of snow before morning. And to the fore, beyond snowy trails and many a barren flat across which the storm would boom, Lander was sixty miles away.

"Get-up, boys," Reb spoke to the mules. He pulled up his collar around his ears and settled to the long, hard drive.

Chapter XII

A RACE WITH DEATH

S NOW began to fall as night closed in. It came on
a rising wind with a freezing, knife-like edge.
Had it not been from behind, Reb soon felt he
could not have kept the mules going.

The thickening dark was an impenetrable pall. In
it the snow was only a muffling gray curtain, shifting,
impalpable, yet with a deadly threat. A dozen times
in the first ten miles, Reb stopped to test its depth on
the ground and to shake free the tarpaulin covering
Jube Cameron's prone form.

"This is goin' to be bad, Reb," the latter whispered
once. "Mebbe yuh should've waited till mornin'. If it
gits worse it'll be the end fer both of us."

Making sure the other was wrapped securely, Santee spoke only in gruff encouragement. But as he
climbed back to the seat and clucked to the mules he
realized that Jube had voiced perfectly his own fears.
He cared nothing for himself. His own safety appeared
an insignificant matter; but how inexcusable to lose
Ronda's father in the storm—perhaps to become directly responsible for his death!

The snow, neither heavy nor wet, nevertheless was
piling up. The wagon began to wallow, though the
mules still pulled strongly. It was steadily getting
colder. Reb had got out of the Basin at last, and the
wind keened down Wind River valley as if it were a
corridor. Had it not been for that he would have considered turning back while there was time. But it

would be useless now. And to pull up behind some
protecting barrier would be equally fatal. In his feverish condition Cameron probably could not withstand
the cold for another half-dozen hours in any event.

Reb was turning his plight over in his mind with
slow persistence, when a pin-point of light to the fore
caught his attention. While he did not minimize
its significance, he hailed it coolly. His unbreakable
luck had not yet let him down. So he was thinking.

Ten minutes later he pulled up beside the black
shape of a ranch house. Banging brought a bewhisk-
ered man to the door who directed him in an annoyed
tone to come in at once.

"I got a sick man here from the Basin," Reb told
him, shouting to make himself heard. "Reckon you'll
have to take him in till the storm blows out."

The rancher changed his tune in a hurry. While Reb
staggered to the house with Cameron's bundled frame
in his arms, he slipped into a sheepskin coat and volunteered to look after the team.

"Yuh jest made it in time!" he declared when he
stamped in again, shaking off the snow. "Man, this is
no night to be out. It's gittin' wicked."

Reb was making Cameron comfortable on the floor
beside a roaring fire. "It'll be slower this way—but
mebbe just as shore for Cameron, here, if we get storm-
bound," he responded grimly. "He's got to have a
doctor mighty soon."

Indeed, Jube's chest was more congested than ever.
He coughed and gagged. Fever made his carved face
unnaturally red, his eyes dangerously bright.

"Sho'! That's hell," exclaimed their benefactor with

ready sympathy. "I got a leetle whisky here that may help."

Reb had brought some himself. It revived Cameron somewhat. But Reb would not leave him untended during the night. For hours the wind howled around the little ranch house. Jube fell into a troubled sleep. The two well men watched over him, talking little. It was the rancher who prowled restlessly about.

"Storm's over," he announced, toward morning. "The stars are out. But that wind won't let up. It's shore powerful cold out!"

Reb could feel it, no more than a dozen feet away from the fire. Had he not found this haven, he knew Cameron would be dead now, frozen. But if the snow imprisoned them, making it impossible to move the wagon, it could be only a matter of time. Cameron's condition was even more serious than anyone had supposed.

Dawn found Reb still beside him, sleeplessly vigilant. The man who had taken them in had succumbed to weariness. He dozed in a chair, but roused himself as Reb stirred to build up the fire.

"Wind's dropped," was the first thing he said. "It's still blisterin' cold. Mebbe the sun'll fix that. . . . Glory be!" he ejaculated, from the window. "Will you look at this!"

Santee moved to his side. Beyond the frosted pane they could see that the wind had blown the dry snow heavily. Patches of ground showed almost bare.

"That gives me a slim chance," Reb said unemotionally. "There'll be big drifts. I'll jest have to keep clear of 'em."

The rancher made coffee, which they drank hot and black. Jube Cameron awoke to sip a little of it. Reb gave him more whisky as well. Soon after, he cared for the mules and got ready to push on.

"Better hold off till it warms up a mite," the rancher warned.

Reb only shook his head. "Every hour may mean somethin' to Cameron," he declared. "I ain't wastin' a one."

There was nothing but the cold to delay him now. The frozen sky, though metallic, was clear. Just as the sun flashed over the white-shrouded heights to the east, the mules hit their collars and Mrs. Farragoh's wagon, carrying the sick rancher, rolled down the flats bordering the glittering band of Wind River.

It was a hard trip. Opposite Black Mountain Santee was forced to cross the river. One of the mules fell on the ice. It cost a precious half-hour to get him to his feet. They went on, making time on the barren stretches, losing it when Reb was compelled to turn back and go around. His impatience with these delays got him bogged in a snow-choked draw more than once. But unremitting persistence wore away the miles.

When Cameron's skin turned blue with cold and he began to mutter, Reb abandoned his steady southern drive and struck out for a ranch in a hollow of the hills. More coffee, whisky, and vigorous chafing seemed to revive Jube.

"You'll have to go easy on them stimulants," a grave-faced range-boss told Reb. "One o' these times he won't come out of it."

"How far is it to Lander?" Reb countered abruptly.

"Fifteen, eighteen miles," was the answer.

Reb pushed grimly on. Once again it was late afternoon when Lander hove in sight across the snow. He saw the white plumes of railroad smoke, made out the mottled clutter of buildings, and half-an-hour later rolled into a side street.

His first objective was a doctor's office. Jube was still breathing, but he seemed in a coma. Reb lost no time getting him into a bed under the physician's care. Then he hurried out to locate Ronda and her mother.

"Why, Reb!" cried the girl, running to him at once when she saw him walk into the lobby of the hotel. "How in the world did you— What is it?" she broke off, seeing his soberness.

"It's all right, Ronda. Leastways, I think it is," he amended with difficulty. "But you'll have to tell yore mother." Laboring with his words, he told of her father's illness and the trip he had undertaken to get him to town.

Tears stood in Ronda's eyes when he finished. Without hesitation and without artificiality, she kissed his cheek. "Reb, I can't tell you all that is in my heart. Perhaps that will express a part of it." Her shining eyes begged him to understand.

Reb's own heart swelled. His hands trembled. "Gosh, I—" he stumbled about for something to say; "it wasn't nothin', Ronda. I mean I . . . But yore mother—"

Ronda left immediately to break the news to her.

Stabling the mules and taking a room in a hotel, Reb decided to remain in Lander for the present. A few days would determine Jube Cameron's condition. That Jube was fighting for his life, he knew. But the next day Ronda told him her father had rallied. There was an even chance that he would pull through. With this, Reb's tension relaxed.

In the long periods of waiting between reports, he found Lander an excellent place to be in. Friends were not hard to come by. A poker game in a place down by the tracks netted him almost a hundred dollars. It enabled him to slip the curb and enjoy himself unstintedly. Every afternoon he saw Ronda for a few minutes—seldom longer, for she appeared to find many occupations here, to meet many calls on her time. Except for these meetings, Reb had little to do save what he could dig up.

He was seldom at a loss. It was easy to forget other things when he was hitting it up with a few congenial spirits. This had been his first opportunity to kick over the traces in months, and he took full advantage of it. On the third night of his stay he went further than he intended. It began in a dance hall. The girls fluttered about him continually, and he could neither resist them nor take them seriously—but they succeeded in filling him with liquor, after which things took their natural course.

Lander was not unduly moved when Reb filled an old stage coach with tinseled beauties, hitched on a few unbroken broncs, and rumbled hilariously up and down the main street, shooting out lights and rendering realistic wolf-howls at intervals. The populace was amused, to be sure; but it had been amused before, if not in exactly this way. There was no harm done, except possibly to Reb himself.

He was taken down from the box at the end of his wild ride by a marshal tight of lip but with twinkling eye. He had to pay for the lights; and it was strictly his own fault if he had not enough money left to pay his fine. He spent a day in jail and missed his meeting with Ronda. But the news traveled over town, by word of mouth even before the newspaper printed it, so that she knew why he had not appeared.

Err in haste; repent at leisure. Reb repented sincerely, for he knew his escapade had hurt him with Ronda. His crinkly grin had returned when he saw her again, but it was a shamefaced one.

"Reb, I know you won't do such a thing again," she told him, genuinely hurt. "You remained away from town too long. I don't need to be told you've earned your fun; but must it be that kind? There's so much better stuff in you."

Reb was abject, impatient with himself. But he showed no more of it than he could help. He asked after her father.

"Father's coming along fine," Ronda said, her whole manner changing. "All he needed was expert attention. He ought to be around in another week, the doctor says." She went on to relate how Jube had laughed over Reb's exploit, which had gotten even to him. "He said he was just such a scapegrace himself when he was young," she confessed.

Reb accepted the suggestion with a grain of bitterness. Cameron's willingness to see the humor in the stage coach incident warned him that the rancher had never considered him in the light of a match for his daughter, and was unlikely to do so now.

"Well," he said slowly, "there ain't nothin' to hold me, now he's nearly on his feet again. I'll hit back for the Basin."

He could not leave without receiving Jube's thanks, and those of his wife. Ronda spent most of his last afternoon in town with him. She was as friendly as she had always been; but something had gone out of Reb. He covered it with jests, and got away at last with real relief, hoping time would allow the girl to forget.

"This is somethin' new for me," he mused soberly, heading back for the Basin in the wagon. "It ain't all fun when yuh got somebody else to consider." It had been his first experience of hurting someone beside himself.

By the time he rolled through the Gap late that afternoon, he had regained his good humor. It was March; the storm that accompanied him south had not been repeated. The crew at the winter round-up camp, having recovered, had driven the drifting cattle back to the Basin and were with them now, somewhere up on the bare slopes to the north and west. Reb drove on to Washakie Point.

He reached the store in the evening. Mrs. Farragoh greeted him with real pleasure. There was much to tell her, though he skirted the stage-coach affair by a wide margin. She would not be content with less than a circumstantial account of all that had happened to him during his trip through the storm.

"An' how's Ronda?" she asked more than once, when assured that Jube was safely past his crisis. Reb thought she showed more interest in the girl than in Jube.

He had his own questions to ask, and learned that with the fold-up of the winter riding, Billy had got himself a new job. He was working for Doc Lantry. It left Reb speechless for a moment.

"Lantry's repairin' his fence; I hear he's fixin' to take on some steers this spring," said Mrs. Farragoh.

It had been planned that Reb should stay the night; but he made his excuses now and, saddling his roan at Mrs. Farragoh's corral, rode furiously to Ghost Creek.

Doc and Gloomy and Billy were in the dugout. The boy greeted Reb effusively, but Doc was reserved.

"Wal, do yuh figure to stick around a while now?" he demanded, with thin patience.

"Shore," said Reb easily.

Lantry had little to say, but he remained close at hand. It was not until the next day that Reb found the opportunity he sought for a word with Billy.

"How come yuh landed here?" he queried.

Billy read beyond his lazy inflection. His smile faded. "Why, it will mean a few more dollars toward a year in Lander, where I can study law in Judge Hamer's office," he responded. "I thought it would be nice, being near you, too. Don't you like the idea, Reb?"

Reb didn't. He was determined that Billy should not make the same mistake he had made. But he said nothing of this to the boy, turning him off with an evasion; nor did he mention the matter to Doc, fully aware of the stand the outlaw would take. Lantry had little real need for Farragoh. He would claim that he was simply following Reb's example of putting himself solid with the inhabitants of the Basin. What his real object might be was more obscure.

But that Santee continued to think about Billy's need of money was attested by his abrupt opening a few days later. Doc was away. They were planning the repairs for the creek dam before the break-up in the hills brought the water down.

"How much money do yuh need?" Reb asked.

Farragoh readily discerned the drift of this. "Five hundred dollars," he replied, making the amount sound like five thousand.

"If yuh get it, I s'pose you'll leave right away," Reb went on.

"Sure," Billy grinned. "But don't worry. I won't get it—"

"How'll it be if I loan yuh the five hundred?" Reb persisted. There was something in his tone the other could not fathom, but he chose to make light of it.

"Get out!" he laughed. "Where'll you get that much yourself?" It took considerable persuasion on Reb's part to convince him that the offer was made in good faith. "But how will I ever be able to repay it?" he exclaimed then, in perplexity. "No, Reb; I can't see it—"

"You'll pay it back some day. I ain't got any fears of that."

So it was finally arranged, not without some hesitations on Billy's part. Had it not been for his long-standing admiration for Reb, and his faith in the other's ability to accomplish difficult things with ease—even to the point of finding five hundred dollars to spare at need—he would never have consented at all.

As for Reb, he came out of the exchange with mingled feelings. He had offered to lend Billy the amount without the slightest idea where it was to come from. It was up to him to make good. The money would have to come from somewhere; but where?

Chapter XIII

THE FORK IN THE TRAIL

IT was two days later that Doc Lantry put in an appearance, on a jaded horse. His dark features were keen, his movements abrupt, as he unsaddled. Something was on his mind.

There had been little enough to do during his absence. Billy Farragoh, who already had conceived a dislike for his rough tongue, expected a quizzing about the work. But Doc didn't so much as look in his direction. No sooner had he got a meal under his belt than he and Santee drifted apart. Standing in a corner of the pasture fence they talked for a long time in low tones.

"Wal, Reb; we been waitin' fer spring," was the opening Doc rasped out; "but there's no use holdin' off any longer. I've lined up a job fer us." There was more cool, unmistakable challenge in the words than Lantry would have been able to convey in an angry shout.

Reb's normally serene blue eyes became hard. "What is it?" he asked, as business-like as the other.

Doc announced that he had found it possible to get through Crazy Woman Pass, which would give them access to Idaho. He had just come back from Castle Gate, a coal camp in the Wasatch Range, after working out the plans for sticking up the paymaster for the coal mine. "It's a cinch," he averred. "We c'n knock off a nice haul an' be back here on Ghost Creek in three days. What do yuh say?"

There was no confusing the issue here. Doc had chafed for months, now, with a doubt of Reb's position twisting in his calculating mind. He was bent on deciding the question once and for all. In a flash of insight Reb saw the step to be even more far-reaching than this: it would mark his first major activity outside the law; definitely it would make him a hunted man, with a price on his head.

He scratched the hair under his soiled sombrero as these things passed through his brain. Then, before Lantry could read indecision there, Reb's eyes squinted in an easy smile as he thought of something else.

"We'll ride over an' have a look at it," he decided. "It sounds good, anyway."

It had struck him, with a sense of relieved discovery behind the discomfort, where he was to get the five hundred dollars which he had promised to Billy Farragoh.

Unaware that Reb was already decided, Lantry was inclined to argue with his caution. "We can't lose," he pointed out. "There'll be guards with the paymaster, but at this season they won't be lookin' fer no trouble. They won't know the Pass is open till it's too late, an' we'll put out that we're Idaho cowmen. It's cast iron, I tell yuh!"

They talked it over from all angles. At length Reb professed his satisfaction with the set-up. Since Doc said the payday for the mine fell on Tuesday next, they would get away early the following day, and be back before anyone in the Basin knew they were gone.

"All except young Farragoh," Reb reminded, with deep cunning. "He's got a head on him, Doc."

"Don't worry," Lantry scoffed; "I'll take care of

him." On the spot he devised an errand which would keep Billy away from the ranch for nearly a week. "I been thinkin' of buyin' in a small herd fer looks," he announced. "Gloomy's been complainin' of too much to do, an' that means he needs more, anyway. Farragoh knows the men in the Basin with stuff they'll let go. It'll be natural, sendin' him to scout out a likely bunch."

Although Gloomy was sulky and suspicious, aware that something was afoot which he was being left out of, Billy Farragoh evinced gratification at Doc's decision. He absorbed the latter's crabbed instructions, unruffled, and the next morning got away with the dawn. Half-an-hour later Reb and Doc swung into the saddle and set off to the west.

Fresh snow had fallen during the night at Crazy Woman Pass, which they reached that afternoon. Doc Lantry expressed satisfaction with the circumstance. "If the same thing happens after we git through, on the way back, we'll be safe as a church," he declared.

A solemn hush held all the high country. They spent the night at an abandoned line camp in the hills below the lofty Tetons. In the morning they came across a horse herd that had wintered at a sheltered flat nearby. It gave Santee an idea.

"We'll switch hosses right here," he said. "That'll give us strange brands to ride with, an' a relay on the way back."

Doc grunted over his particularity, but acceded to the suggestion. Their own mounts they left in an old corral at the head of the flat. Willow and cottonwood bowered the place. It had not been visited for weeks.

They rode on. It was afternoon again before Doc said they were drawing near to Castle Gate. He was in no agreeable mood, for the horse he had taken from the flat had already fallen lame.

"Take it easy," Reb advised him, paying no attention to his fuming. "We got till tomorrow—plenty of time to get a nag. I want to look this place over, anyway."

It was decided that he should go into town alone. Lantry had been there, and had no desire further to fix his identity in curious minds. Reb was content with the arrangement. He was not really inclined to as much caution as he pretended, but he did want to check up on Doc's judgment.

"Bring back somethin' to drink," Lantry told him before he left.

"Okay; gimme the price," Reb responded. "I ain't got a cent on me."

There was unabashed calculation in the way Doc peeled a hundred dollars from the roll he always carried with him. "Yuh c'n pay me back after we do the job," he said. "An' don't forgit, Santee—spot me a good hoss."

Reb pocketed the money and rode off.

Castle Gate was situated in a high-walled canyon. It consisted of one long street, of stores, saloons and miners' shacks, extending from the railroad crossing up toward the hills. Across the tracks from the station stood the two-story stone building which housed the office of the coal company.

Reb satisfied himself about these things and others. He looked over the breed of men they would have to deal with, and in the early evening, a hearty meal inside of him, dropped in a saloon at the lower end of the street.

A desultory poker game was in progress between the Salt Lake gamblers who were waiting for the morrow's harvest. Reb had found no other amusement in the waiting town. He sat in. Always a good poker hand because he smiled in success and adversity alike, to-night he found himself at a loss. The cards were against him consistently. One hundred dollars is not much at such a time. His cheeks were set in lean hardness, but his gaze was as serene as ever when, two hours later, he pushed back from the table.

"That's all of it, boys," he said. "I'll have to punch a few more cows, I reckon."

The gamblers expressed conventional regrets. Reb waved them off. Moving to the bar, he flapped a hand to the proprietor.

"Few of the boys are camped outside of town," he explained; "an' they sent me in fer somethin' to drink. How about it?"

The proprietor knew an easy-going puncher when he saw one. Reb was genuine from his turned-over heels to his battered hat. He was good for future sessions at the cards, no doubt about it. Half of his present hundred dollars, moreover, would go to the house. The saloonkeeper set out three bottles of Old Crow.

"There yuh are, feller. That 'nough? . . . Tell the boys it's on me."

Reb delayed. "Yuh don't get it," he said mildly. "I'm right willin' to pay."

"Okay, cowpoke. Yuh c'n give it to me the next time yuh ride by."

Reb nodded and walked out, the bottles clinking under his arm. He found Doc huddled over a pine-knot fire a brace of miles out of town.

"Where's the hoss yuh was goin' to bring me?" he demanded contentiously, sampling one of the bottles.

"Never mind," Reb answered him off-handedly. "I've spotted a real one for yuh. It needn't be missin' till yuh want it."

"What if it ain't there then?" Lantry snapped back.

Reb put him aside indifferently. He knew Doc's nerves were cocked for the job they would do tomorrow.

It was only Lantry who slept badly that night; and he because of impatience. They made leisurely preparations in the morning and rode toward town at an easy gait.

"The train pulls in at eleven," said Reb. "We'll be on the side of the tracks toward the stone buildin' when it comes."

"An' that hoss fer me?" Doc growled.

"We'll pick it up now."

They reached Castle Gate by ten. Reb led the way toward the lower street, and at a point near the saloon where he had lost Doc's money, turned in at a vacant lot between tumbledown shanties. A hundred feet in from the board walk he pointed out a long-barreled, rangy roan racer with keen, pointed ears, prancing about a corral in the rear of the saloon, with half-a-dozen lesser animals.

"How's that suit yuh?"

Doc made no reply, unless the sudden glint of his eyes was one. Getting down, he handed Reb the reins of his useless pony and walked to the corral. A cautious look around revealed no spectators to his actions. With quick movements he let down the corral bars, and walked away. It was not until the ponies in the corral found their way out and began to wander that Lantry put his rope on the sleek roan. He had his saddle on it in a moment, turning the lame pony loose with the others.

"We better be gittin' on," he muttered tightly, swinging up.

They circled the station and pulled up in back of a shed beyond the coal company's office. "Plenty of time," Reb remarked, taking a look up the street across the tracks. Lantry looked too.

"This ain't so good," he said, noting the miners beginning to line up along the buildings. "We'll have to make our play while the train's in between."

They waited. Doc's tenseness caught him up in a rush when Reb lifted his hand. Back in the mountains the long-drawn scream of the locomotive whistle echoed and re-echoed. Men were gathering on the station platform.

A few minutes later the train pulled up with a grind of brake-shoes and a hiss of escaping steam. The conductor opened doors, calling out. He got down the steps of a car on this side with his little stool; following him came a man with a leather bag in each hand, accompanied by two other men wearing heavy gun belts. One of them bore a badge of some sort.

"Now!" Doc Lantry grated.

"Hold on," Reb warned him sharply. He had seen the paymaster stop to speak to the conductor. The engineer, leaning out of his cab, was looking back at them. The payroll guards listened.

"Dammit all, that train'll be pullin' out jest when

we want it there!" Lantry exploded, in a fever of impatience.

"You keep yore shirt on," Reb told him. He was as cool as ice, still waiting.

By the time the paymaster made a laughing remark over his shoulder and started for the office building, Doc was on tenterhooks. The locomotive bell had begun to clang. The train would pull out in a moment.

"Now we'll walk our ponies out there, easy like, as if we'd come in by the trail," said Reb.

Doc cursed under his breath. They started. One of the guards flicked a glance at the two careless punchers, but the paymaster was exchanging remarks with the other. They were all at their ease when Reb and Doc came abreast of them.

"Reach, boys. Make it high," Santee suggested, his smile prominent. Even as he stepped down he put a gun on them before they got a good look at him. "Okay, Doc," he said quietly.

Lantry got to the ground with alacrity. Reb took a step forward. No one had as yet noticed that anything was wrong. The locomotive was belching large puffs of smoke, its drive wheels turning. Taking charge of the leather money bags, Lantry fastened them hurriedly to the saddle of the racer.

The train pulled away from the crossing. Reb stood facing his three victims, his gun held low. But the raised hands were a give-away. Sudden disturbance occurred up the street, across the tracks. A man called out. A gun cracked.

Lantry swung into the saddle. "Let's go," he snapped to Reb. "We gotta git out of here damn quick!"

Santee said nothing, his freckled face unruffled. Without taking his eyes off the scowling guards, he backed toward his horse, feeling for the bridle. There was a clatter from the building behind him as a clerk ran from the coal company's office to the head of an outside stairway. He carried a rifle which he brought up quickly and fired. The slug ripped the dust, and Reb's pony shied in fright.

"Steady, boy," Reb soothed, backing toward him. "Take it easy."

"Hurry up, will yuh?" Doc bawled, already half-a-dozen jumps away. More shots came from the street; the miners were running in this direction.

"Shucks," Reb told his partner coolly, over his shoulder; "them birds can't shoot fer sour apples."

He was still feeling for his pony, clucking reassuringly. The clerk fired again; but Santee had a way with horses. When he backed into his pony and laid a hand on its neck, the pony trembled but stood still.

"Watch it, now," Reb told the guards. In another moment he was mounted, his gun still covering them.

Lantry was swearing luridly, and Reb laughed as he swung toward him. "We're leavin' now," he said. Bullets sang past them as they galloped down the street and out of town, but their luck held.

"Gimme one of them bags," Reb directed, when they had gone a mile or more. "No use of you carryin' all the weight."

Doc flashed him a stare, but complied. They pushed on.

They were pursued, as they knew they would be. A posse set out from town without delay. Telegraph wires hummed, another posse started from below the line in Utah. But no one caught up, and the next morning they pulled in on the little flat under the Tetons.

Making the exchange back to their own horses, they pressed ahead. Lantry regretted the roan, but Reb made him turn it loose. Late in the day they crossed Crazy Woman Pass and rode down into the Basin.

Back in Castle Gate, feeling over the robbery ran high. None was more vociferous than the saloon proprietor whose horse had been taken.

"I spotted both of 'em, soon as I heard," he declared angrily. "They had us all sized up; they even drifted my hosses so's the roan wouldn't be missed right away, dang 'em! An' not only that, but that nervy white-haired feller tapped me fer some whisky, too. Gad, whut gall!"

But some time during the second night the roan racer returned of its own accord. They found it the next morning, grazing near its home corral. Ten dollars of the payroll money were twisted in a paper tied to the roan's mane, and on the paper was scrawled simply, "For the three bottles of Old Crow."

"Cripes!" swore the saloon keeper in amazement. "Whut do yuh know about that!"

Chapter XIV

HEART OF GOLD

A MILE below Crazy Woman Pass, with the Basin spread out at their feet, Doc Lantry insisted on stopping to divide the proceeds of the robbery.

"We'll never be safer, or more to ourselves, than we are right here," he declared. "These leather bags have got to be burned up, too."

"What's the idea?" Reb queried curiously, a thread of amusement in his voice. "Why not go on to the ranch an' do it?"

"Because I say we do it now!" Lantry snapped.

"Well, don't bust a cinch about it," Reb told him lightly.

"I'll bust whatever I have to, to head off yore damned arguments," Doc retorted tartly. "We'll do this thing the way I want it done."

Perceiving suddenly how the land lay, Reb let it go, content to give Lantry his way in small matters. It was one of the few opportunities Doc had left to save his pride. He didn't need to be told by this time that any real argument with Reb was unlikely to be won by himself.

The truth was that since the hold-up in Castle Gate, Doc had been struggling to alter the situation between them. Trails were taken because he wanted to; things were done to suit his taste. He believed that Reb's taking the definite step into outlawry would remove any grounds the latter had for assuming superiority; that it set them on an equal footing, wherein as time went on he could reassert his natural right of authority. Reb read the thought in him. He bided his time, without troubling to correct Doc. Experience, however slow, is a sure teacher.

They divided the money. Doc lit a small fire and burned the paymaster's leather bags. Then they went on.

Gloomy Jepson was in solitary charge at Ghost Creek when they rode in. One look at his long, dissatisfied face as he followed Doc Lantry's self-complacent movements about the dugout told Reb why Doc had insisted they split their booty before arriving at the ranch. He did not intend that Gloomy should share in their haul in any way.

Later in the day Reb peeled seven hundred dollars off his roll—his own share amounted to several thousands—and seeking out Gloomy, he handed over the sum.

"This is yore cut, Gloomy," he said easily.

Jepson took it suspiciously, his melancholy eyes suddenly sharpened. He did not know what to say. "I s'pose Doc—" he began.

"He knows," Reb put him off, to save his feelings. "Yuh don't think Doc'd make a haul without lettin' yuh in on it, do yuh?"

Gloomy did not say what he thought on that head. "Doc's all right," he averred defensively. There was a hint of jealousy in his voice as he added: "The money don't mean so much t' me. But I shore would'a liked to go 'long—"

"I ain't got nothin' against Doc, myself," Reb assured him, pleased by his loyalty; "but Gloomy, I think I like you better, all the same."

It was so much like something Gloomy had heard before, yet so much more generously put, that he could not help being struck by the comparison. He asked diffidently what had happened, and where. Reb told him, rather slighting his own part than otherwise. By his way of it, the job had been incredibly easy and everything had gone according to schedule.

Riding back from a survey of the pasture—and a scout for roving peace officers—Lantry caught them talking together. At least he thought he did. His somber gaze, suddenly heavy and hard, shifted from Gloomy to Reb.

"Braggin' already?" he remarked caustically.

It was not the crude attempt to insert a wedge between Jepson and himself that Reb took note of, here. The very form of Doc's bitter wit was a confession that he had played second fiddle in the Idaho stick-up. Santee found it worth a smile. Doc did not wait for his lightly-voiced rejoinder.

He said: "Gloomy, there's half-a-dozen wabbly posts young Farragoh didn't git to, on the north side of the pasture. Better git out there an' tamp 'em down."

Jepson nodded. Without response he moved toward the corral. Lantry followed him to elaborate on his instructions. Reb looked after them, unmoving, a new light in his crinkled eyes.

"I reckon it's no news that Doc is jealous of me," he mused. "But if he thinks he's gotta keep Gloomy away from my wicked influence it's gettin' to a point where I better begin to do some thinkin'."

He had not forgotten Lantry's endeavor last fall to undermine him with the Logans and the rest of the Wild Bunch. Still fresh in his mind was the outcome of that attempt. By a quirk of fate Doc had won then, in a left-handed way. But it was wholly unlikely that this would weigh against his accumulating resentment.

"I hope Gloomy keeps his mouth shut about that seven hundred," Reb thought on. "Doc'd shore figure I was tryin' to buy the man."

What he would do with him when he had him, was something Lantry would not pause to ask. The first impulse of his enflamed jealousy would be retaliation. Impotent, foolish as Doc's rage was, it went without saying that it would take the form of treachery.

"I'll jest keep an eye on him," Reb told himself, and thought no more about the matter.

Billy Farragoh rode in two days later. Lantry queried him brusquely concerning his survey of purchaseable cattle. Doc was still riding his high horse. Despite Billy's expressed belief that he would have no trouble in gathering a herd, his whole manner was one of implied criticism.

"Lay off the rough stuff, Doc," Reb was moved to interpose, before this had gone far. Billy's done a good job for yuh."

They were in the dugout at the time. Lantry slammed down a fork, the handle of which he had been using to scrape out his pipe, and glared at Reb.

"Why the hell shouldn't he do a good job?" he retorted sharply. "He knows everybody in the Basin, don't he? What do yuh think I picked him fer?" He delivered himself of further remarks in questionable taste. "Where *d'you* fit into this?" he broke off pointedly.

Reb's mouth had relaxed; but when he looked at Doc in a certain way, the latter was never sure whether the glint in his eye was the light of humor or of something else. He took an easy step now, and fronted Doc, not three feet away from him.

"What I'm gettin' at," he explained temperately, "is that everybody don't know yuh like I do. Billy's liable to think, from yore tone, yuh got somethin' against him. He don't know yo're takin' out a private grudge on the first handy man. But I do, Doc."

"The hell with you!" Doc burst out violently.

Billy Farragoh stared at them both in amazement. "What's this all about?" he inquired. "My skin isn't as thin as you seem to think, Reb—"

Suddenly he became aware that Santee was not listening to him. Nor was Doc Lantry. The two measured each other as if they were alone in the dugout, alone in the world, with a difference to be settled. Reb was grinning at Doc with an ease that amounted to ridicule.

"Yuh don't mean that, Doc," he said softly. "I won't even ask yuh to take it back."

Not even Billy needed to be told that here was dynamite.

Doc exploded into nervous curses, his leaping apprehensions at his throat. What was Reb getting at? His innate, deep-hidden cowardice before this man, alone among all men, corroded his soul like an acid.

"Yuh know whether I mean it or not," he ground out. "An' Santee, if yuh think yuh can make me take it back, or anything else, why don't yuh try it out!" It was the open break. He did not care what he said, grasping any pretext to vent his bile.

Reb understood him. "Gwan!" he returned with thin

scorn, not yet angered. "Take yore hot head outside an' cool it. This is a nice show yo're puttin' on here."

It drove Doc to frenzy. He made noises in his throat, starting forward. Reb stopped him with an upraised arm across his chest, the fingers biting into his shoulder. They paused, toe to toe.

"Better think it over, Doc. If yo're bound to make me bust yuh, I will."

He flung the man back as easily as he would have brushed aside a willow branch. Doc slammed against the table. It supported him, its legs scraping. His face blackened, his lips drew up.

"Damn yuh!" he flared, his voice trembling. "It's no mystery what yo're drivin' at, tryin' to make a fool of me! Yuh can cover Farragoh now, an' yuh can git around Gloomy's soft side; but it don't fool me. I'll make yuh sweat one o' these days, an' mebbe some more o' yore fine friends, too!"

He was backing toward the door, glaring his implacable, unveiled hatred. He kept his hands wide of his belt. The watchfulness faded out of Reb's eyes as Doc sidled crab-wise through the door and was gone. He had held his breath with a tautness which must have communicated itself, for fear Lantry might blurt something that was better left unsaid in this moment. That danger past, he was himself once more.

Billy Farragoh was no less mystified than before. He turned to Reb inquiringly.

"What made Doc blow up like that?" he queried. "Do you know?"

"Well, I reckon it don't bother me, why he did," Reb stalled competently. "But yuh heard me tell him. He's had it in fer me. . . . Shucks! It don't amount to nothin'," he added. "Tell me how yuh found folks while yuh was away."

They discussed this and other things.

"Some of the ranchers aren't home yet. I had to change my plans somewhat on my trip," said Billy. "I stopped by here, Sunday, but you were away." He did not see the sudden covert look Reb shot him. "Gloomy said you and Doc had gone somewhere for the day."

"Yeh," Reb lied easily, catching himself; "we was lookin' out the lower range." It gave him a twinge to deceive Billy even in such a manner, but he did not hesitate. Better to cut off the boy's curiosity at the root than to get involved in some elaborate explanation of a prolonged absence. "Now yuh done what yuh could for Doc," he went on, anxious to change the subject, "I suppose as soon as yuh get yore five hundred, yuh'll pull out in a hurry."

"I expect I would." Billy did not ask if Reb had the money. "I've decided to quit anyway," he confessed. "I have no intention of making trouble between you and Doc."

"I told yuh that didn't amount to nothin'," Reb rejoined; "but this'll make that scarcely worth while arguin' about." He pulled out a bandana into which he had previously knotted the five hundred dollars, in a variety of small denominations so that Billy would think he had saved it.

"Gee, I—" Billy was dumfounded, looking at the bills. "This is just swell. Reb, you're the tops with me!" he exclaimed fervently.

"That ain't why I'm doin' this," Reb told him gruffly. "I want to see yuh do what yuh want. Yore mother deserves it. Yuh both do, I reckon."

"Golly, won't mother be pleased!" Billy's enthusiasm lifted him up. "I'll be in Lander in another week! Mother'll be as proud of you, Reb, as she is of me. And Ronda—"

"Don't tell her!" The ejaculation was jerked out of Reb before he could stop it.

"Why not?" Billy looked puzzled. "Nonsense! Why shouldn't I tell her?"

"Well—" Reb temporized lamely. "Maybe it would be all right. Only I . . ." He stopped. It gave him a turn that Ronda should think he had done this fine thing, while as a matter of fact the money had been stolen. Even if she didn't know, the idea of the thing—

"I can see through you," Billy grinned, relieved by his own thoughts. "You don't want folks to know how good you are."

Reb let him have it so. But he was troubled. "If Ronda or Billy ever found out where that money came from, they'd never look at me again," the new thought bored in, shocking him like the bite of a steel trap. These things went on and on, without end. He told himself that without Billy's need, he would never have turned to outlawry; that now the necessity was gone, he would not be weak a second time. It was cold comfort, but it was all he had.

Billy told Lantry that evening that he was quitting. Doc accepted the news with a grunt. He asked no questions.

"You're going to ride to the Point with me, aren't you, while I tell mother?" Billy asked Reb, as he saddled up.

"No," Reb decided reluctantly; "not now. But I'll prob'ly see yuh again before yuh leave."

There were more protestations of gratitude on Billy's part, and then he was gone. Reb stood in the doorway, watching him ride away.

"Wal, are yuh satisfied now?" Lantry snarled from behind him.

Reb seemed to awaken from a reverie, turning.

"I know what yuh think, Doc," he said with a wintry smile; "an' it ain't true. I didn't tell that boy to get out. You drove him out! . . . I dunno what yuh was thinkin' of. If it was anybody else, yo're blowin'd soon be all over the Basin. I tell yuh, I'm about sick of it."

"Wal, it won't be long before yuh have somethin' else to worry about," Doc flung back, almost with relish. "In 'nother month yuh can forget young Farragoh, an' the rest of the Basin, too!" He was referring to the return of the Sundance Kid and his crowd.

To be reminded thus, while he still had no inkling what his future course would be, gave Reb something to think about, indeed. But he did not forget Billy Farragoh. Nor, it appeared, had Billy forgotten him. He rode out the day before he left for Lander, and found Reb riding across the range.

"Reb, I don't like to think of your staying on here with Lantry, for some reason," he said, during the course of their talk. "I don't want to mix into your business, but he certainly doesn't appreciate you. Why don't you go riding for some other outfit?"

"Well, it suits me here," Reb responded. "Doc don't bother me."

"Jube Cameron has returned home," Billy went on with studied casualness. "He wants to see you some time before long."

Reb's attention was caught. "What about?" he asked. And after a moment: "Does he aim to offer me a job?"

"I think he does." Billy did not want to explain that he had had a talk with the rancher about Reb's unenviable situation, or as much of it as he understood. But to Reb it was as plain as print that this was what had happened.

For a moment there came over him a desire to chuck the whole business; to take the job with Cameron and defy Doc and the others, expose them if necessary. He could win through somehow, he thought. But the impulse did not last.

"It wouldn't be square," he told himself soberly. "It's too late, anyway. Doc would squawk about that Castle Gate business, an' I'd be on the run. He'd see me behind the bars before he'd see me inside the law again."

"No," he said aloud; "I don't reckon I'll take a job with Jube, nice as it is of him to want me. But I'll go over an' see him," he added. "I can do that much, anyhow."

They left it at that.

Chapter XV

GOD DISPOSES

"IT ain't simply because I owe yuh my hide that I'd like to have yuh on my payroll," said Jube Cameron persuasively. "I might's well admit my aim is partly selfish. I know whut yuh can do, Reb; yores is the kind of stock savvy a man needs."

They were on the C 8; Santee had ridden over to see how the rancher was getting on. Jube lost no time in coming to the subject uppermost in his mind. It irked the flaxen-haired one no little, for while there was something about the prospect of a job with Cameron that appealed to him strongly, he was unable to make up his mind to accept.

"I can't offer yuh nothin' better than punchin' right now," Cameron went on; "but I am free to say my foreman's sort of took up with the idee of a spread of his own. That'll leave me shorthanded, an' I'm thinkin' about a man who'll step into his boots without stumblin'. I figure yuh can do it, Reb; anyway, yuh got first bid when the time comes." He ended with the air of a man who has laid his cards on the table.

This was a strong inducement for any man. Reb's eyes crinkled with pleased gratitude; nevertheless, he still remained dubious.

"Cameron, Billy Farragoh never said he had a talk with yuh about me," he said frankly; "but I know he did, an' I know what about." He shook his head decidedly. "Yuh both got it all wrong. I ain't got a thing

146

to complain of, right now. I shore thank yuh for thinkin' of me, but—"

"Hold on!" Jube exclaimed, his expression inquiring. "What's this yo're sayin', now?" Reb said it again at more length. Cameron gave a negative shake. "Unh-uh," he denied forcefully. "Billy come to me jest before he went to Lander," he lied smoothly, "an' told me he knew jest the man to replace my foreman, if I could git him. It was you, Reb; Billy said so, an' that's all he did say." He went on to elaborate his innocence of any planning to do more than acquire the services of a man he wanted, knowing this was the line that would get him the farthest with Santee.

It did alter Reb's mind materially. After all, there were a good many reasons why he would like to work for Jube Cameron. He affected to listen with deferential regret, while he thought it over again.

"I got a letter from Ronda yesterday," Jube changed the subject craftily, reading Reb's mood. "She says Billy's studyin' in Judge Hamer's office right hard. She does git to see him occasional, though. . . . But she'll be comin' home in a few weeks, now— her an' the Mrs."

It was an even stronger argument with Reb, unconsciously as it had been put. To work on the same ranch where Ronda lived, to see her daily. . . . To prove to her what he could do—and prove to himself that what had happened to Dan Morgan's money, down at Moab, had been an accident. . . . It certainly had its attraction.

Reb thought of Doc Lantry then, and of something else. The return of Ronda in the spring would coincide with that of the Wild Bunch, expecting the redemption of his promises to them. He couldn't throw those boys down altogether, not with what Lantry had on him. But a new thought came—perhaps the responsibilities of a job with Cameron's brand would excuse him from taking part in their activities for a time.

It didn't take him long, after this, to arrive at his decision.

"I'll go yuh on that job, Cameron," he said abruptly, grinning to cover his reflections.

"Fine. I was hopin' yuh would, Reb. Yuh can drag yore war-bag over here jest as soon as yuh want."

Jube took it calmly, with no sign of his relief at the success of his endeavors. It was a way he had, of carrying even a small conspiracy through to a finish. Billy Farragoh had drawn no flattering picture of Doc Lantry in his talk. Any man, the boy declared, was fortunate to escape from Doc's employ, on general principles. Well, Jube owed that much to Santee. Nevertheless, Billy's very vagueness about Doc had left him more than a little curious.

"What kind o' man is Lantry, Reb?" he could not help asking, as they walked back toward the house from the corrals. "I mean, how is he to work for— He's so damn shy o' being neighborly," he added apologetically.

Instantly on his guard, Reb affected casualness. "Why, Doc's got some rough edges," he admitted. "I reckon he's had a hard time of it. Makes him difficult to deal with—Billy prob'ly found that out. But we get along."

"Been a hoss-dealer long, has he?" Cameron persisted. "Where'd he come from, anyways?"

In these questions and others the rancher evinced a

desire to learn something of Lantry's background that warned Reb like a red flag. He built up a circumstantial past for Doc, spotted with appropriate blanks; for he knew better than to seem to have Doc's history too well at his command. A few artistic touches tended to make the man appear innocuous, a dyspeptic recluse.

Still Cameron hung on conversationally, as Reb settled into his saddle for the ride back to Ghost Creek. Why didn't Lantry see a doctor? Maybe it was something that could be cured. "No need to say that if doctorin' would make him more like you, it'd be worth tryin'," Jube smiled.

"No," Reb sparred; "Lantry's set in his way, Cameron. It's ingrained in him—he wouldn't listen to no sawbones, nor to me neither. He'd rather rock along as he's doin'."

"Mebbe if me, or somebody else, was to turn up over there an' drop a word to kind of set him thinkin'—" Jube offered queryingly.

Reb shunted him away from that in a hurry. He didn't want any of the Basin men taking an exaggerated interest in Doc Lantry, on whatever count; and it went without saying that Doc didn't either.

"Doc's crabby on the subject," he said, frowning down the rancher's suggestion. "It's only askin' fer grief to talk it to him."

"Reckon that's so," Jube nodded comprehendingly. "It's still purty good medicine to leave a man to his own concerns. . . . Wal, then I'll be expectin' yuh, soon as yuh git straightened out over there, Reb."

So the subject of Lantry was passed off lightly; but as he rode away, Reb experienced a revival of the apprehensions which Cameron's earlier cunning had allayed. *Had* there been talk of Lantry between the rancher and Billy Farragoh? Certainly Jube had been doing some thinking about Doc, at any rate. All these seemingly idle questions—Reb couldn't get away from the feeling of a deeper purpose behind them.

"Mebbe somethin's come out about them hosses Doc was sellin'," he mused uneasily. "It can't be much; but it wouldn't take much to grow into a sneakin' suspicion. . . . An' Cameron wantin' to get me away in a hurry. Why don't he wait till his foreman quits?" But after all, it might be his own awakened vigilance that made this look ambiguous.

"Dang it all!" he burst out, grinning at his fears; "this is what Doc's damned shady life leads to. The wild, free way of livin'! I'll be spooky as a bronc if it goes on much longer."

Seen in this light, the matter receded to its proper proportions. But later, when he mentioned to Lantry casually that he had taken a job with Cameron and Doc objected, Reb's thinking came back in a flash to help him.

"Dammit all, Santee!" Doc exploded. "Yuh can be depended on to jam things up! The Kid an' the others'll be comin' along soon—yuh won't have time to hold down no job!" He ran on with quick acerbity.

"Are yuh done?" Reb inquired, when he stopped for breath. "Well, then, look here: Do yuh think the money means anything to me? No! So when I do somethin' like this—"

"I s'pose yo're tellin' me this job is another clever way of divertin' suspicion!" Lantry cut him off disgustedly.

"What yuh don't know don't hurt yuh—right

away," retorted Reb sententiously. "But Doc, what *I* know bothers me." There was shrewdness in his humorous eyes as he gave an accurate account of Jube Cameron's inquisitive questions.

Doc was inclined to be indignant. "Where does he git off, with his nose in my business?" he barked.

Reb laughed at him. "Yuh mean where'll you get off," he corrected. "No, Doc; you'll never get done coverin' up. No use tryin'. Now, my idea is that somethin's come out about them hosses we drove up here. An' if yuh want to know, I'm takin' a job with Cameron to try an' find out what's known, an' who knows it."

Lantry thought this plausible. He had lost some of his assurance now. "What'll I tell the Logans, though?" he queried, when they had talked it over.

"Why—tell 'em jest that. It won't be for long, maybe. If the Kid ain't satisfied, I'll ride over some night myself."

Doc was displeased with his leaving, but there was nothing he could say to any point. He wanted to stay on at Ghost Creek, for he had seen its advantages. Reb's move might help him to do so. Masterfully at ease, Reb stuffed his war-bag, and the next morning rode off to work for Cameron.

Spring drew on apace now. The dirty snow was melting off the levels, the Wind River feeders began to swell, the ice to pile up. It was a season of swift rises in temperature. The C 8 cattle were being held on the high slopes, where last season's cured grass lay bared, but taking his place with the boys, Reb found no sinecure awaiting him. Steers had to be tailed up through the thaws, kept out of the dangerous draws;

weaklings needed looking after, which generally meant moving them down to the ranch by wagon, where they could be regularly tended.

One day Cameron rode out with Reb to see how his stock was shaping up for the coming beef cut. The air was balmy. The snow had almost disappeared. New grass was peeping up through what was left of it.

"Yuh ought to get a cut of a hundred an' fifty," Reb said, as they rode along. "It ain't much, but I wouldn't dig into my two-year-olds if I was you." He jerked a thumb toward the white-faces grazing the slope below them. "They'll be mighty hefty, time the grass gets strong. There's 'nother bunch over the hump, here."

Jube nodded, his gaze turning as he took in the spread of Shoshone Meadows, dotted with his cattle. "Yore estimate of the cut agrees with Pat's," he said. Pat was his foreman. "It removes any doubts I might've had about yore ability, Reb."

They talked on, until Reb broke off to discourage two young steers inclined toward belligerence. "Don't pay to have 'em fight off no beef," he commented, riding back to join his employer after his swift maneuvers.

Jube smiled quizzically. "Yuh was born to raise cows, Reb," he responded.

It was true. Reb loved the work. He became absorbed in it. It came over him with a surge that he could ask nothing better of life than to go on like this. The money in his pockets meant nothing when he had good horseflesh under him and the wide sky overhead—steers to think about. The Sundance Kid was due back any day now. For a moment Reb hoped to make the break with his bunch permanent. Cameron would need him through the round-up. Logan and the others would become impatient with waiting, drift away. . . . The picture had its bright aspects.

It was late that afternoon, and Reb was riding alone down Rock Creek—Cameron had returned to the ranch long since—when he saw a solitary rider racking forward. He stared at the other, caught by something in the man's posture, and then grunted. His eyes hardened as the two drew together, but his grin was easy.

"Takin' a chance, ain't yuh, Logan?" he queried.

The Sundance Kid pulled up. "Howdy, Reb. I knowed it was you. . . . How's tricks?" He was his old, cool, impudent self.

"Well, I'm doin' some scoutin' on Lantry's account. Workin' for Cameron."

The Kid's lips parted, drew upward. "Doc told me," he admitted. "But o' course you'll drop that now."

"No. Not yet," Reb returned. He told the other why, though he was sure Lantry had explained this also. "Doc don't scarcely take enough pains for his own good," he concluded. "Somebody's got to, if we go on usin' Ghost Creek. I'm doin' it."

The Kid didn't quiz, didn't press him. Not openly, at least. He evidently had heard about the Castle Gate job. And he showed a respect for Reb's judgment that had not been in him last year.

"Have to keep up a front with the C 8," he agreed, "till yuh git what yore after, anyway. But yuh can fix it up to git some job that'll let yuh off now an' again without anyone knowin'." His tone implied that there was no question of this.

"Well, I dunno." Reb had been taut and guarded since the Sundance Kid's appearance had jarred him.

Outwardly he was as free as ever. "Grass'll be gettin' strong right soon now. Reckon I can't find much excuse for shirkin' the busy season."

"You do what yuh can," Logan urged, when they had smoked and thrashed it out, to Reb's advantage as far as he could see. The Kid unhooked his knee from his saddle-horn. "We're all primed to go into yore scheme, Santee. I'll look yuh up again in a day or two."

"You'll find me in the thick of Cameron's boys, an' damn busy, too, if I know anythin' about it," Reb thought to himself, as the Kid rode off in the direction of Ghost Creek. He knew the crisis in his affairs had come. Before, he felt, he had been driven by circumstance. The Castle Gate robbery had been a product of fate. But if he went into anything further of the kind, he would have no such excuse; there would be no answer save his own weakness. And he was not weak. He had always gloried in his strength.

He rode back to the C 8 determined to give the outlaws a wide berth for a few days, until chance or wisdom pointed out his proper course of action. There was no inkling then that fate was to strike again, with the sharpness of lightning, within a few hours.

Jube Cameron called him into his office from the supper table.

"Reb," he said without preamble, "I'm goin' to put yuh out at the Upper Shoshone camp fer a few weeks."

Reb nodded, thinking it fell in precisely with his own plans. "Who do yuh want up there with me?" he asked.

"You'll be alone, Reb," the rancher answered slowly; "an' I'll tell yuh why. I wouldn't even put a man there to keep the cows out of the Rock Creek bog, if it was only that; but there's a handy corral there, an' I need some extra broncs broke fer the round-up. You'll have yore time to yoreself, wrangle the hosses, an' keep an eye on the bog, without any trouble at all," he went on pleasantly, with no idea of what he was doing to Reb. "I'll send the boys up with the cavvy tomorrer—an' the wagon with yore grub, too."

Reb's agreement with this arrangement was a masterpiece of outward control. Inwardly he groaned. "The Sundance Kid'll find me wide open now, with no way to turn," he thought bleakly.

Chapter XVI

THE WILD, FREE LIFE

IN a sandy wash near the Union Pacific tracks, a few miles west of Wilcox, half-a-dozen men waited. It had rained heavily during the night, but now the rain had stopped; the world was still, breathless, dank. Dawn was near at hand.

"Hark!" said Lonny Logan, pinching at his cigarette. "Is that it?"

They listened intently. Among them were Lonny's brother, the Sundance Kid—Flat Nose George, Bob Leigh, Carver, Doc Lantry. Plans had been laid to rob the through express. The brains behind the exploit and the real daredevil of them all, Reb Santee had ridden into Cheyenne—the nearest stop to the east— the night before to board the express. He would take no companion. It was incredible, but true. His plan was to reach the engineer by some means and stop the train at this point. The Wild Bunch was waiting to see whether he would make good.

They had argued the matter pro and con, but now they were silent, expecting the express any minute.

"That's it!" exclaimed Bob Leigh, a moment later.

They all heard the distant, attenuated roar of the train across the plain. Five minutes later a dark shape rushed forward through the first faint light.

"He didn't make it!" cried Doc Lantry disgustedly. "It's goin' right on by." There was nothing here to indicate a proper anxiety for Santee. As a matter of fact, Doc hoped for the worst.

Even as he spoke, however, the scream of the air brakes split the deeper rumble of the locomotive. Slowly the train ground to a stop.

"All right, boys!" the Sundance Kid jerked out swiftly. "Reb done his part. It's up to us to back him!"

They ran along the train. Pullman windows banged up; heads were thrust out. As the outlaws swung aboard, a shot echoed from the rear of the train—another. The Kid returned this fire in a flash. "Yuh got 'im!" Bill Carver called out. It discouraged further argument. The heads of the curious were hastily withdrawn.

"Take a look ahead," Logan directed Flat Nose George. "See what the smiler's doin'."

This was answered a moment later when Reb stepped down from the cab, herding the engineer and the firemen before him.

"Here, you!" he called, avoiding Curry's name. "Put a gun on these two."

Flat Nose George complied. Reb strode back along the train. Several of his companions had gathered at one end of the express car.

"Got that stick of blastin' powder?" he grinned at them as he came up. Bob Leigh handed it to him. "Watch the caboose," he said, and walked to the door of the car. Angry exclamations sounded from behind its grating, but crouching down, he paid no attention. The slugs from a six-gun, fired at an angle, could not reach him.

Bill Carver crawled under the train to guard the other side. The sky was bright in the east now; figures could be distinguished vaguely at some distance. As

Reb worked at the closed door a brakeman with a rifle jumped down from the caboose and knelt on the ballast. His weapon came up. It was Doc Lantry who blazed away at him. The rifle was never fired. The brakeman wilted down.

"Yuh didn't have to do that!" Reb flung at Doc. "Couldn't yuh smoke him back inside?"

Lantry began to swear, but Reb wasn't listening: he touched off the blasting powder, ran to the car-end, ducked. The explosive let go with a roar that rocked the car. The outlaws dashed forward. The car door hung in splinters.

Santee was the first inside, gun in hand. But the way was clear. The express guard and the mail clerk were both dazed and half-conscious, shocked and hurled back by the explosion.

"Bring our hosses," Reb told Lonny Logan, while the Sundance Kid and Bob Leigh attacked the safe in the upper end of the car. "Take one up to the engine, too."

Leigh slipped away. Further occasional shots rang along the train as Bill Carver and Doc Lantry put an abrupt end to investigations by the trainmen and angry passengers.

Blasting powder ripped open the express safe, blew aside the crates with which it was shielded. The Kid and Leigh knelt to stuff saddle-bags with currency, gold, a little silver.

"Okay," said Santee coolly from the door, as they stood up. "Let's light out of here." He kept an eye on the reviving express guard as his companions walked to the door and jumped down. Then Reb swung out also.

All except Bill Carver and himself were in the saddle. Ahead, Flat Nose George awaited their starting before he released the engine crew.

"Let's go, Bill!" Lantry called under the train.

"Shut up, you fool!" Reb lashed out at him.

Doc glared a species of frenzied exasperation. "Damn yuh, whut're yuh pickin' on me fer?" he snarled.

"Let it go!" the Sundance Kid told him fiercely, and Lantry subsided.

A fusillade of shots scattered them as a man at the caboose opened fire with the dead brakeman's rifle. "Shove off!" Reb ordered them harshly, returning the fire without aim; but he did not himself move, holding the reins of Carver's pony. The rest started away. A rod apart, however, the Sundance Kid wheeled his mount.

"Dammit," he ejaculated admiringly; "that's guts, fella, but it ain't brains—"

Reb waved him on. Carver was coming now. He dragged one leg. Reb got down to help him mount. In a moment they came on. Guns cracked along the train after them, but they were soon beyond range.

"Bad hit, Bill?" Reb asked Carver.

"Naw." The latter was disgusted. "My own fool fault. I whaled away at a flash—an' stood still myself. He got me in the thigh." He was busy trying to tie up his flesh wound as he rode.

"Reb, yuh don't even need us birds," the Sundance Kid said, with a grin. "That was clean as a hound's tooth. How'd yuh do it?" He referred to the stopping of the train single-handed.

"Why, I walked forward through the cars an'

climbed over to the cab, is all. There wasn't nothin' to it."

Others looked their homage, and Reb was pleased. He had surprised himself, be it said. But there was little time for these reflections now. The sun was up. They struck off across the high Laramie Plains.

An hour before noon came the words all had been expecting.

"They're after us!"

A band of riders could be seen coming down from a break in the Laramie Mountains, four or five miles to the east. They were not from Wilcox. This meant telegraphing—a general alarm. The fugitives swung west and pushed on.

It soon became evident the posse had fresh horses. Steadily they drew up.

"We got to stand 'em off, or git fresh nags ourselves!" Doc Lantry burst out excitedly. No one answered him. There was no ranch in sight. There wouldn't be. The answer was plain.

The pursuers were only a half-mile behind now, spread out like Indians. They came on with deadly intent.

"Cowboys," gritted the Sundance Kid tersely. "Joe Hazen's gathered 'em from around Casper."

Within the hour the first shot was fired from behind. It went wide, but its warning was unmistakable. Reb Santee's face was as untroubled as ever, but his mouth had hardened. He led the way into a rocky ravine and pulled up. There was a little pool, a few pitiful tufts of grass.

"Get in the rocks," Reb directed.

There was no time to waste. Grimly ready, they

crawled away, four of them with rifles. Lonny Logan stayed to guard the ponies. Santee worked back to a large rock overlooking their trail. A rattlesnake buzzed and he circled it, all his attention fixed on the matter in hand.

He had almost reached the rock when the smash of a gun brought him around, crouched. A group of horsemen were outlined against the sky on the southern edge of the ravine. They had circled with incredible speed, and were firing down. A rattle of hoofs took Reb's glance to the horses of his friends, brought a grunt to his lips. The shots of Hazen's men had scattered the ponies. They all clattered out of the defile except one, fighting the bridle to which Lonny Logan clung desperately.

A volley from several points in the ravine dispersed the posse. They ducked away, while powder smoke drifted among the rocks; but the damage had been done. Lonny's pony kicked him, tore loose. Logan picked himself up and lunged for cover, cursing. They were afoot.

It did not daunt them. The cowboys fell back and set up a raking fire on the edges of the ravine. The outlaws replied with interest.

Bill Carver crawled near Santee, his bloody leg awkward. "Dang it all—now I am in a mess!" he growled ruefully. "I couldn't git away if I had a fifty-foot road an' a week to do it in."

"Keep yore chin up," Reb advised him, sighting at a far movement and firing quickly. "We're safe, holed up here."

"Yeh," Carver returned dryly. "It won't be lead that gits us."

This was proved as the afternoon dragged by. Slugs slapped the rocks and screamed away, the fight was hot, but no one was hit. It was Joe Hazen, the deputy sheriff, who, just before sunset, fell to the rifle of Doc Lantry. It angered his companions. They made a determined rush on the ravine, their guns flaming, but were staved off.

"We can't keep this up much longer, Reb," the Sundance Kid declared. "We're half-starved now. An' there'll be officers here—mebbe fifty men— in a few hours."

"We don't need more'n half that time, for what we'll be doin'," Santee responded. The twinkle grew brighter in his eye as his men grew more dejected. He knew just how tight this spot was: it could not mark him.

To add to their discomfort, clouds blew up with the dusk, rain began to fall, light at first and then in a deluge. An hour later the sky, the night, were inky black. It was still punctuated by red flashes. Cartridges were running low in the ravine.

"Gather the boys," said Reb quietly, at last. "We're leavin'."

Before long they had collected at the upper edge of the ravine. A deep gash in the rock led away. "Now we got to duck an' run for it," Reb murmured. "An' there won't be no noise."

They understood him. One by one they started off. Carver had no complaint to make, but Reb knew how he felt. He helped the man, a hand under his arm.

More than once they froze, ready for anything, in that stealthy advance. They dodged, they wormed ahead like serpents. They mistrusted every shadow.

But they were not challenged. A quarter-mile from the ravine, Reb felt sure they had slipped through the cordon. Still the rain came down, soaking them— covering their escape.

"Now all we need is wings," Flat Nose George muttered.

Reb thought it over. "We'll hit north," he decided. "There's a freight road near the river."

They were weary when they reached it. The men took turns toting the saddle-bags containing their booty.

"What'll we do now—walk back to Wind River?" Doc Lantry broke out sneeringly.

"You hold on," Reb told him thinly. Bill Carver was the one he was worried about. The man was suffering, feverish, but tight-lipped. He had to he half-carried.

It was Bob Leigh who stopped, a mile farther on, probing the darkness. "There's a camp, ahead there," he whispered.

"Shore," returned Reb easily, softly. "Freighters."

Suddenly they saw his plan.

"Wal, by Gawd!" Harve Logan breathed his gratification.

"Quiet, now," Reb warned. "There can't be no slip here."

Cautiously they located the freighters' horses, staked to graze. Their hides were sleek and wet. Reb released them and led them away, one by one. No sound, no movement came from the wagons under which the weary freighters slept.

"They'll be one surprised bunch, come mornin'," Bob Leigh chuckled, when they all held the hackamores of unsaddled mounts.

"We'll hit the Platte, cross, an' strike west," Reb murmured his instructions. "Don't try to run these plugs till we git well away."

Softly they rode riverward. When they reached its bank, Doc Lantry burst out unguardedly: "Hell's fire! It's runnin' a flood!"

The Sundance Kid whirled to blast him with invective. Before a word came, a disturbance sounded a hundred yards down the bank.

"Who's there?" the challenge rang out—a voice of authority.

"Officers!" Reb bit off, cursing Lantry in his heart. "Into the drink, boys! We got to make it!"

They plunged in. Shots split the night behind them, excited cries echoed. The storm-swelled Platte swept them along with a silent, treacherous current. But the heavy draught horses swam powerfully.

Twenty minutes later Reb climbed his mount out on the north bank. The Sundance Kid followed. Bill Carver showed up, gasping but game. Soon they were all together again.

"This is too hot fer comfort," Reb told them soberly, taking one of the heavy saddle-bags. "Here's where we split up. We'll go our own way, get good hosses wherever we can, gather on Ghost Creek as soon as possible, an' divvy. Okay?"

They chorused low agreement, intent on nothing so much as getting out of the country. None needed to be told it was up in arms—that danger hemmed them in on every hand. A few minutes later they had separated, riding in different directions, and the night-cloaked bank of the sullen Platte was deserted.

Chapter XVII

DOG EAT DOG

THERE were further exploits after the safe return to Wind River Basin, crowded one upon another. The Sundance Kid and the rest of the boys professed themselves royally pleased with Reb. Bill Carver, cared for in camp until he was around again, swore by him.

One by one Reb put them in debt to him until, although there was a freemasonry among them which took no open account of such things, he was their acknowledged leader.

He was at their head always. He planned and executed the daring bank robbery at Kemmerer; he passed on the advisability of the job at Burnt Creek, Montana, the stage station halfway between the mines and the railroad; it was he who vetoed the wholesale rustling by which the Logans proposed cleaning up the Basin in a burst of glory.

For his own part, Santee's cleverness amazed him no little. In his jovial moments—and they were many—he was not above expressing a laughing admiration of himself: "Hell of a note to be a natural born outlaw, an' never find it out!" It went farther toward self-justification than any of his hearers realized, such was his easy philosophy of life.

Everything seemed to be working out fine. More than once, two bunches were in operation at opposite ends of the Outlaw Trail at the same time. Through his knowledge of the Utah and lower Colorado range Reb worked out cattle drives too far away for him to attend to himself: an activity which gave Gloomy Jepson and the lesser luminaries of the Wild Bunch occupation.

As a result, Doc Lantry's pasture on Ghost Creek began to show a fresh and growing band of horses to sell. Doc was not wholly satisfied with this. He had come to perceive the magnitude of his connections and the need for a secure position; to cement it he carried out his word and acquired honestly a herd of steers.

It gave Reb an idea which he was not long in broaching.

"Look here, Doc," he said to Lantry one day in the presence of the others; "this stock end of the game is growin' top heavy. Why don't yuh turn business manager an' handle that side of it altogether?"

"Whut the hell are yuh drivin' at?" Lantry scowled, not at all pleased. "Yuh tryin' to git rid of me?"

As a matter of fact, Santee was. Experience had long since taught him that Doc was undependable. In the routine grind of handling stock he was brutally efficient; but the temperament which left him habitually morose rendered him excitable and jumpy in a pinch.

Unfortunately for Lantry, the Sundance Kid agreed with Reb. "Somebody's got to do the work, Doc," he pointed out. "Yo're good at it—we'll have to depend on yuh as much as yuh do on us."

"Shore," Reb inserted easily. "Stuff's showin' up on the Trail regular. The boys'll be keepin' yuh busy a big share of the time."

Between the two of them they persuaded Lantry, against his will, to attend the menial end of their activities at least for the present.

Doc knew what has happening. His jealousy of Reb became a naked flame. He never once identified the quality which made Santee so popular with the others; he could never have emulated it, in any event. Meanwhile Reb went his irrepressible way, riding off to his rash adventures with no diminishment of the grin and the flashing humor which endeared him to his companions.

There was the time Gloomy Jepson begged to be taken on a bank robbery and Reb, able to resist few pleas, consented. It was at Buffalo. An alert citizenry, augmented by cowboys as rollicking and daredevil as Santee himself, surprised them in the act and they were forced to fight their way to their horses for a swift retreat. Lead flew through the enclosed alley, the contest was in grim earnest. Lonny Logan sagged in the saddle of his rearing horse with a punctured shoulder; others were grazed. But Gloomy got a spur caught in his tapadero; his pony started away with fervor and Gloomy, clinging desperately to the saddlehorn and yelling lustily, hopped a considerable ways on one long leg, banged this way and that, frantic with the fear of being dragged.

It was too much for Santee. Danger or no danger, he burst into a bellow and laughed until he was weak. The last his fleeing comrades saw of him he was swinging belatedly into the saddle, guffawing recklessly in the face of the charging town. Half-an-hour later he caught up with them, unharmed, all his impatience at the failure of the haul dispersed by his still bubbling mirth over Gloomy's predicament.

Curiously the Kid did not frown on these capers, serious as he knew the danger of identification to be.

It irked him that Reb stuck to his employment with Jube Cameron; perhaps he hoped for it to end. It did not; and Reb's fortune in timing his trips was so good that it was never guessed he was away from the Upper Shoshone camp.

He was hasty enough in his work. Few broncs were broken with greater dispatch than those he wrangled. Often he took the chance of employing Flat Nose George, who had been a bronc peeler, and they spent a feverish day catching up, so that the round-up should find sufficient cow ponies for Cameron's need. Yet such was his luck that on the afternoon Sheriff Ward rode up on a cold scent, hunting the now notorious Wild Bunch, it was to find Reb serenely employed, alone, in his corral.

Santee was neither curious nor incurious concerning his activities and Ward left with the conviction that Reb knew nothing nor had seen anything of his quarry.

The weeks rolled by quickly. The grass was tall; the sun showed signs of summer ardence; almost the only chill in the air now came at dawn, when the early draughts blew down off the melting snow on the Wind River Peaks. One day Cameron rode out, to find the line camp deserted. Reb had been miles away to the north for three days; he found Cameron's tracks an hour later, and read them accurately. He caught up with the rancher before he got back to Rebel Creek.

"Where yuh been?" Jube inquired.

"Fool bronc threwed me yesterday, a ways from camp," Reb grinned without hesitation. "Made me so mad I dogged an' caught him. Then I give him a real run. . . . I found yore tracks."

Cameron nodded, passing it off. "Round-up time," he said briefly. "I'll be needin' yuh in a few days."

Reb gave him a long, slow look of questioning, but his voice as they talked over the plans for the work was even. That afternoon, having returned to the Upper Shoshone camp, he rode on to Ghost Creek. Most of the boys were spending a few days in idleness at the old shack of Lucas and Tapper, in the Owl Creeks, but the Sundance Kid was there, checking up with Lantry.

Reb told him what was afoot. "I owe it to Cameron," he said simply. "I promised him."

"Yuh got to go through with it, o' course," the Kid agreed. "It'll only be fer a few weeks."

Reb was oddly grateful for his understanding, so different from the black, stabbing look from Doc Lantry; there was a ready acquiescence to the range code in Logan which Doc wholly lacked. Reb had by now given his liking to the Kid, as he had at first liked Lantry, but in a new way. He told himself that *his* code would bring him back to the Wild Bunch as soon as he was free. He had gone too far to draw back, his scruples were paper, and not only that but there was something unexpected about the life, some secret thrill of challenge. . . .

He reckoned without the tug of that other life, however. On the morning he rode back to the C 8 spread, the day after he talked with Jube Cameron, he had scarcely hit the corrals before, from the ranch house, a small, trim, well-remembered figure came running—

It cost Reb a pang to smile into Ronda Cameron's shining, trustful, upturned face. *"Reb!* How good it is to see you!" There was a note of gladness in this lilting voice, deeper than ever before. Reb's heart bounded and stopped, then began again heavily. His own hopeless devotion rushed up to enmesh his confused thoughts and enslave his senses.

There was much to talk about. He didn't have to ask after Billy Farragoh. Ronda had seen the boy just before she left Lander. He had been cramming steadily and was almost ready for his bar examination, she announced. "Isn't that just fine, Reb? Aren't you proud of him?"

A moment later Ronda was off on another tack: "And aren't you ashamed of yourself, young man, for staying away from Mother Farragoh ever since you did so much for Billy! She's provoked with you. . . . Oh, I heard all about your sprees together at the Point, during the winter while the men were sick."

She laughed over the legerdemain Reb had practiced on the Shoshones; commented on her father's return to health and a dozen other topics, with freedom and animation, and did not note Reb's troubled silence.

He had retired into himself for once, more than a little upset. Ronda! Good God, how could he have forgotten her? Her trust and frank affection, the light in her fine eyes, washed over him like a bitter accusation. Useless to hope for her love now! Wasn't it? He found no answer to his panic and beat back away from it with shame, only to have it engulf him afresh at every turn of the girl's head, every gesture of her arms that sent the fire of longing racing through his veins.

How he got through that afternoon he did not know. Ronda noted nothing strange about him, but it was almost with relief, and a wild, tormenting sense of loss, that he rode away to the round-up. He threw himself into the work with the vigor of three men and if the C 8 hands noted any slackening of his humor they attributed it to fatigue.

It was too great a strain for a nature such as his not to revolt. During the week Cameron sent him east to rep through the badlands outfits, Santee's exuberance broke out one day when he met Bill Carver riding an isolated range. Reb turned his back on the round-up and together they rode south twenty miles to get a drink from the stock of Big Foot Sal.

It was a small place, a freight station run by Sal's husband at Soldier's Crossing. The liquor was bad and Hank Breen was morose; but Big Foot Sal, a bent and aged harridan, could swear more luridly than any freighter who stopped there, her stringy hair hanging over her beady, snapping eyes and her jaw clacking like a nut-cracker. Her fame had a currency worthy of the best entertainment.

It was accordingly not without intent that, having tested the solace of her liquor and found it wanting, Santee stood in the station yard and shot the heads neatly off a dozen of her scrawny, scratching chickens. At every crack of the unerring six-gun Big Foot Sal emitted a fresh outburst of blistering invective, weird and thrilling, until Reb was doubled over with mirth and Bill Carver rolled on the ground in his glee.

"Dang it, Reb, yo're a card!" he gasped weakly.

Big Foot Sal corrected that impression. With staggering inventiveness she explained exactly what Santee was, and it was plenty. She waved her skinny arms at him and stamped her feet, on which were worn boots at least half-a-dozen sizes too large for her.

"Well, Sal; it's worth somethin' to have the cards read on me like that," Reb laughed, when she was out of breath. With magnificent abandon he tossed her a double eagle for each decapitated pullet.

Big Foot Sal subsided in momentary astonishment, her toothless jaws working feverishly, but her cupidity saw to it that she gathered up the golden coins with the promptitude of a miser. They disappeared within the folds of her tattered, voluminous dress. She could not bring herself to fawn, however. As if wishing to clinch the validity of the bargain, she treated them to a parting blast of vituperation as they rode away.

But the relief of such a lapse from grace, for Reb, was only temporary. The next day, chastened and on the job once more, his thoughts were as gloomy as ever. He could not forget how low he had sunk. What would Ronda say if she knew? What was he heading for?

It was Doc Lantry who undertook to answer this question for him, if not wholly to Reb's satisfaction. During the round-up season the Sundance Kid took his men off from time to time, and did two jobs which Reb had planned in neighboring counties. Lantry received his cut, but it was being left behind that rankled with him. He said as much.

"Whut yuh belly-achin' about?" The Kid retorted with scant consideration. "Santee's out of it too, ain't he?"

"Yeh—an' if it's up to him, I'll always be out of it! I know he's puttin' the skids under me with the rest of yuh!" Doc knew it was the worst thing he could do, to admit his knowledge that he was in eclipse; he could not help himself. There was more of it, and of the irksomeness of his monotonous employment. It had grown on him with passing time that not only were they letting him out, but he was being used. He blamed it all on Santee and it fanned his resentment to the pitch of fury. "I tell yuh it's got to stop!" he shouted, the veins bulging on his forehead. "I won't have it!"

The Kid gave him a smoky-eyed look of contempt.

"You'll stay right where yuh are an' do what yo're doin'," he gave ultimatum with a clipped thinness. "If that don't suit yuh, settle it with Santee."

"I will," Doc yelled. "By God, I'll settle it with him one way or another!"

But later, when he had cooled off, he knew that he would have to devise some means of getting rid of Reb without incriminating himself, and the first step was to make it appear that he was ready to forget.

"Reckon I was a little hasty," he said to the Kid craftily. "It's jest the nag of this damn work, an' not knowin' if the rest of yuh are all right. I'll rock along as I'm doin'."

"See that yuh do," Logan nodded. "There ain't none of us gits what we want, exactly."

He was expressing a truth which all outlaws know to their secret sorrow; but as he turned away, Doc told himself, square-jawed that he would change this in his own case at least.

"Damn sudden an' complete," he added, his hatred of Reb flaming afresh. "Santee said it was dog eat dog in this game. He had a gall! I'll show him a few fangs of my own."

That was the way Doc saw the situation. All that remained was to find the means.

Chapter XVIII

HAIL AND FAREWLL

"HERE yuh are then," said Mrs. Farragoh portentously, stepping to the edge of the porch. "Come up an' let me get a good look at yuh." Her good-natured, bullying tone commanded obedience.

Reb grinned at Ronda as they dismounted before the steps. He moved forward sheepishly, doffing the big soiled sombrero.

"Shucks, ma'am, I been powerful busy," he said apologetically, "or I'd have been here sooner. Miss Ronda said yuh had a piece of news that couldn't wait."

"Yes; and I practically had to waltz him over here myself, to make sure he came," Ronda inserted smilingly.

Mother Farragoh ignored Reb's lead for the moment. She examined him critically, as a woman might a mannequin, and then turned to Ronda.

"*Is* this the plausible young rip who's been backin' my son?" she inquired. "I don't seem to reco'nize him. Let me see. . . ."

Her manner further confused Reb, who chuckled his embarrassment. He had a good deal of explaining to do to justify his long absence; but when he had managed this, Mrs. Farragoh changed abruptly.

"Reb, my boy's passed his bar examination." Suspicious moisture stood in her eyes, her blunt old warrior's face seemed soft. "He's close to bein' a full-fledged lawyer." Plain to be seen that the knowledge left her heart full.

"Ma'am, that's—fine! I reckon yo're right proud of him." Reb shuffled, but his manner was sincere.

"Wal, I am. I'm proud o' you, too, Reb. It was you, got him to take a chance an' go to Lander right off." She was husky now. "He was farther along 'n anybody knowed."

There was more of this. It got to Reb, beyond his diffidence, with unaccustomed warmth; it made him feel *good*, with Ronda standing there, smiling at him, yielding all her good will: possessive, too, as a girl will be.

"Billy wants us to come to Lander," the boy's mother went on, folding her thick arms. "There's goin' to be a kind of celebration. He says he won't take no excuses."

Reb looked at her blankly. "Us?" he repeated, taken off his guard.

"Shore. Reckon we c'n do that much fer him." She was scrutinizing him keenly, asking a question. "*I'll* go if I have to wear an Injun bonnet."

"Yes, and you too, Reb," Ronda added. She was laughingly in earnest. "The round-up is over. You have no reason to refuse."

"I—well, I—" he began.

"Don't yuh say no!" Mrs. Farragoh warned. "I don't want the job of explainin' to that boy why yuh didn't come. Why, he's a *man* now, Reb! None of our doin's is more important than his."

The prospect of such a trip threw Reb into uncertainty. All his gay self-command threatened to desert. But he clung to one thought.

"Are you goin' along?" he asked Ronda.

"Yes." A faint tinge of red unaccountably touched her cheeks as she made answer.

It decided him. He did not pause to question the cause of that flush, appropriating it to himself. "We'll all go, then," he said simply. Vaguely he knew that the sojourn to Lander would have its painful aspects for him, but he experienced a delicious clandestine thrill in anticipation of Ronda's company that made him put the knowledge aside.

There were plans and suggestions. They had no great length of time to spare. The next morning they started off in the spring wagon which Ronda had been driving when Reb first met her.

"Seems queer not to fork a hoss, after the round-up," he confessed, as they headed south down the Basin. "But I been wantin' to buy me a new saddle. I'll do it in Lander."

He was in excellent spirits this morning. He joked and laughed with them until they were in stitches. They thought they had never seen him in better form. At any time during that long drive he was likely to burst into song. Mother Farragoh's humorous jibes— she treated him much as a man would have done— found no chink in his impudent armor.

She was dressed stiffly today in bombazine and black ribbons to do honor to her son, her seams bursting, and even Reb was decked out in a new shirt and kerchief and a nearly clean hat, and carried a coat which he obviously disliked to put on. As for Ronda, she was a vision, ravishing in a gown of sheerest blue under her coat, which she said was evening wear, for the party—"We must look our best for Billy, you know, from the minute he lays eyes on us."

But she had a smile for Reb as she said it, and there was no lapse of her attention for him throughout the day. Her proximity intoxicated him. When she brushed against his shoulder or he caught a whiff of the aroma of her hair, a glimpse of the soft skin at her throat or temples something laid hold of him with almost physical violence. He wanted this girl, as he had done from the first—but more insistently now, a desire with a fierce sting in it. There was no real reason on earth, he told himself with heady assurance, why he could not have her. And once he did, anything would need to have wildcat ferocity to come between them. . . .

The truth was that familiarity with his situation, plus a little honest sweat, had gradually restored to him his self-respect. Other men had dealt with these things. There was no goal beyond whatever barrier that he could not reach if he strove mightily enough. . . . The wine of Ronda imbued him with unconquerable spirit. His gaiety increased, if anything. Ronda joined with him as in a conspiracy, her cheeks glowing and her eyes bright; and if Mrs. Farragoh bent a wondering glance on Reb occasionally he did not notice it.

They arrived in Lander in the early evening in a gale of merriment. It seemed odd to them all that the town was not decorated, that folk on the street went about their concerns calmly; for there had been much talk of Billy, and had that individual heard their praises he would have lost something of the quietly grinning poise with which he met them at the hotel.

"Don't eat a thing," he told them at once. "That will come later. Just get yourselves ready."

The women retired to their room for this purpose. Billy evaded the offer of a drink, but handed Reb a cigar as they stepped back to the dusky veranda to talk while they waited.

"Well, Reb," he said with controlled exuberance, "I've got my foot on the first rung—thanks to you."

Reb congratulated him. He found a change in Billy. a touch of maturity, of self-possession, that had not been there before. He was surprised when Billy handed him a small packet of bills.

"What's this?" he got out.

"You'll find that adds up to two hundred dollars," Billy replied in a pleased tone. "I didn't need the whole five hundred, Reb. I thought I could give more of it back, but I found—"

Reb cut him off with protests. He would have urged the other to keep the money, but on reflection he stuffed it into his own pocket. It somehow made his secret offense against Billy lighter, if only by a little. And Billy was so pleased to be able to cut down his indebtedness by this much that Reb had not the heart to deny him.

"Judge Hamer and a few colleagues have arranged to admit me to the bar tomorrow," he announced, as they talked on. "I'll stay in the Judge's office for the present. He says he wants me. . . . He's giving a little party for us at his home tonight."

The little party proved to be quite an affair. A number of Lander's prominent figures were present, with their wives. Mrs. Farragoh commented to Reb *sotto voce* that she felt like a fish out of water in such company, and Reb was in little better case. He wondered what would have been said if all these highly respectable people were to recognize him in his true colors. They treated him, however, as one of themselves, and his ability to mix readily with all comers stood him in good stead.

Even Judge Hamer—a big, bluff, hearty-voiced man with eyes as piercing as Reb's own—had known the pound of saddle leather in his youth, and passed a word about the range. Santee was not long in perceiving that Hamer had taken a fancy to Billy Farragoh and meant to put his political influence behind him without reserve. Billy would go far, that was assured.

Later in the evening, after a prodigious meal, with appointments of silver and china and a flutter of napery such as Reb had never before seen, he suffered his first twinge of misgiving as he watched Billy and Ronda Cameron dancing together. It was not their smooth rhythm, suited perfectly to the music, or entirely their graceful complement of each other, as if they had been made to dance together—to live and breathe together —so much as their rapt engrossment in each other, to the exclusion of the entire company, that disquieted Reb. A thin blade of doubt slipped into him which he laughed away uneasily at the punch bowl.

But it was the next morning, at court, that the blow fell. Ronda and Billy had together accorded Reb much attention after that dance; they had talked late, and gone to bed weary and content, all three. In the court room, however, after the sober rite in which Billy was admitted to the Wyoming bar, it was only for each other that the two had eyes. Ronda won to Billy's side even before his mother: she lifted up her arms, put them around his neck and kissed him.

Even Reb knew there was some special significance

in that frank, whole-hearted kiss. A lump in his throat choked him at once, a great blur blinded him and left him dazed and groggy. He stumbled to the door and out, and something seemed to burst in his chest. Ronda loved, not him, but Billy Farragoh! The knowledge had come as a staggering surprise, and it was devastating.

"Why couldn't I've guessed?" he groaned. "Her always bein' with him—comin' down here, an' all." But even that foreknowledge would not have made his way any easier.

It was Billy who sought him out later, with a clap on the shoulder. An exultant light beamed in the younger man's eyes.

"Well, Reb—we've done it!" he declared, and there was deep gratitude in his voice as well as pride. "Now all you have to do is to bring your troubles to me."

Reb found the irony of it hard to bear.

Ronda approached them. Billy turned to her with a fond smile. "Now I can announce my engagement to the future Mrs. Farragoh," he said, with no knowledge of how the words tore.

It was Ronda's hand that slipped into Reb's then. "Reb, you're glad, aren't you? Doesn't it please you?"

There was an appeal here that Reb could not refuse, sick as he was at heart. "Shore, I—I reckon I'm tickled to death," he managed, his grin masking the ache. "You two are made for each other," he went on gallantly. "I seen that last night."

Neither noted how late the knowledge had come to him. For his part, only his loyalty to their faith in him could steady him now. With a pang he found himself ranged against the fondest wishes of the two persons he loved most in the world. He drew back from that treachery precipitately. That it was treachery to himself to see it thus did not come to him till long afterward. He had been betrayed earlier, by his own hand, he felt, and he was man enough to admit it.

There was more celebrating that day. Reb found it impossible to enter into the spirit of it. Mother Farragoh alone noted his quiet and talked with him a good deal in a gruff tone that was like a tonic. She had plenty of opportunity. The two young people—he saw their youth now, for he felt like the Old Man of the Mountain—were wrapped up in each other and in the happiness that opened out before them. But when they turned to him, as they did unexpectedly from time to time, he met them bravely, with a ready sympathy. He was still a great spirit to them, whatever he was to himself.

It got to be a kind of nightmare at last from which he was glad to escape. The merest possibility of these two ever discovering him in his true character opened a pit before him like the yawning chasm of death itself. "I've got to get along back," he said, announcing his intention of returning forthwith to Wind River Basin. "Soon as I get me a new saddle I'm on my way."

It was a different saddle in more ways than one, from the tree he had straddled so long. The very world itself looked different. When he cinched up the blue roan, which had trotted to Lander behind the spring wagon, and headed out, it was with no intention of returning to the duties on the C 8 the others supposed him to be thinking about. His eyes were bleak and he was face to face with the emptiness of existence.

"Reckon I'll make Cameron my excuses, tell the

Bunch to go to hell, an' ride out of Wyomin'," he muttered his thought without awareness.

There was no suspicion in him then that he would have difficulty performing any of these things. His heart was haunted by the gray eyes and black tresses of the girl who was lost to him forever; he was able to dwell on nothing else for long, unless it was the dull determination to put unnumbered miles between himself and the scene of this catastrophe.

Chapter XIX

COYOTE OR WOLF?

DUST raised up in clouds and settled in a thinning golden fog as the last of the steers lowed and trotted past the ranch on Ghost Creek. Doc Lantry waited only to see that the boys pushed them on toward the Owl Creek Mountains and then swinging his pony back, rode in to hitch it at the ranch corral and walk toward the dugout.

The Sundance Kid waited there, fiddling with a dead cigarette, a frown on that good-looking thin face that could turn so sullen. Doc saw him, but he affected nonchalance. The Kid wouldn't let him get away without a brush.

He said: "Look here, Lantry. That stuff was drove off right here in the Basin, wasn't it?"

"Yeh. But don't worry—I broke the trail."

"Yuh was with the boys all the time, was yuh?"

Lantry assented gruffly.

The Kid spoke in a wintry voice that carried a biting flick. "Yuh planned the raid yoreself, too, I gather. . . . Don't scowl at me like that, Lantry! What did Santee tell yuh about layin' off here near the hide-out?"

Doc's gusty wrath exploded into nervous fragments of words. The hell with Santee! He was gone, wasn't he? Let him give orders and ride off—and see where it got him! Didn't this place belong to Doc himself? . . . Well?

If it was wholesale challenge that Lantry flung out, the Kid accepted it. As Doc attempted to walk past him into the dugout with a morose independence, Logan's thin, iron fingers whirled him back sharply. The lowering face he found thrust into his own was hawk-like.

"Don't try that with me, Lantry!" the dead level voice bit out. "I know Santee can shrug an' pass off yore damned orneryness, but I ain't good at it! From here on out yuh can mutter an' glare all yuh please— but you do as yore told. That means keep yore paws out of the rustlin' an' let Santee decide what's to be run off. Savvy?"

Doc began to fume, all the skin visible above his rumpled open collar turning a lobster red.

The Kid cut him off: "I know how yuh feel, mister! But git this: it's eat crow now or lead later! An' if you'll have yore lead now, I daresay I can square myself with Reb. Do yuh git it?"

Lantry got it. What was more, he saw Santee's hand all too plainly behind it all. They were trying to oust him from the Bunch; they *had* ousted him, they were making him the goat all around. Without the interference of the flaxen-haired one it would never have happened. Doc cursed the day he had fallen for Reb's treacherous smile. It was a laugh that that one didn't know what he was doing, as Doc had once thought— he knew!

But Doc didn't laugh. This ceaseless iteration of his curse was driving him crazy. Crazy with rage.

"I got to walk shy—an' act quick," he told himself, sweating, as soon as he was alone. "Santee's been watchin' me an' now he's got the Kid doin' it." He cursed feverishly as he realized that he didn't know what minute he was under surveillance. It made him stealthy, suspicious as a coyote, venomous as a snake.

He rode into the Owl Creeks to get away from Logan and to make sure the stolen bunch of steers had gone its appointed way. But the boys didn't have much to say to him when he caught up; he thought they looked at him funny. He gave up and rode back to Ghost Creek in a savage temper.

The Sundance Kid rode away the next morning on business of his own, and after that Lantry breathed easier. But not for long. Two different times during that afternoon he thought he got a glimpse of some skulker watching the ranch.

"Dammit, I'll put a stop to this!" he raged under his breath, the second time it occurred.

Swinging into the saddle, he was ready for anything. He knew he ran the risk of sudden attack the moment he smoked out the man who was shadowing him. But his hand was clammy with desire for the six-gun grip; he was sick with determination.

Heading at a run for the spot where he had last got a flash of the skulker, he rode on past, topped a crest and then, out of sight, followed an eroded gully which circled around to a point on his back trail. There he waited, crowded into concealment, ready.

He was not kept long in suspense. Within the minute a cautious advance could be heard, the dull clink of hoofs on soil. It lit a flame in Lantry. His temples pounded. So they had a man on his trail, did they? By God, he'd let them find the fellow dead! That would bring them up short.

The trail led down the cut bank into the gully, across

at an angle, and up a little path to the other side. Lantry crouched, dismounted, under the over-hang. His six-gun was out, his thumb white on the hammer. His lips were drawn back from the tobacco-stained teeth in a vulpine snarl. When his pursuer's pony slid down into the gully on bunched hoofs, Lantry reached out to yank down the curb-chain, thrusting his gun up. As the pony stamped, the two men exchanged leaping glances, looks clashing like flint on steel.

Doc's jaw dropped. The man was no member of the Wild Bunch at all. It was Ike Lucas, chased out of this country months ago by a grim-lipped posse. He looked as if he had been on the dodge ever since. His stubble was long, his hair unkempt, his clothes ragged and weather stained. Just now he was taut with petrifying surprise, his low brow knotted in anticipation of violence.

Lantry's eyes were opaque with uncertainty but his harsh voice grated:

"Whut're yuh doin' here, Lucas?"

A change swept over Ike, like flooding relief.

"Gawd!" he gasped. "I thought yuh was—someone else."

There was too much surprise here for it to be in-sincere. It increased Doc's lingering doubt of the man's object. That Lucas was not one of Sundance Kid's crowd disjointed all his expectations. For the moment he didn't know what to think. He did not relax his vigilance.

"Yuh was trailin' me!" he charged. "Whut fer?"

Lucas expostulated: "I wasn't layin' fer yuh, Doc, honest! I was after—" He stopped, sucking in his breath as if his tongue had betrayed him.

Doc's eyes narrowed. "Yuh was after Reb Santee, wasn't yuh?"

Lucas's startled look was acquiescence enough.

"Figgerin' to knock 'im off?" Doc went on inexorably.

"No! I—I wanted to take it out of his hide, fer what he done to me an' Stony. That's all, Doc, I swear!" Lucas's words were hurried, nervous, persuasive.

Doc was not deceived. Ike thought he was on Reb's side—that he would tell Reb, perhaps get him killed if he didn't do it himself. Ike was at bottom a coward, he knew. In the same instant, another side of Lantry's brain leaped in calculation. He saw his great chance. He could use Lucas. Ike was the perfect engine of revenge—a man who hated Santee! Doc didn't even have to prime him. All he had to do was help, see to it that Ike got his chance.

All this flashed through Doc's mind in a second. He heard himself saying: "Yuh don't have to lie to me, Ike. I know how a man can hate Santee! It's all right. . . ."

There was a good deal more of this, cunningly put, for Lucas was cagy, his fear of Reb Santee was genuine, as strong as his hatred. Lantry played on him as upon an instrument. Even after he was convinced that they saw eye to eye, however, Lucas still could not understand why Doc had not taken his own revenge before this.

"Never mind," Lantry told him. "It'll all come to yuh in time, Ike. I'd be marked, can't yuh see that? I got a place here I don't want to ride away from— the Wild Bunch would crack down on me in a hurry." He waggled his head shrewdly.

"How 'bout me?" Ike queried suspiciously.

"Nobody knows yo're here but me," Lantry pointed out. "Yuh can do yore job an' drag it, an' who'll be the wiser? Whut's more, I'll see that yuh have all yuh need, an' a little stake to start away with."

They talked it over from all angles. Lucas finally agreed to stick around until Santee returned—he was at Lander just now—and shoot him down. It was decided that the only safe and sure means was for Ike to bushwhack his man from cover. Flame leaped in his eye as he spoke of it. Lantry didn't know whether to trust him or not; but whatever doubts he had of Lucas's nerve, there could be none concerning the validity of his intentions.

"In the meantime, yuh better hole up an' lay low," Doc advised smoothly. "I'll let yuh know when Santee gits back."

"Where'll I go—up to our old place in the Owi Creeks?"

"God, no!" Lantry didn't want the Wild Bunch to so much as dream of Lucas's presence yet—though there was some hazy hope in his crafty brain that he could manage to have these deadly men bring down the dry-gulcher later on, and thus clear himself of any suspicion of complicity. They'd see it all quick enough: the story of Reb's dealings with Lucas and Tapper had got around.

Doc told Ike of a remote hide-out in the hills, warned him to go there at once and remain, and started him off towards it forthwith.

"Wait," was his parting word; "yuh got a damn good rifle, ain't yuh? . . . Okay. I'll bring a box of shells;

but Ike, yuh better know now, yuh won't have time to use more'n one of 'em!"

"Don't worry!" Lucas's eyes were wicked. "I'll do the trick slick an' clean, the fust whack. What I want the exter shells fer is what comes after."

There was a sinister note in this not easily to be mistaken. In a way, Lucas was conveying a warning and a promise. There was to be no dirty work beyond what they had carefully planned. He well knew the hornet's nest the slaying of Reb Santee would stir up, and he was preparing for it.

Lantry was quick to read the danger to his own plans. It made him wary. At the same time it answered his question of Ike's efficiency. The man was a mad wolf now. He said nothing, nodding carelessly, hoping Lucas would not too soon awaken from the false security of bitter hate which Doc himself had induced.

Without further words they parted, Lucas to strike back into the hills with the alert caution of a wild thing; Lantry to return to Ghost Creek, savagely content.

"Now we'll see where mister Reb gits off," he nodded grimly to the empty, peaceful and embracing range as he rode.

Chapter XX

THE CAREFUL MAN

Y O'RE makin' a big mistake," said Jube Cameron seriously. "It ain't because I'm losin' yuh,
Reb. I don't need to tell yuh that. But a man
that turns down a chance like this don't know what
he's doin'."

Santee shook his head again, regretful but decided.
It struck him how seldom a man—in this case, his employer—could be so completely wrong when he believed
he was absolutely right.

Jube had just offered him the foremanship of the
C 8 ranch. It was just one more straw added to the
heap of ironies that ringed the puncher about. Reb
said no; he voiced his intention of leaving altogether,
and offered a dozen excuses which Cameron declared
to be evasions and refused to accept. After that, Reb
ceased to explain himself, but he stood pat. Now he
was meeting the arguments the rancher advanced why
he had to remain. He owed it to Ronda's father at
least to listen.

"Does anybody else know whut yo're aimin' to do?"
Cameron bored in. He was genuinely concerned, studying Reb shrewdly. "Have yuh told yore friends, Reb,
or have yuh stopped listenin' to 'em?"

This searching barb, and others, failed to find lodge-
ment in Reb. "I told yuh, Cameron, I'm driftin' on,"
he said patiently, his smile harassed, a little worn. "I
might better take it on the loose now, than let yuh
down later when yo're dependin' on me."

He clung to that doggedly. All the cunning the rancher had exercised before, and that he thought had given him power over Reb, could not move him now. Jube knew better than to lose his temper. His face became heavy, his manner ponderous.

"Are yuh feelin' sick?" he probed insistently. "Is there somethin' the matter with yuh? . . . Yuh don't look any too happy since yuh got back from Lander."

This was too close home for comfort. Reb's ingenious countenance lengthened. He assumed a woebegone look.

"Cameron, now yuh mention it, I *don't* feel so good," he confessed. "Reckon I need a change. I—I got aches an' pains regular since I been workin' fer yuh steady, an' sometimes my head feels light." He heaved a sigh.

For a moment Jube looked at him searchingly: then without warning he fetched Reb a blow on the back that staggered him, and burst into a guffaw of rumbling mirth.

"Dang yuh, yuh near had me that time!" he roared, his features reddening as he shook. "Reckon I ought to know yore breed if I'm ever goin' to, yuh footloose young scallawag. . . . Come on up to the office an' I'll give yuh yore time, it that's what yuh want. We'll have a drink on it an' yuh can look me up the next time yuh drift into the Basin."

Half an hour later Reb rode away from the C 8, jobless. He sang a song and affected light-heartedness as long as Jube Cameron's eyes could follow him. After that he relaxed imperceptibly under the shadow that had come to him so suddenly in Lander.

"Reckon I had to lie to Jube," he thought soberly. "I'm havin' to lie more an' more to everybody. It ain't much—but it's hell when I don't want to."

He had taken the best course with Cameron, he saw now. The rancher had insisted on some good reason why he was quitting. Santee had been forced to play his cards with cunning. They seemed to sum up to the fact that he had no reason he could put a name to. Cameron drew the inevitable conclusion that he was simply irresponsible, a drifter, driven on his aimless way by the restlessness that was in him.

Six months ago that would have been true of Reb. Had it not been for the peculiar and telling force with which the Basin country had hit him—his meeting with Ronda Cameron—it would have been true now. But he had concealed these things beneath a laughing armor, absorbed and buried the impact which the girl and her home had had for him: perhaps even she and Billy Farragoh would believe in the lame reasons for leaving which Reb had given his employer. They would feel sorry to see him go but they would understand, and after a time they would forget. . . .

"That's the greatest kindness I can do Ronda now," he mused bleakly. "Lettin' her forget all about me."

He was riding toward Ghost Creek as he thought these things, paralleling the willow-garnished border of a creek feeder at several hundred yards. It was summer now, rich and lustrous: the grass was deep and green, the sky smiling, the air soft and balmy. Flowers dotted the slopes, wild sweet scents assailed the nostrils; but Santee was oblivious of his surroundings until something tugged sharply at his shirt-front and buzzed away with an angry note.

Reb jerked backward away from it by instinct; and as his mind leaped to the present with a jar, he allowed himself to slip on, tumbling out of the saddle with lax grace. He knew what it was that had come so close to him, even before the belated crack of a rifle report followed. He had barely struck the ground when he found his feet; an instant later he gripped the pony's bridle and peered under its neck, six-gun in hand.

His movements from the time he had leaned back in the first flash of awareness had not taken more than five seconds, yet already the white puff of rifle smoke was dissipated, for he could not locate it. A minute passed—another—while he scanned the line of willows from which he believed the shot had come: and now the hundred minute sounds and scents of the peaceful day drove in upon him.

He paid them no more heed than before, a dread alertness on him. Although he could not suppose the hidden marksman to believe his attack successful, there were apparently to be no more shots despite the fact that a determined man could have dropped his pony and made it hot for him—perhaps sooner or later got him.

"Somebody with no guts," he muttered, his lips twitching with a cold, sardonic amusement. "Reckon it's jest as well for me."

He did not swing astride the roan and ride straight for the willows as he might have done could he have trusted the bravery of the man who lay there still, or else had crept away. Leading his mount and remaining shielded by it, he angled toward the treacherous cover, waiting for the moment the would-be assassin might believe to be another sure chance.

It never came. Reb reached the willows unmolested. No pony stood tethered on the other side. When he swung up and rode forward there was no sign to be read, nothing. Reb pursed his lips and squinted, looking away.

"Whoever done that was a damned careful man," he mused. "Now what feller like that do I know who's got it in fer me?"

It was a rhetorical question. As a matter of fact Doc Lantry had leaped into his mind at once. For an instant he felt the impulse to get to the dugout in a hurry—he felt sure he would find Doc there before him—and face the man out. Then he shook his head.

"No," he said, "I won't do that. Lord knows I got reason enough. But I ain't shore it was him: an' if it was, somethin' drove Lantry to this, an' I know what it is. He's jealous. He'll get over it when I ride away. An' I'll go at my own pace. I don't figger to be chased."

He knew what the result of a clash between himself and Lantry would be. There could be only one—death for Doc, blood on his own hands. He didn't want that.

When he rode up to the dugout later on, Lantry was there. Reb unsaddled deliberately and stepped in. Doc was fiddling with his pipe. He looked up with a show of interest.

"Back, eh?"

Reb was preoccupied. "Where's the Kid?" he countered.

Doc was watching him furtively. His tone was too hearty, overbold. "I dunno, Reb. He's been gone a couple days."

"Yuh shore? Yuh ain't been away yoreself?"

"No."

"Rest of the boys around?"

"No, they're away too."

They talked on, Lantry never turning his back. Wariness kept him from putting the questions Reb guessed were burning on his tongue. He hummed to himself, pottering about. Reb paid no attention to him directly.

The truth was, something else weighed on his mind. He would have to wait now for the Sundance Kid's return to tell him of his decision to leave. He didn't want to. At the same time, he recognized that he didn't want to tell the Kid and the boys that he was pulling out at all.

A new thought came—one he would not have entertained before. Why throw up the Wild Bunch even now? The Kid at least was a faithful friend. The jobs they did together were an occupation. He could perhaps persuade the Bunch to leave with him and they could operate elsewhere. The attempt on his life, little as it had bothered him, warned that he could never be wholly safe again; it was just enough to supply the spark of stubbornness needed to bulwark this resolve.

Curiously, the change in the direction of his thoughts made a difference in his feeling about that shot on the range, too. Like a match to powder, his deciding to stick it out with the boys awakened a resentment against the intended murderer that strengthened the longer he thought about it. Somebody trying to put him out of the way, eh? It brought him to life in a way he had not thought possible when he had said good-bye to Ronda.

He went outside, and without caring whether Lantry watched or not, looked for the heated pony Doc must have recently released if he had fired that unwarning shot and then ridden hard to be here first. He didn't find it. Doc's favorite mount dozed in the corral: it had not worn a saddle for hours. It proved nothing, but it served further to remind Reb of Lantry's shrewd caution.

He said nothing, but instead went about using his own method to produce results. Pointed and contemptuous indifference was something Doc was not constituted to withstand for long. For the rest of the day he stuck close to the dugout. He and Lantry watched each other in an unremitting cat and mouse game. Though Reb seemed as cool as ever, it set up a tension in Lantry which the arrival of Gloomy Jepson did nothing to relieve.

Gloomy came into the dugout with the air of an accomplishment and flung down his saddle.

"Wal, Doc, we got 'em away—" he began; and stopped abruptly, when Lantry made agitated signals for him to be silent, behind Santee's back.

Reb turned around. "Got what away?" he queried.

Gloomy had been about to discuss the steers which had been run out of the Basin: a matter Doc emphatically did not want Reb to know anything about until it could no longer be avoided. He knew the towheaded one already suspected him of something—else why had he kept so silent about the attempt on his life which Ike Lucas had promised to make today? Anything— such as this rustling in the Basin—might serve Reb as an excuse for the explosion Lantry sensed to be boiling up in him.

"Some frisky young bulls pawin' an' fightin' out near our east fence," Doc inserted suavely. "I sent Gloomy an' a couple others out to push 'em away before they knocked down the wire."

Reb saw through this. He could have riddled the evasion in short order, but he let it go, glancing at Gloomy. Jepson was examining a torn rope-callous on his palm. He shook his head when he caught Santee's eye.

"Well, Gloomy, better pour a little whisky on that. I reckon yo're about ready to collapse."

"I'm about ready to do somethin'," Gloomy returned cryptically. After Reb smiled and turned away he shot a resentful stare at Lantry.

It was a strange evening the three passed. Little was said. Two of them, at least, were waiting—and perhaps all three, for Gloomy read a note of suspense in the atmosphere, stolid as he ordinarily was. He followed his usual custom of aloof indifference. Doc Lantry was the last to roll into his bunk, and that only after Reb had decided the Logans would not return tonight, and Gloomy had long been snoring.

In the morning Reb saddled up and rode away without a word. He returned to the scene of his close call and circled it at a distance of a mile. Still he found no suspicious sign—but on the crest of a swell a brace of miles from the dugout he did find a set of tracks he was unable to recognize. He followed it for a ways, his interest growing.

"Looks like a hombre with mysterious business, whoever he is," he murmured. "I'd say he was watchin' fer somethin'—or somebody."

For the first time it came to him that it might not have been Doc Lantry who had fired the shot at him after all, despite his willingness to give the outlaw a break. "Here I was huntin' fer proof that it was him—

an' now I'm provin' it wasn't," he grinned. "Maybe," he added after a moment.

He intended to find out the answer. Without ado he set off on the trail he had discovered. It led for miles in a series of loops around the Ghost Creek ranch, and then struck off toward the Owl Creek Range. Reb pursued, his brows knit in speculation.

"He shore hemstitched our range fer fair," he mused. "But who in time is it?"

The solution to the riddle lay somewhere to the fore. Santee pushed on into the Owl Creek rises, keeping a keen watch ahead, on each side and to the rear. At no time was the trail easy to follow; nowhere did it fade out altogether.

He was tracing it across an open space in a wooded valley, miles from the Basin range, when, looking ahead, he saw in the rocky walls beyond, a narrow canyon crevasse he felt sure the unknown had been headed for. He drew up and eased himself in the saddle, considering.

"That's no good," he thought. "I can't get in there without bein' seen. This's a real out-of-the-way place all right—he's prob'ly holed up." He turned it over thoughtfully, while the blue roan cropped grass and looked around. "I'll watch," he decided.

He left the trail, heading for cover. The man was bound to come out some time. If his business took him toward Ghost Creek, he would come this way. Reb nodded over this, his eye-corners crinkled, and settled to wait.

He was prepared for a long vigil, but as it turned out it was but a short one. In ten minutes' time another rider appeared roughly in the direction from which he had come, and headed for the canyon. Doc Lantry's gaunt, hard frame was easily recognizable.

It fetched a grunt from Reb. "I wasn't so far wrong about him, after all," he told himself. Only the sharpening of his blue eyes would have told what this meant to him.

Doc rode on. After a little he disappeared in the mouth of the canyon. When the rattle of his pony's hoofs ceased on the bare rock, Reb came out of his concealment. All his movements were precise now, his muscles driven by a brusque compulsion not of the mind. He climbed the roan carefully up a rocky shoulder to a point from which he could look into the little canyon.

At first he saw nothing. Then he made them out against the dun background—Lantry standing beside his horse in the cuplike hollow, talking to a second man, ragged of appearance, with eagle vigilance and a rifle slanting in his grasp—Ike Lucas. Even at several hundred yards Santee recognized him instantly. Something caught him up then, bitter and uncompromising. It was the crisis—not for Reb, not so much for Lucas—as for Doc Lantry. Santee knew what had crawled in the man's brain for so long, and what Doc had done about it at last. His mouth hardened.

"So that's the way of it!" he gritted.

In the instant that he recklessly pushed the roan forward to slide to the canyon floor, Lantry and Lucas looked up, startled by the clatter of small stones, and saw him.

Chapter XXI

WITH HIS BOOTS ON

IKE LUCAS'S rifle came up with convulsive swift-
ness. The ringing shot echoed in the rocky
crevasse. It did not stop Santee. He leaned back
in the saddle as the roan took the slide, yanked his hat
down and came on.

A series of crashes from Doc Lantry's six-gun
banged out. Then he was clambering hastily to the
saddle. He knew what to expect at Reb's hands, the
second he laid eyes on him.

Lucas had disappeared behind a large rock. He re-
appeared, mounted. He and Lantry jumped their
horses up the narrow canyon gorge. Reb had hoped
to corner them here, but after a flashing glimpse of
Lantry's face, white now, the eyes like coals, they
turned up a cleft and were gone. The hoofs of their
horses clattered in a fast run.

Reb took the corner. There they went, up the
choked gully at a gallop. His eye darted ahead. He
saw then that they'd have a fair chance to escape, at
least for the present. Half-a-mile above the canyon
gave upon a maze of radiating gullies which worked
up into the hills.

Fear drove them to flight—it seemed to drive the
ponies also, for they pulled ahead. But Santee was
playing his own game. There was something grim in
the way he came on, undaunted by Ike Lucas's wild
shots, neither drawing up nor losing too much, his gun
still in the leather.

Lucas and Lantry broke from the head of the canyon to more open ground. Still they attacked the slopes, climbing higher and higher. They hugged the aspens and the young pines, as if losing Santee to sight just across a grove were an aid to flight. At first they tried doubling back to gain time, or to lay an ambush, but as Reb doggedly pursued, glimpsing them from time to time, they straightened out and rode their hardest. Soon the tumbled folds of the Owl Creek Mountains were gathered all about them.

It had been at noon that Santee drove the fugitives out of the hidden canyon. It was four o'clock when he drew up on a high pass and saw the two sets of fresh tracks pointing straight over the gap and on. Behind lay the rugged backbone of the Owl Creeks. To the south and east, Wind River Basin fell away, spreading out and out down there, a vast panorama marked with rich shadow like water rising in a bowl. Ahead, over the pass, rose yet higher ground: a jumble of peaks stretching away west, gray, massive, silent, towering against the late afternoon sky as though they would hold it up.

"Strikin' fer the Teton Peaks," Santee mused, his mind fixed solely on the riders he followed. "I'll hand it to them, they know what to look for when we meet."

Nor was there any further hesitation on his part as to what it would be. He would crush them both as he would have smashed an insect. Neither had any claim on his mercy. Lucas had been warned to stay out of the country: he had not only returned, but proved he would take Reb's life without compunction; and as for Lantry, he had engineered the attempted assassination, that was plain. He had confessed it by running. Moreover, Reb would never forget that it was Doc who put him outside the law. He would pay for it. It suited Santee's plans that payment should be exacted, by Lantry's own choice, deep in the wilds, where only the carrion birds would share the secret.

The trail led on and ever upward. Sunset came up like thunder, a blood red pageant that isolated the Teton Peaks in awful grandeur, melancholy with the aloof silence of death itself. Reb had not seen his quarry for half-an-hour when dusk fell. He was content to let them wear their horses out in the inexorable altitude.

"No chance of overhaulin' them tonight, anyway," he muttered. "An' I don't want to scare 'em into splittin'."

Fortunately, the throw of the lofty slopes gave him an accurate idea of the course the two would take for several hours. He pushed on in the early darkness, rendered bleak by the lofty pines. Midnight brought him to a point at which he had thought he should have to pull up until daylight; but the palely brilliant light of a waxing moon discovered to him the trail he followed. He went on until it waned in early morning, and then drew up, unsaddled and hobbled the blue roan and himself sought rest.

He was on his way with the first streaks of dawn. Lantry and Lucas, he soon discovered, had not pulled up at all. Their tracks were three hours old or better, but as the morning lengthened, their lead diminished.

It was nearing mid-day when Reb saw them again. They had got above all but stunted timber now, clinging to the rocky slopes. With eyes turned constantly to the rear, they descried him almost as soon as he came in view.

Lucas swore luridly. "He hangs on like a buzzard!" he spat out. "Dammit, Lantry, yuh said we'd shake him in a few hours!"

"I thought we would," Doc retorted. "Yuh needn't jump me about it. Yuh ain't hopin' fer it no more 'n I am!"

Both of them were keyed to the pitch of jumpy nerves. Moreover, they were tired from the unremitting grind. Their breath came short; and the ceaseless wind which boomed over the high wastes snatched from their lips what little they had.

They pressed on in morose silence for an hour, watching closely that ominous blot behind them which they seemed incapable of shaking off. It was Lantry who opened the subject again, rasped by Lucas's first explosive accusation.

"We wouldn't be in this fix if yuh'd done yore work in the first place," he snapped suddenly. "Lucas, if this is what yuh come back to the Basin fer, yo're a blessed fool!"

Ike's skin darkened under the ragged stubble. His darting stare was malignant and distrustful. "What would yuh call yoreself, then, fer leadin' Santee straight to my hideout?" he flung out bitterly.

Doc denied that he had done so. "Don't pass yore mistake off on me!" he growled. "Although I ain't shore whether yuh can or not, this time. . . . If I ain't mistook, it's li'ble to come yet to the point where yuh shuffle off with yore boots on fer it."

Ike's suspicions leaped to life. They wrangled fiercely, then fell silent again, to strive onward and up in the desperate struggle to lose their relentless nemesis.

Reb, two miles behind them, watched carefully where they went but otherwise paid strict attention to the ground underfoot, grasping the chance of saving the roan by a switch-back or by heading a gully. Although born and raised on the untamed range, he had never ridden so lofty a trail; he knew he was fighting nature, no less surely than he meant to fight his quarry: that the outcome depended on endless care for details.

Wild and mountainous Wyoming lay about him in trackless confusion. No man, he told himself, had ever trodden these waste spaces before; no man would follow, perhaps for years. It lent an austere nakedness of human passions to the chase that only steeled his will.

Lantry and Lucas had disappeared over a rocky, barren shoulder which seemed to jut out into space. They were virtually on top of the world, and they were not hastening now, if they were wise, and neither was Santee. He toiled on, occasionally dismounting to lead the roan over a rough patch. His lungs felt tight, his thoughts hazy. The unceasing wind roared in his ears, tugging at him, hampering his advance.

"It's as hard fer them as it is fer me," he reminded himself, panting. He felt hot and worn out, the sweat evaporated from his flesh as fast as it formed, but he knew the two ahead were in no better case.

He reached the crest of the bulge. The pair were nowhere in sight. The ground fell away sharply, caught itself a mile or two ahead, then soared in breath-taking majesty, the way apparently blocked off by impassable cliffs of granite.

"They've run into an alley now!" he breathed. Something leaped in him, a violent readiness. "They can't get past them rocks. Even a fly'd break his neck there."

He plunged forward, ready for the show-down, until he realized what he was doing. Then he pulled in and went on at a more moderate pace. A quality in this thin keen air set up a grim elation in him. It could only be a matter of minutes now—five or ten at most.

He found the tracks of the two and followed them closely. The trail was faint, the ground was so flinty: a scratch here and there on stone, an occasional gouged fragment of moss. The way led over and down, unaltering, and worked along a slope of increasing steepness. Reb still could not see the fugitives, but broken upended rocks gave sufficient promise of cover for men at no great distance. He advanced warily now, the gun loose in his holster.

There came a time when Reb would have said that horses no longer could cling to the acclivity, that they must turn back. Still the marks of driven hoofs led on. They had been made only minutes ago. Yet no sound drifted back, nothing but the cold, lonely boom of the wind. Reb did not hesitate. His lips drew back in a grin which his foes would have found wolfish.

"Reckon I can't follow if they take to wings," he thought. "But I can make a stab at doggin' 'em anywheres else they're likely to go."

Even as this passed through his mind, the trail petered out. He turned back patiently to his last glimpse of sign, spotted it, and worked forward again, without result. Then, dismounting for a closer scrutiny, he saw it—the unbelievable wild scratches where clawing hoofs had raked straight down over the bulging rock.

Reb straightened and stared. The drop, a few yards down, was almost sheer. He could see nothing—no sign of the fear-ridden men who had taken a desperate chance of escape here, whatever it was. He shook his head, frowning.

"It can't be!" he ejaculated. "They couldn't go ahead. They didn't go back. Yet it's plain enough— unless they jest fell over the edge—they couldn't give me the slip in such a spot!"

But a careful search of the place revealed only that that apparently was what they had done.

When Ike and Doc passed over the crest of the barren hump, they were not far from panic. They could see the way quite evidently cut off to the fore. Massed jumbles of stone rose in their path, edged them to the south along the ragged slope.

It grew steadily rougher and more sheer. A dozen times in as many minutes Lantry was on the point of pulling up, seeking some other road; only the knowledge of the fate dogging his pony's steps urged him forward. But the time came when his innate caution told him it was folly to go on. The declivity was so steep that it offered only disaster. He reined in.

"This is crazy, Ike!" he burst out. "We got to do somethin' quick, if we don't want to git stuck, an' face that devil here on the edge of hell!" He shuddered at the prospect.

Lucas turned with a snarl. "We can git on," he declared bullingly. "It's better, yonder a piece."

It wasn't: hope was speaking, but still Ike raked his

pony ahead. The animal stumbled and slid a yard, crouching like a cat. Ike hurriedly dismounted and, bridle in hand, essayed to lead onward. The pony balked. Lucas yanked impatiently. The shod hoofs flew four ways at once; the bridle was yanked out of Ike's hand, and with a scream the horse slipped over the edge, pawing futilely in a last effort for a footing.

No sound came up of the beast's fall, thousands of feet below. Only the ghastly silence, humming to the wind.

"Yuh damned fool!" Lantry raged. "Now where are yuh? Afoot, by God! I told yuh where you'd wind up!" He got out of the saddle himself, trembling.

There was a desperate light in Lucas's scared face. He glared for a minute, then caught himself.

"Jest which way are yuh figgerin' to leave here on a nag?" he flashed. "Because if yuh go back, yo're goin' alone!"

Doc's worried eyes deepened. He looked back, driving himself to frantic thought, but said no more. A moment later, planting his feet carefully, he set himself to lead his mount straight up the slope. The pony slipped and caught itself, struggling gamely. It was no easy task; it looked impossible, but as the minutes passed Doc's efforts began to show a gain. Lucas watched him disappear behind a bowlder and then started to clamber after.

They were out of sight and hearing when Reb reached the spot where Lucas's horse fell. They were acutely aware of him somewhere near, however. They fought on. After a time they came to safer, if slower going. Lantry still led toward the frowning cliffs which appeared to cut them off. When they came to a little open space, Doc mounted and rode. Ike stumbled along at his side, sullen and wordless.

Fear surrounded them now like the endless rocks, for they knew they were making no time; but with it all, suspicion and distrust crept in too, and they watched each other furtively. The same thought was in the minds of both: one horse between the two of them. It was of little use now, but when it was—?

It was Lantry who made the discovery, at a time when they had all but resigned themselves to the inevitable—a narrow, humping ledge winding along the face of the cliff. He struck out for it, head up like a scenting dog. Even Ike's face brightened. He seemed for the moment to forget his more fortunate companion.

"If we c'n only git around that fust shoulder, there, before Santee sees us—" he muttered. Hope was like strong drink in his tired, trembling limbs.

They started up, and now the horse was a real menace to them, delaying them, threatening to drag them into space, to fall forward on them and topple them off. Still Lantry clung to it stubbornly. Evening was drawing on when they completed the first leg of the precarious climb. They reached the turn and looked beyond.

"Gawd!" Lucas gasped. "Nothin' but a crack to hang onto!"

Still they pressed on, climbing indeed like flies, until the cold, blustery dark closed in. They holed up for the night in a crevice barely large enough to accommodate them. Now Lucas became optimistic, for Santee had evidently been lost at last. He whistled softly as he broke up the gnarled branches of a dwarf pine.

"Don't light no fire here!" Lantry rasped out. "D'yuh want to bring that hell-cat down on us fer shore?"

Ike stared at him. "Lantry, I've been itchin' to tell yuh a few things fer a long time," he retorted insolently; "an' this seems like as good a place as any. I don't eat, an' I don't ride," he went on hardily, "but by God, I warm myself, if I know anything about it! Yuh c'n git warm with me, or yuh c'n go to hell—I unnerstand it's plenty warm there!"

He dodged, at the end of this belligerent speech—but not quick enough. There was a flash and a bang, snatched and whipped away in an instant. Doc Lantry punched out the empty shell and stared down at the death thoes of his companion.

"Yuh had that due yuh, Ike," he said coolly to the empty silence. "Maybe it'll save yuh grief, comin' now."

But his hand shook as he sheathed the gun.

Chapter XXII

TRAIL'S END

DOC LANTRY closed his eyes only fitfully at best that night, and then against his will. Thin and bony and with an undermined constitution, he had no reserves of stamina. It had often been said of him that sheer cussedness made him tough; but no amount of morose fortitude could help him now. Tortured nature made his head drop on his knees in a shivering doze; dread of the unknown jerked him broad awake a dozen times.

It seemed to him that dawn would never come. Yet when its first gauzy tentacles streaked the east, he was sorry. It meant that he must go forward again, while the freezing night and the terrors of solitude had so weakened and demoralized him that he was afraid to move.

Gradually the sky became gray and the formless granite stood up about him with its cold menace. He went to the mouth of the crevice and stared gloomily at the narrow ledge which he must negotiate. It was so bad ahead that he doubted whether he could manage to pass it himself, let alone with his pony.

"I can't go back," he muttered perplexedly, his teeth chattering. "It was bad enough gittin' here—the hoss'll never make it back down that slope!"

He was loath to part with the horse. It meant continued freedom—perhaps life. Indecision kept him chained to the spot, while the light strengthened. A wind-blown rattle of loose shale along the ledge trail brought him up short. He darted a stealthy look. Reb Santee appeared some distance down the ledge, advancing carefully and steadily. He was without a mount.

Lantry sucked his breath in sharply. His last hope—that Reb had been eluded—was gone. A recklessness surged up in him like brutal anger: he flung up his six-gun and from the corner of the crevasse sent three wild shots at the advancing figure.

Wind whipped the faint cracks away, but Reb heard the dull smack of slugs on the granite, the fierce buzz as they tore glancing into space. It told him his quarry was near. He looked ahead coolly, marking the spot whence the shots had come, and without hesitation, without haste, continued to work his way forward.

Gripped by rising panic, Lantry fired again, feverishly attempting to steady his aim. His muscles were flabby. His thoughts were so scattered that he gave the wind no heed. He yelled a warning at Santee. He could see the other's face clearly as he punched out the used shells and fumblingly reloaded: to his consternation Reb looked as if he were serenely occupied with some endeavor of particular interest which he had no thought of abandoning.

"I'll smoke him off that ledge!" Doc raged wickedly.

He fired again rapidly. Reb shrank together and waited for it to end. Then he came on once more, inexorable. He did not even have his gun out of the holster, using both hands to pull himself over the uneven obstructions in his path. Plainly he meant to pursue Lantry into his crevasse, to force him into the open where they would have an equal chance at each other.

Doc had never seen an exhibition of sheer nerve to match it. It left him in the grip of a cold grue which he was unable to fight off. Drops started out on his forehead, his breath came in gasps.

"Gawd!" he ripped out. "Nothin'll stop 'im!"

He fired a third time, holding the gun hard on Santee's compact frame and driving the bullets with concentrated hate. When the smoke whipped away, Reb still clung there, the tightness of his lips visible now. Lantry lashed himself into a frenzy, thrusting head and shoulders forward around the rock.

"Go back!" he bawled. Then, with a wild endeavor to command himself, he thought: "Why tell him that? I *want* to polish him off! Let him walk into it!" But he could not whip up the lethal determination, the iron-cold rage he craved. The ague in his limbs told, if his heart did not, that he feared this white-haired puncher as he had never feared anyone or anything in his life.

If Reb heard Doc's wind-shredded warning, he gave no sign that he intended to heed it. In plain sight he threw up his head and, incredibly, tauntingly—laughed. It was the laughter of the devil, of a madman, immune to the impulses of caution and bent only on destruction—or so it seemed to Lantry. He jerked back and made frantic supplication of the steely morning sky, the cold gray rocks. There was indeed no way for him to turn.

Santee was scarcely more than fifty yards away now. Doc shrank from the moment when he should close in. He flung down his six-gun, sprang for the rifle in its boot on the saddle of his horse. That would tear Santee loose from the rocks, tumble him into space, with no

more ceremony than that with which Doc had disposed
of Ike Lucas's body.

Even as he tugged at the gun-stock a rattling clatter
sounded near the mouth of the crevasse. He could not
see the ledge to which Santee clung, from here; but it
was easy to imagine the other's impending arrival.
Doc's shattered nerves were ready to account for anything to his inflamed brain, darkened already with the
portent of disaster. He had no way of knowing Reb
had thrown a fragment of rock forward, and he
wheeled, expecting to see that hated face behind the
threatening guns on the instant.

For a moment the forces of stark insanity tugged
the man this way and that. He knew his hour had come
—was about to strike. There was no way on earth to
avoid it. The only clear thought that came to him was
the wild hope that he could take Santee with him to
his doom. How was it to be accomplished?

In a satanic flash he had it. He gathered his frame,
facing the mouth of the crevasse and the ledge, as he
made ready. The instant Reb showed himself, silhouetted against space and without any inkling of what
was to come, Doc meant to fling himself forward,
grapple his enemy, and carry them both over the
gaping edge.

His eyes were distended now, his knotted expression
less than human. His breath came in rasping gulps to
feed his racing pulse. . . . Again came that nerve-
tearing clatter on the ledge. A pebble stirred at the
side of the crevasse mouth, as though kicked. Lantry
drew in a sharp breath and plunged, his legs driving
him forward, intent on smashing into Santee before he
had time to pull trigger.

He came to the mouth of the crevasse hurtling like a rocket. There was no one there, no whip-hard body to oppose. Doc's eyes widened in horror. His frame stiffened, he tried to stop himself on the ledge. For a bated breath he tottered on the brink—then with a piercing, wind-whipped scream he lost his balance and plunged downward, arms and legs flying.

Twenty yards away along the ledge, Reb Santee leaned back against the rock in a squatting position and gaped, his jaw dropping. He had expected no such result after he had tossed that second rock. Now, sitting there curiously bereft of object, he pieced it out in his mind, reconstructing as he had done before the steps by which Lantry had slowly and surely approached his fate.

"I'll be damned," he said softly, when he saw it all.

It was three days later that Reb rode out on the high crest of the Owl Creek Mountains and let his gaze run down the broad trough of Wind River Basin. He had taken his time on the return trip from the Teton wilds, making his way by easy stages, for the pursuit of Lantry and Lucas had taken a lot out of even him.

It had taken so much out of him that there was little left, for the time being, save a fixed idea: to wait only for the return of the Sundance Kid to the Basin and then pull out of Wyoming forever.

For a week he had dwelt grimly on nothing but the perfidy of Doc Lantry and on the settlement Doc must meet for his mistake. That account was closed; with the backwash came all of Reb's old problems and disappointments. Had it not been for the Logans, he would not have returned to the Basin at all, for there was just one thing that country meant to him now—Ronda Cameron, soon to be Ronda Farragoh.

He planned not to see her again. That would be the best way, despite his aching desire. Accordingly, it was a shock to him when he rode down into the Basin late that afternoon, that the first person he met should be Ronda herself.

It was on the grassy divide that marked the boundary between the C 8 range and that of Lantry's ranch, that Reb saw the girl riding forward. She had seen him first, and advanced with some driving urgency in her demeanor.

"Reb!" she burst out, when she came close. It was an exclamation of relief. "I have been watching for you."

"For me?" He scanned her features closely, too tired to exercise his smile; noted the faint lines of care at her brow, the steady, troubled regard of her gray eyes. She hesitated over her next speech.

"Reb, a good deal has happened in the Basin while you've been gone," she began in a regretful tone. "I scarcely know how to tell you—"

"What is it, Ronda?" They were riding toward the wooded course of Rebel Creek. The late sun cast their long shadows far ahead. "Nothin's gone wrong with yore dad, I hope?"

"No, it's a rancher over west. . . . Have you heard that over fifty head of Star A steers were rustled last week?"

Reb hadn't heard. He elicited the details, a sober gravity on him. Easy enough for him to determine where the blame rested! There flashed through his mind the memory of a speech made by Gloomy Jepson, days ago: "Wal, Doc, we got 'em away—" Stolen steers were what he had been talking about, not fighting bulls.

"And that's not all," Ronda went on. She faced him squarely. "You have got to go away, Reb. It's why I've been riding over this way every day—to warn you." They had reached the line of willows. She drew up in that cover, turning her pony as she spoke.

He stared at her, arrested at hearing from her lips that he must leave. "What do yuh mean?" he got out quickly. "What is it?"

"Reb—" her voice broke in spite of her—"the Ghost Creek ranch has been taken over by Sheriff Ward. He is waiting there, with his deputy, to arrest you and Mr. Lantry!"

The blow had fallen, in some incredible manner. Reb looked away, his face slowly whitening, the freckles standing out. But arrest was not what he feared in this moment. He scarcely thought about it, gripped by the realization that Ronda should be the one to warn him; that she should know—

"The Star A steers were traced almost directly past the ranch and into the hills," she hastened on. "Three men have been caught—Mr. Jepson among them. They would tell nothing, but Sheriff Ward says he is certain of you and Doc Lantry. . . . Reb," she burst out, "isn't there some way you can prove your innocence of this rustling? I am sure you know nothing about it!" She was taking it as hard as he did, pleading with her eloquent eyes.

It was a sad moment for Reb. He hated to trust himself to say anything. But silence would not do. "No," he managed slowly, "I don't know the first thing about this rustlin' business, Ronda." It was easy to comfort her that much, for it was strictly true. But how much would she learn later—how much would come out about other things, if he were to be apprehended?

Ronda studied him worriedly. "Reb, I don't know what to say," she returned; "what to tell you to do. I believe you, of course; but it doesn't quiet my fears. I meant to beg you to leave at once, but it would be terrible if you were captured before you got away. Nothing would convince a jury that you were innocent then." Her face brightened momentarily. "But you've many friends who will stand by you. If you will give yourself up, Billy will defend your case—"

Reb shook his head. What she suggested brought back the old stab once more, a hundredfold sharper. "I'm afraid I can't see my way to go that far," he said, trying to keep his eyes away from her soft, appealing face. "I'll never be tried for rustlin' if I can help it."

"Throw up yore hands," commanded a masculine voice behind him, with startling distinctness. "This is one time, mister, you ain't goin' to be able to help it."

Ronda gasped, the blood draining away from her cheeks. Reb's hands started to move in a flash; he caught them in time. They paused, and went up slowly until they were level with his shoulders. He kneed his pony around. Bob Calverly, Ward's deputy, pushed through the willows with a gun trained on him. His grin was good-natured.

"Oh, Reb!" Ronda cried. "What have I done to you?"

"You didn't do nothin' that could've been avoided, Ronda," he assured her quickly. "Just forget about it."

"That's right," Calverly seconded. "I didn't depend

on yuh, ma'am. If it wasn't this way, it would've been some other way." He seemed very assured in his tanned young strength, but Reb was grateful to him at least for the relief his words brought to the girl.

The deputy relieved him of his gun. "Wal," said Calverly comfortably, as he resumed his horse, "now we're all here, what've yuh got to say to the law about this rustlin', Reb?"

But Reb was not saying anything. His lips had drawn into a thin line; he shook his head shortly, his eyes bleak, revealing nothing of the hurt behind them. Even when Ronda left hurriedly to carry the news of what had happened to her father, and he was taken to Ghost Creek where the sheriff waited, he kept his peace. Ward proved amiable if cynical, Calverly joked with him; but no questioning could draw from Reb the whereabouts of Doc Lantry. It was decided finally that he should be taken to Lander.

Ward remained on Ghost Creek; it was Calverly who accompanied the prisoner south. Reb loosened up then; they smoked cigarettes and chatted as they rode. Late the next day Reb was lodged in a cell. He had been doing a lot of thinking behind his cheerful mask on the way to Lander, and he was not easy in his mind. He knew it would be only a matter of hours before Billy Farragoh visited him at the jail.

The night passed, and Billy did not appear, although a number of other friends stopped by to pass a word. Few men seemed to hold it against him that he should be in custody.

In the morning Reb was arraigned and his trial set for the following week. Still Billy did not come to him, but Reb found some relief in the fact that the charge against him was for rustling—a crime of which he need have no hesitation about declaring his innocence before any man. He wondered whether it might be a technical charge, on which they would hold him while they sought grounds for prosecuting his real offenses.

There were half-a-dozen cells in the Lander jail, containing three other prisoners at the time. On his return after arraignment Reb found them buzzing among themselves. When things quieted down a bit he asked what it was about.

"D. A. died las' night," said a strapping cowboy who had been picked up for being drunk and disorderly. "Apoplexy, I hear. . . ." He went on to give details.

Reb thought fast. "That means that trial dates'll be shoved back," he mused aloud.

"No they won't. They appointed a man already to fill the D. A's office."

"Who?" Reb could not suppress a quiver of premonition as he put the question.

"Young Farragoh."

The name fell on Santee's ears like the clang of a knell. The district attorney dead—Billy Farragoh to fill out his term of office! It was like an added stroke of fate. There no longer was any mystery why Billy had not come to see him. He would not come at all, now. The next time their eyes met it would be across a counsel table, and Billy would be marshaling his forces to obtain a conviction of his friend.

Chapter XXIII

FOR THE PROSECUTION

NO trace of Reb Santee's profound reluctance was revealed in his manner as he walked into the court room on the morning of his trial. Men spoke to him kindly; the bailiff poked him in the ribs and cracked a joke. But for him these things were like a dream, he was so intent on the questions he asked himself.

Would Ronda Cameron be present to-day? What would he see in Billy Farragoh's glance? To think that he should ever have known these two at all, and have the association come to this, made him feel wretched.

But it was Judge Hamer's eye that Reb found heavy on him when the jurist walked in and took the bench. The murmuring and low laughter ceased; boots scraped and a man cleared his throat explosively in the taut quiet. Hamer stabbed Reb once with a bleak, unreadable glance that served unmistakable notice: whatever you are, whoever you know, you get simple justice here, no more, no less. Hamer could not have said it plainer.

Reading it, Reb did not know whether to rejoice or sorrow. As far as the rustling charge went, he felt he ought to clear himself easily; but he hadn't an idea how deep Hamer's promised justice would cut. If it went to the heart of the matter he might get life and a day; and in the travail of his heart he was not above admitting that in all probability he deserved it.

Ronda and her father, he soon saw, were not going to be present and he heaved a small sigh of thanksgiving for that. For Billy's part, the boy treated Reb to a single quick look and a nod he strove mightily to make casual. There was the uprightness of a soldier obeying a fatal order in the stiffness of his back, the carefully schooled composure of his face. Then he looked away quickly, and apparently wasn't going to look at Reb again until he had to.

Reb saw the manliness in him, fighting to conceal his deep feelings. Billy was heart-broken. For him this was an hour of pure tragedy, as it was for Santee. The scales had dropped away from his young eyes with awful completeness now; he rightly suspected that Reb had stolen the money which had helped to pay for his education; in fact, he was convinced that Reb was guilty of even greater crimes than the one on which he was being tried. Word had trickled in, unmistakable to his ears, of the intrepid smile of a man who had robbed trains and banks with reckless courage in the past few months. Billy thanked his God that men were not sentenced on such convictions of the heart.

It was a nightmare court session for the newly appointed district attorney. He stuck valiantly to his guns, however, and in short order succeeded in convicting Gloomy Jepson and two of his companions and sending them to the pen on the rustling charge.

Reb's case, on a slightly different status, since the evidence against him was entirely circumstantial, was called. A new jury was impaneled. It was impossible not to notice that while these twelve good men and true had nodded and grinned before, in the jury box

they scrupulously avoided Santee's eye, as if aware of
the danger of being corrupted by his well-known smile.

Even Billy, when he squared on Reb and began to
bombard him with staccato competence, was beginning
to show the lines graven on his features by the necessity to do this thing. It had been his idea to try Reb
separately, for unquestioned fairness; but he did not
relax his own vigor in the prosecution. Reb's fascinated
eyes dwelt on him in pity and self-condemnation; in
the pathos of the moment he almost forgot to answer
questions; he made irrelevant responses, until his
counsel—a bony, middle-aged lawyer with a red, hard-
eyed countenance—cleared his throat loudly, trying to
recall him to himself, and even attempting to interrupt.

It was the sight of Lonny Logan, the Sundance Kid's
brother, seated alone in the crush of the court room
with his burning gaze fixed on him, that awoke Reb
to his situation. He knew the Kid was bringing pressure to bear in this trial—that he was doing all that
could be done. How the Kid had escaped Sheriff
Ward's net and learned of Santee's position; what he
would be able to accomplish, Reb didn't know. But
Rasher, the lawyer, had been sent to him by a mysterious agency, evidently the Kid's man, though it had
not been mentioned. Rasher was putting up a stiff
fight, too.

But to little avail. The Wind River country was getting cynical and hard-headed about these things. Reb's
stout defense of himself crumbled when he refused to
declare where he was and what he was doing at the
time of the Star A rustling. He honestly did not remember. Prop after prop Billy knocked out from under him—establishing his intimacy with Doc Lantry,

proving that Lantry had quite evidently fled, making it darker and darker for Reb until Rasher ranted in anger, weakening his own position.

With the case turned over to the jury, and those men charged by the judge, Billy Farragoh wiped his forehead with a kerchief and sank into a seat, weak and white. Reb knew it was not feigned. Billy had done his duty like a man and the puncher felt sorrier for him than he did for himself.

Judge Hamer evidently had a good idea the verdict would not be delayed, and court was not adjourned. It was just as well. In twenty minutes the jury filed back to the box and a hush descended over the room.

"Gentlemen, have you reached a verdict?"

"We have, your Honor."

"Please instruct the court as to your findings."

The jury foreman was a big man, broad-shouldered, with blunt features. He turned an inscrutable glance on Reb and said:

"We find the defendant guilty as charged."

It was no more than Reb had expected. Innocent as he was in fact, he knew himself guilty in spirit: it was at bottom a just retribution; in fact, fate had overtaken him in a remarkably lenient mood, one such as he had no right to ask. He found no comfort in it. It was acid to his soul to stand up before Judge Hamer, under Billy Farragoh's eyes, and listen to the level, impartial voice:

"You are sentenced to serve one year at hard labor in the penitentiary at Laramie City."

Hamer paused deliberately, then added on another note: "I'm not sure, Santee, but what this is the best thing that could happen to you."

That was the human note creeping in, which few of these men had lost for him despite their adherence to the hard ritual of justice. It made Reb feel more wretched than ever. But there was more of it. Now that the trial was over, his duty done, Billy Farragoh came to Reb without hesitation, placed a hand on his shoulder. The pain in his eyes was unashamed, his voice husky:

"Forgive me, Reb!"

It took Reb off his guard completely. For a moment he fought for control of himself. Then his old grin flashed through, indomitable. "Shore, Billy." His bitterly mastered tone was easy to the ear. "Yuh done what yuh had to. . . . It was a nice job."

He hadn't meant to say exactly that and he could have bitten his tongue out. But it was too late to withdraw. Billy looked stricken as he turned away, all the young resilience gone out of his frame. Reb cursed himself for his clumsiness throughout the rest of the day, during the trip east with Bob Calverly by rail, south around t̄ie bend to the main line, and up to Laramie in the gray light of the following morning.

But only when the iron gates of the prison clanged to behind him did there come to Reb a full realization of his position. Then it crashed in on him like toppling walls. In the eyes of Wind River Basin he was an acknowledged and convicted felon. Ronda, Jube Cameron, Mother Farragoh, the dozens of fine friends he had made there—they all knew him for what he was— for what fate had made him, he corrected himself, never what he had meant to be.

Doc Lantry had paid the supreme price for his destruction of a man's life, but it was too late now—Reb could never go back. With the associations he had made he could not hope to win back to all that meant the most to him in the world.

"I was a maverick," he told himself with pitiless insight. "This is my own fault. The first man branded me that got to me—an' I let him."

Well, he was out of circulation for a year, now. Plenty of time to think over his wrongs and his mistakes. And nothing else to think about, as he faced the iron prison routine.

But as time dragged on he found a new care boring into his consciousness with increasing insistence. It was the deadly confinement of stone walls. Born and bred to the open sky, he came to know in time the true nature of his punishment in this intolerable place, and it was terrible. Day by day he dragged through his duties with growing dejection. His old smile, the occasional flashes of wit, were unfailing still. His fellow prisoners found in him a source of infinite relief and entertainment. The warden liked him and made his lot easier. Occasional packages, small sums of money and the like found their way in to him to comfort his hours, remembrances of the Sundance Kid. But there was nothing that anyone could do to ease the imprisonment that cankered his wild, rash heart. Stone walls, meals, work!

"God!" he groaned one night on his cot, at the end of three dreary months. "If I'd known it would be like this, Calverly never would've taken me alive!"

The warden, who knew range men, assured him that time would be knocked off his term for good behavior. Reb smiled and wouldn't crack. Then one day he had a visitor. The sight of Billy Farragoh's face at the end of the gray corridor picked him up off his cot without his awareness.

"Great God—Billy!"

"Reb, old man! How are you?" Billy entered the cell and reached for his hand.

It was a hard interview for them both, strange with an unaccustomed tenderness which neither would confess. Billy was his same old self, warm, deferential— if anything, more sympathetic than before. Reb wondered what had brought him here, but it was not until considerable constrained talk about the Basin, Reb's condition and other things had been gotten over, that Billy began diffidently:

"I expect you know that Judge Hamer was preparing to run for governor at the time of your trial?"

"Why, yeh." Reb didn't see the connection. "I was expectin' to vote fer him myself." He grinned weakly. "Was he elected—?"

The gravity of Billy's nod suddenly told Reb what this was all about, whither it tended. "Judge Hamer is to be the next governor of Wyoming, Reb. I suppose I scarcely need to tell you that I've already begun to work on a pardon for you."

Reb's face lighted up, then clouded. "Yuh oughtn't to do it, Billy," came from him after a moment. He swallowed hard. "Yuh done yore duty an' it ought to be let go that way." It cost him a good deal to say and nothing but his loyalty to the stalwart young man before him would have induced him to do so. But Billy saw it a different way, shaking his head.

He said: "The state's satisfied, Reb. Nothing in the world need hinder the governor's pardoning you, if he sees fit. I've seen to it that Mr. Hamer realizes your word is as good as your life."

Reb was looking at him steadily. It hurt him that Billy did not refer to the rustling charge on which he had been sent up. If he would only ask in confidence whether Reb was guilty or not, it would be so easy to set his mind at rest on this one point at least. Reb found himself jealous of every scrap and shred of honor, now, before this boy.

All this passed through his mind in a moment. Another part of him was grappling with Billy's meaning. It eluded him.

"Your pardon," Billy went on evenly, "depends on your word, I'm sorry to say. I couldn't manage it otherwise."

"What do yuh mean, Billy?"

The other's tone was studied. "I've got Mr. Hamer to consider granting a pardon on the grounds that you agree never to molest the State of Wyoming again."

The moment dragged out and Reb said nothing. There seemed nothing that he could say. The very wording of Billy's statement—the drift of its meaning—told him the worst. He was considered a confirmed evil-doer. What the terms of this proffered pardon suggested was not rehabilitation, not a return to better things, but simple amnesty.

Billy must have seen something of this in his face. "That's easy enough to guarantee," he attempted to soften the blow. "You know cows, Reb. I heard about the offer Jube Cameron made you. I don't know how he feels now, but if you want, I'll see to it that you get a good position in some other—" He halted miserably, feeling worse every second.

Reb came to his rescue. "No," he said; "I reckon I don't know jest what I'll do if I get out. But thanks all the same, Billy. Yuh can tell Judge—that is, Governor Hamer, I said 'yes' to what he proposes. . . . An' I'm mighty grateful to yuh for goin' to all this trouble."

They talked it over at some length. Reb's face told nothing of his feelings, now that he had got a grip on himself, saw where he stood. Billy spared him the truth—that to persuade the state executive to consent to a pardon on the mentioned terms, he had assured Hamer that Reb was potentially responsible for most of the worries of stockmen and others. Not even the governor had any doubt that Reb would keep his word in this fantastic promise—it was a day when such things were valid, the one way men of widely different status, but of one caliber, could deal with each other and preserve a mutual respect.

At last Billy got up to go. "Mind, I don't want to promise anything, even now," he pointed out. "I'll admit I'm the prime mover in this. The Judge isn't even in office yet. But I think I can bring it off. Nothing would afford me greater satisfaction, Reb." He spoke with the dignity and caution of an older man.

They were stiff and a little formal with each other now, without meaning to be. There was too much between them to be taken lightly. They shook hands, looking away, and Reb's grip said a lot.

The turnkey unlocked the cell. Billy stepped out. Reb stared at his back. "Billy—" he exclaimed suddenly, as if it was dragged out of him.

Billy turned. "Yes, Reb?"

Santee made a hopeless gesture. "Never mind. . . ."

Billy Farragoh, who was no fool, had an inkling of what was in his mind and he thought about it as he walked soberly out of the jail. All during their talk Ronda's name had not been mentioned. Reb had burned to ask after her, to know what was in her heart toward him. More than once he started to speak. But in the end he found himself unable to speak the words.

The days passed once more and became weeks. Billy did all he could, and Reb waited. He grew in time to believe that his friend had failed. It came as a surprise to him, not immediately significant, when one afternoon early in the third week following Billy's visit a keeper accosted him at his work with the announcement that the warden desired to see him immediately.

Something familiar in the warden's face greeted him as he stepped in the prison office—the look of a man glad that he is able to do something for someone he likes.

"Well, Santee," he opened up gruffly; "here's somethin' that'll make good readin' for yuh!" He handed over a legal document.

Even as he opened its folds, Reb knew what it was. Billy Farragoh had succeeded in procuring his pardon. He read a few words and his grin widened—the same old grin that made him friends wherever he went; that made it seem more than worth while to do these things for such a man.

"Free!" was all that he said, but it expressed much.

Chapter XXIV

"I GAVE MY WORD"

WHEN Reb made ready to leave the Laramie Penitentiary it was his old range clothes that he elected to wear instead of the new but shoddy suit the prison provided. His sombrero and his laden belt were like old friends. He thought he was afoot, however—having made the trip from Lander by rail—until, just before he walked out at the gate, the warden told him:

"I've had word that yo're to stop at Dern's livery, Santee, on yore way out. Sounds like a hoss to me. . . . You'll soon be foggin' the range again, boy."

He had given Reb the usual talk on being released: an affable exhortation to better things. Reb good-naturedly accepted it all. It was his way. But he wasn't listening attentively. No longer could he earnestly agree as of old. Inwardly he knew himself radically changed. There was even bitterness in him, if he would admit it. Had the warden dreamed of the terms on which pardon had been granted, he would have saved time and breath by giving curt directions for the shortest trail out of the state. So Reb told himself.

But walking away from the prison at last in the clear, bright sun he gave way to feelings of another order. It was spring once more. The air was balmy, rich with the odor of dust and grass. And he was out in it! The world was his! He could do what he wanted to! . . . No, not that last, he corrected, with leaden heart. The things he most wanted to do had long since been closed to him—long before Governor Hamer granted the truce forbidding the things he and others thought Reb wanted to do.

"There's still a few things left a man can turn to," he mused, tightlipped. "I'll manage to keep busy."

At Dern's stables, he found the blue roan waiting for him. His eye lit up. "Billy thought of that," he told himself. "It's jest like him." Cinching his own saddle on, he led the roan out through the barn.

"How'd Farragoh get the hoss here?" he asked the liveryman interestedly, feeling better in spite of himself.

"Who?"

"Billy Farragoh. The Lander district attorney."

The barnman stared a moment, then laughed long and heartily. "That's a good one!" he gasped, red in the face. "But mebbe yo're lucky, at that, he didn't send yuh an escort."

Reb withdrew into himself, secretly hurt. The glow in his heart vanished. But he laughed with the man, too, affecting a wise air; all the while probing for knowledge. The fellow displayed a surprising intimacy with Reb's history, seemed proud in a cheap way to be associated with him. He knew things Reb hadn't supposed anyone but himself and the Logan's knew.

"The Kid said to pass yuh word the Bunch is down at the Park," Dern muttered before Reb swung up to ride away. "They're expectin' yuh."

Reb nodded, his glance serene; but his thoughts were instantly in a whirl. That a liveryman in Laramie should have cognizance of the Sundance Kid—that he should know Logan and his crowd were at Brown's Park—was startling. But there was more to it than that. Suddenly Reb knew it was by the agency of the Wild Bunch that his roan pony had been waiting for him. Billy hadn't thought of it.

He started away from Laramie's life and bustle, riding west. It was soon left behind. A mile out on the trail over the rolling prairie he heard a clip-clop of hoofs behind that brought him around. A man rode up almost warily. It was a deputy sheriff Reb had got acquainted with in prison.

"So yo're ridin' out, eh, Santee?" he opened up.

Reb gave him a grin and a ready response. The other was no longer as friendly as Reb had come to know him, however. His lightness of manner was a thing of the past. There was an awakened challenge in him that said they were henceforth strangers.

"I don't know how yuh worked it," he said; "but don't make no mistakes in Albany County, old boy."

Reb's grin faded. "Reckon I don't savvy that," he said slowly.

The deputy's eyes were hard. "Yuh savvy all right," he contradicted. "Jest tell the rest of the Bunch what yuh learned while yuh was with us."

Reb cut the talk short with a touch of grimness and rode on. Just a fool kid lawman on the make, he told himself—trying to impress him. But as he thought it over he knew better. That deputy had done him a real favor. No longer was there any doubt that his connection with the Wild Bunch was widely known. It was what that liveryman had hinted at broadly enough. It was—Reb gulped—it was why Billy Farragoh had engineered that strange bargain for the pardon. Billy *knew!*

Reb's faith in Governor Hamer's humanity abruptly

died. Hamer was being shrewd. Had Reb's sentence run its course in eight months or less Wyoming would expect to have his outlawry to deal with once more. But by commuting the sentence and extracting Reb's promise Hamer thought to gain immunity.

"He'll get it!" Reb grunted decisively. "But it's lucky fer him I promised Billy Farragoh to lay off, instead of himself!"

He could not forego this outburst of incensed spirit as he saw what had been done to him. Hamer cared nothing for his future. All men conspired to put him outside the law—except Billy. Reb's faith in Billy's sincerity alone endured.

There was no question, however, of where he would go now. There was but one place to which he could go. Three days later found him at Brown's Park after a ride across the desert. The Sundance Kid was away, and most of the boys were with him, when Reb arrived. Only Flat Nose George Curry was there. He lay in one of the cabins recovering from a wounded thigh, with a surly, low-minded companion to tend him.

Curry greeted Reb effusively and said the boys would be back in three days. And they were. Late on the third afternoon they pulled in at the fag end of a hard run and set up a shout of satisfaction when they saw Reb. The Kid slapped his back and pushed him about and seemed genuinely glad.

"How'd yuh manage to git out so soon, Reb?" he demanded. "We expected yuh late this fall, but here it's only nicely spring. Tell us about it." He could not withhold a certain mystification.

"Well, I—I knowed the right men," Santee answered evasively. He didn't want to tell about Billy—cheapen their friendship. Something held him back from openly claiming that friendship now, anyway. But it was sacred. It was his tie with Ronda Cameron, too—the only one left, tenuous as it was, he realized.

The Wild Bunch put on a celebration for Reb. Lonny Logan was there, wanting to talk about the trial; Bill Carver, Harry Lonabaugh, Bob Leigh, others.

"Reckon Lantry's faded," the Kid said casually. "We ain't had no trace of him fer months."

Reb said nothing, his face wooden. Logan chuckled. "I expected yuh'd feel the same way about it that I do." If he knew more than he had said, he kept it to himself.

Flat Nose George had been unable to tell Reb exactly where the Bunch went on their last jaunt. Reb asked the Kid himself. The latter replied that they had grabbed a payroll east of Worland, Wyoming. Reb frowned. He said nothing at the time, but later, taking the Kid aside, he began bluntly:

"Kid, I find I got to tell yuh how come I got my pardon." He told of his promise not to molest Wyoming again.

The kid missed his confident expectation of understanding agreement. "That's good!" he laughed. "Wait'll I tell the boys."

"Yuh don't get me," Reb interposed patiently. "I gave my word, Kid."

Logan eyed him shrewdly, arrested. "All right," he said coolly. "What of it?"

"I expect to keep it."

The Kid thought. "Well, yuh can work other places,"

he said finally with unusual callousness. "I'll take care of Wyomin' myself."

Reb's easy manner tightened. He didn't want it that way. "Reckon I promised fer the Bunch," he pointed out quickly. He proposed that they leave for the Robbers' Roost, or ride north to Idaho.

Logan was no longer as ready to agree as he had been before. In Reb's absence his plans had been put into effect with good results. The Kid was of no mind to give it up.

"Yuh spoke too soon, Santee, if yuh promised anything fer us," he retorted shortly. "We'll go on as we been doin'." Nor would he retire from this position.

Reb let it go. He had to. But as time passed he found the Bunch more and more willing to follow where the Sundance Kid led, less and less disposed to listen to himself. They were as free and friendly as ever. But they went their own way. Reb realized that he had relegated himself to practically the same position that Doc Lantry had been forced to fill the season before.

He accepted it more reasonably than Doc had done. He loved the cattle trail. He knew that he would in all probability never again ride for a respectable brand. The rustling of small bands of stock from the south and east was at least a substitute for the past.

On the trail his mind went back often to Wind River Basin. He relived the horse-breaking for Jube Cameron, the rigors of the winter round-up. Ronda loomed large in his melancholy reflections at that time. She had been his golden dream, his star of guidance which he had failed. To escape these saddening memories he ranged even farther back, wondering what Steve

Cabanus and Gif Inch were doing now, around Moab —and if careful Pony Clark had become a ranch foreman.

One day he returned to the Park from a long drive out Kremmling way, east in Colorado, to find the Sundance Kid just back from a raid. He and the boys had robbed the Union Pacific at Medicine Bow, getting away with a good haul, and were puffed up with success.

"We had a little brush with the deputies," said the Kid carelessly, his soft black eyes gleaming humorously. "One of 'em asked after yuh."

Reb jerked alert. "What did yuh tell 'im, Kid?" he probed.

"We, we told 'im yuh was back holdin' the hosses," Logan grinned impudently.

Reb exploded with impatience—the nearest to an exhibition of resentment the Kid had ever seen him betray. "That's a hell of a spot yuh put me in!" he wound up. "Ain't yuh got no brains at all?"

The Kid stared. "Dammit, Reb—"

"Never mind! If I pass my word fer a thing, whose business is it besides mine? I know I'm blame easygoin', Logan, but don't get the idea there's nothin' else to me." Reb's sharpness was not for himself, much as he made it sound. He was thinking of the spot Governor Hamer and Billy Farragoh would find themselves in if this sort of thing was going on—if everyone thought Reb continued to pillage in spite of anything. It might be a jest here—but it was one Hamer and Billy would have to answer for to the state.

Logan's deceptive gaze narrowed. A killer without compunction, almost without nerves, he was never one to pass over a challenge, however light. But he had seen Reb in action. The knowledge that Reb spoke the truth was what made him pause, weigh the matter with cold accuracy, and then relax with an easy laugh.

"Get out!" he passed it off. "Yuh don't think I meant that, do yuh?"

"Yuh meant it, all right."

Logan's pupils flickered. "Dammit!" he swore admiringly; "yuh do know, don't yuh? . . . Don't fret, Reb. The deputy I told that to was dead before I turned my back. I wouldn't've let out a peep otherwise."

Judging him sharply, Reb decided this was the truth. "Okay," he nodded. "But it'll be all right with me if yuh understand that I don't like that kind of a joke. An' what's more, Kid, I've decided to argue a little further with yuh about this matter of operatin' in Wyomin'."

"Yeh?" The Kid froze up again. "Wal, yuh can argue."

"An' I can do more'n that!" Reb's voice rang.

"The hell yuh can! . . . If it interests yuh, Santee, we've decided the U.P. won't be expectin' us again fer a while. We're plannin' to stick up the express at Rock Creek next week."

Here was defiance of the most insolent order. Reb and Logan faced each other toe to toe, their faces darkened. It was no moment to slight. More than that, the rest of the boys, attracted by their raised voices, were gathering around. The Kid had cunningly played for this result, Reb guessed. Still he stuck to his guns. He tried scornful persuasion, a thin smile hovering on his lips, addressing them all. They harkened attentively, but shook their heads. No assurance of Reb's that the pickings were just as good elsewhere would move them.

"I don't like it," he told them flatly. "An' that don't mean I'm jest disgusted with yuh, either. Nobody has to tell me when they're throwin' me down."

"We ain't throwin' yuh down! Why, hell, Reb—"

"Let it go," he cut them off. "We can't get nowheres talkin', I see that. We'll jest watch how it works itself out. But mark me!" he faced them squarely: "I say yuh won't knock off that train at Rock Creek, an' I mean it!"

Incredulous mutters sounded. The looks that fell on Reb were cool.

"I'll be damned!" Bill Carver burst out, nonplussed. "Yuh ain't shy about sayin' what yuh mean, are yuh?"

There was a lot more, back and forth, but the Kid summed up the attitude of the Bunch when he finally declared: "Have it yore way, Santee. Yuh called the turn when yuh said we'd see how it works itself out. We will. But I'm sayin' again—we're hittin' that train as we planned. If yuh think yuh can do somethin' about it, take the bit an' go to it." He spoke with a cold, repressed force, in which there was no trace of lingering friendship. It was his ultimatum.

Reb had said all that he intended to say. From the moment Logan had voiced an intention to rob the Union Pacific a second time he had determined to stop it. He knew now that he was credited by all the law-abiding world with heading the Wild Bunch, wherever it went. Their depredations were marked up against him. His carefree, daredevil days when the Bunch had operated from Wind River Basin and he had led them

had put him in a position of responsibility to Billy Farragoh which could not be avoided.

He knew to the last jot the seriousness of what he
proposed doing. The Kid and the others would argue
with him readily enough, deny him and let it drop;
but the minute he put his plan into effect it would turn
the men outside the law against him to the death, as
surely as those who lived inside it were against him
already.

The knowledge could not deter him. He had given
the boys warning as he would have warned any man;
they would laugh it off, believing it was his last argument to stop them; but in his heart he found more
than this at stake. Some trace of respect for him in
the hearts of Ronda and young Billy was all he had
ahead of him now, all that was worth preserving.

He hadn't an idea what those two were thinking
about him. Probably it was pretty hard. But if he
measured up in his own eyes, it would ease the load
a lot. It was what decided him. He would go through
with his desperate determination to thwart the train
bandits.

"They've got to know I mean what I say," he told
himself. "Once they get it they'll swing over to me
an' we'll head out together fer another country—if it
don't come to somethin' worse first."

For all his resolution he did not underestimate the
deadly opposition of the Sundance Kid to what he
proposed doing.

Chapter XXV

THE BATTLE OF ROCK CREEK

ROCK CREEK was little more than a watering tank on the main line. At one time a roaring construction camp, it had dwindled away to a way-station, little used, and a few section sheds. Beside it was the rocky gully which gave it a name. The desert flowed up for miles from every direction, studded with sage and cactus, with buttes and mesas. Beyond, in another world, sere and verdureless mountains, many colored, dreamed in the pitiless drench of the sun.

Reb had been there more than once. He knew exactly how the Wild Bunch would work. They would not board there and run the train down the line a mile or two. There was no need. Only the station agent— he was flagman and telegrapher also—need be taken care of, and the way was clear while the locomotive took on water.

So Reb did not have to nose out the details of the hold-up he proposed frustrating. It was only a matter of awaiting the time, playing his cards for safety and certainty. He debated the advisability of starting off on a cattle trail with some of the lesser lights of his calling, to allay the suspicions of the Bunch; but it was not necessary. The Sundance Kid unconsciously told him so when he joshed Reb as the time drew near. He did not dream Santee meant what he had said, nor did any of the others. They commiserated with him on his decision to take no part in the job.

"Be seein' yuh, Reb," the Kid waved a derisive

hand, as he and the others rode away from the Park the day before their intended coup. Logan had become faintly contemptuous since their clash. He had got a glimpse of the inevitable deadlock between them, and was fortifying himself. It was the ruthless way of his kind.

Reb nodded negligently from where he sat on a pine log, trying to look irritated and indifferent. He had used all his persuasions on these men: there was nothing left but guile. Some of the boys remaining behind with him watched enviously the Kid's departure. Reb held their minds by the discussion of a job of their own. It was three hours after the Bunch had gone before he dared saddle up his own pony.

"I'm goin' to scout out a bunch around Meeker," he said casually, as he swung up. "Be gone a day or so. Then we'll get to work."

They assented—four grizzled range men, thumbing cards in the shade of the pines—for they read Santee's superiority and liked to be with him. They trusted him. "An' here's where I let even them boys down," he thought gloomily as he rode away.

There was a shadow over him, like a weight on his shoulders, as he worked east for five miles and then turned abruptly north toward the Union Pacific, bisecting the desert. He had the greatest reluctance for the job before him. Some deep mood of hopelessness told him that he must somehow fail—that win or lose now, failure dogged his heels and would ride him under before the streak broke. He fought it, as always, valiantly; but bleakness touched his face all that day.

"I'm doin' this fer Ronda—her an' Billy," he told himself. "Nobody else on earth would understand.

But they will, if they ever learn." It comforted him to say it.

It was like armor to know that he was keeping faith with them.

He camped that night at a water hole in the desert, severely alone. Not since leaving the Park had he seen a soul: only the bounding rabbits, the snakes and lizards, and once a slinking coyote. In the morning he went on warily, giving Rock Creek a wide berth to the east, and then, having crossed the railroad tracks, to the north. It was only in the afternoon, when he reached Rock Creek gully two miles to the northwest, that he turned down the defile and drew near the water tank and the brown buildings shining in the sun.

A mile from his objective he dismounted. After that he stole from one scorched curve of the gully to the next, reconnoitered ahead, then returned to lead up the roan. It was always near at hand. It must always be. And now he began to plan his campaign.

He had turned it over a good deal already. It would have been possible to board the express at the next stop east and be ready to meet the Bunch as they boiled aboard—or to warn the railroad people of trouble, as any unimaginative man would have done. Reb had given up the first with reluctance, liking its boldness, but knowing he would be recognized and his object misunderstood. The second he scorned as treachery, defeating his own object.

There was another alternative, however, and one he had decided on. If he could get to the Wild Bunch before it got to the train, he might hold them at the point of a gun until their chance was gone. At best that was most dangerous to himself, and only a delay.

Balked, the Bunch might turn on him and rend him—
they were almost sure to. And that was no gain. So he
had decided to brace them at the moment they reached
the train, ready for their grim work.

"It'll mean an out-an'-out battle," he mused calmly.
"I'll have to bluff the boys plumb in front of their
game. An' they'll rare up." But this was not enough to
discourage him in his plan.

It had, on the other hand, the merit of surprise. It
would disorganize their aims. It would make for deadly
unexpectedness at every turn. And more than that, it
would warn the railroad men, appraise them of their
narrow escape, enable them to guard against a second
attempt at the spot.

It was by far the most perilous course Reb could
have adopted, and by no means the surest. But there
was fairness in it, an even chance for all. Santee trusted
to his nerve and ingenuity to carry him through.

The express from the east would pull in at 8:10—
about dusk. Until then Reb's sole object would be to
avoid the Kid's men, find a way to reach the train un-
detected, and insure his own avenue of escape afterward. To many men the dragging time, the uncertainty,
would have been nerve-racking. Reb was unmoved,
his hand steady, his muscles slack. He knew the Wild
Bunch would shoot him down if they caught him here.
He would mean nothing to them save an obstacle. It
was what he meant to be.

He found a tongue of sage running out from the
creek gully toward the watering tank that would have
to do for his advance. Then he settled impassively to
wait, fighting his desire for a smoke. It was a watchful
waiting, for he had not yet placed the outlaws he now

knew to be somewhere near. At any moment they might stumble over him.

The sun burned low. The desert silence was profound. The last freight had rattled by on the main line hours ago. Reb watched the shadow creep up the gully wall opposite and then, as the sun touched the horizon, engulf the sage. The sky was red, was pink, was lustrous opal, was gray.

Miles across emptiness a faint locomotive whistle keened. It was half-an-hour away, but Reb stood up. The evening lowered rapidly. He filled the last chamber in his six-gun, twirled the cylinder, saw that the gun hung free and then crawled out of the gully into the sage.

Still he had seen no sign of the Kid's men. Had they slipped up—changed their minds—gone elsewhere? Reb's nostrils stirred; his teeth bared.

"No fear," he thought. "Harve Logan's a wolf at this game. They'll get here like they'd sprung out of the ground, when the time comes."

The express was nearer now. Its faint roar ran forward across the desert, a stealing whisper of sound that faded, returned, momentarily grew stronger. Reb crept through the sage, alert to pierce the gathering dusk.

Disturbance broke out at the little station a hundred yards away: a few thumps, an angry cry, a gun shot. Then silence. It dispelled any doubts Reb might have had. The Bunch was here, they were taking care of the agent.

The train ran near. It let out a fresh blast, slowing, and came on, its trucks clacking and clattering over the rail-joints as it passed the station and puffed up to the water tank. The voices of the engine crew were audible.

The shape of the cars was vague now, except for the lights in the windows; the firebox glowed. Reb stood up and walked forward.

Figures ahead of him were suddenly busy around the locomotive. Curt commands cracked: Engineer and fireman—the trainman who attended to the water—climbed down beside the breathing iron monster, followed by a lithe figure with a hard face and a gun in his hand. It was Lonny Logan.

"Line up, here," he growled to the crew. They did so, grumbling, with Lonny facing them. For a moment, stealing close, Reb thought he would have no chance to approach the outlaw.

But the shadows along the engine tender were thick. He followed them, moving quietly but openly. Just as he stepped near, Logan turned. The light shone on Reb's gun from the engine-cab; Lonny thought him one of the Bunch.

"Okay here," he grunted. "Go 'head with the boys. But send somebody up here with my hoss."

Reb said nothing, taking another step forward. The Kid's brother must have had a sudden sense that something was wrong. He stared. Before he could open his mouth, Reb's boot came up in a hard-driven kick.

The boot struck the gun in Lonny's hand. The weapon spun sidewise to strike against a drive-wheel. At the same instant the engineer, a heavy man, but active, realizing what was going on, made a dive for the outlaw. They grappled fiercely.

Before Reb recovered his balance after the kick, Lonny began to curse feverishly. He was wiry; he twisted this way and that in the trainman's grip. Reb's gun flashed up. There must be no outcry here, as he had seen to it that there was no betraying gunfire. The barrel slashed down over Logan's head—just as he lurched about.

Reb's blow struck the engineer instead. He groaned and wilted.

Stifling an exclamation, Reb struck again. Lonny had jerked free; his body leaned as he thrust a leg out to run. The blow fell alongside his ear—tumbled him end over end. He was out.

Reb caught himself and whirled. The encounter had taken a bare ten seconds altogether. No one had had time for other than fleeting impulses. The remaining trainmen had acted on theirs and fled incontinently into the thickening night.

Reb snorted. He had hoped to have the engineer crawl in his cab and pull out at once. It was too late for that now. The man lay groaning on the ballast—and there was other work to be done. Reb strode down the side of the train to the meeting he had known all the while must come.

Cries sounded ahead of him. A shot rang out on the other side of the train. At the end of the second car, a coach, a man bounded off the platform. It was an outlaw: it was Bill Carver.

"Hey, you!" he called gruffly. He grabbed for Reb's arm, to swing him around. Reb's appearance had startled him. He thought he knew where all his friends were; yet even in the darkness Santee would not be mistaken for a trainman.

Reb thought fast. A glance in his face and Carver would give the alarm. Even as he turned, his fist came up—driving straight for Carver's luminous eyes. It struck with a dull smack. Bill sagged, clutched for support. His fingers weakened, and he slipped down.

Reb thought: "That was dumb. I'm goin' to need my right hand bad." He flexed his fingers, moving on toward the express-car.

A blast ripped the night. They were blowing the express-car door open. Splinters showered. Men ran forward. Reb identified Flat Nose George, Bob Leigh, the Sundance Kid. It was the latter who clambered up in the shattered door. Reb had no time to spare.

"Kid!" he ripped out.

Its very suddenness arrested the outlaws.

"Who is that?" an imperious demand flashed back. It came from Leigh, not Harve Logan. He didn't need to ask, he knew.

"Santee!"

The Kid's crackling ejaculation was followed by the smash of a shot as he fired. George Curry, half in the broken door, slipped back and ducked. A gun banged from his position. Leigh had faded too, but not far.

"Come out of the car, Kid!" Reb jerked out. He had not fired as he dodged and weaved, closing in; but Logan and Leigh sent two more raking slugs in search of his voice.

"Be damned to yuh!" the Kid yelled. There was a fierce heat in his defiance.

More yells sounded from down the train. Windows banged up. But no one was likely to come running forward while lead flew. At the moment, Reb was intent on nothing but getting the Sundance Kid out of the express-car. He started for it with reckless abandon.

Curry and Leigh's guns flashed near at hand. Reb silenced them momentarily by letting loose a blast in the air. He had no quarrel with these men that demanded blood. It was Logan whose mind must be changed, violently or otherwise.

He reached the car door and started to swing up. From somewhere within a thunderous detonation sounded; lead ripped the boards near Santee's knee. Then a diversion occurred: the half-stunned express guard blazed away at the Kid from his position on the floor. Logan returned the fire. It was blind fighting— and blind chance that guided a ball which ripped into Reb's thigh as he rose in the door. He wavered, caught himself.

The Kid was cursing in frenzied disgust, somewhere in the dark car. Reb had not fired at him once as yet. He wanted to lay hands on him—fling him out of the car by main force. And he got his chance as Logan started for the door, crying out to Leigh and Flat Nose George to come on.

He and Reb collided fiercely. For a moment they struggled, Reb fighting the waves of nausea that threatened him, sweeping up his trunk.

"Will yuh get out of this?" he bawled into the Kid's face.

"*No!* Damn yuh, Reb—"

Reb laughed abruptly, harshly. "Then I'll throw yuh out!" He jerked violently. Logan resisted with the ferocity of a cougar. They toppled on the splintered edge of the express-car door.

The interference had kindled a blind, hot rage of helplessness in Bob Leigh and Flat Nose George, crouched outside. It was never learned which of them fired point-blank at the two figures in the shadowy door, just as they lost their balance. Perhaps he thought to finish Reb. But it was the Sundance Kid whose back was turned. The slug smashed through his spine, came out through his stomach, and ranged upward into Santee's vitals. Together they fell, not half-a-dozen feet, but into eternity. A dead man landed under Reb on the cinder ballast; a half-dead man rolled from him, struggled a little, and then slumped back. Reb had time for but one thought—he had foiled the train robbery, whatever the cost to himself. The outlaws were effectually scattered. There was more firing, but their bolt had been shot.

He lost account of time. His mind hovered in a dream world while men yelled and ran, and a lantern flashed. He heard hazily the deep voice of a trainman:

"I'll be damned! It's the Wild Bunch—an' Reb Santee leadin' 'em! I reckon there ain't no doubt now that he's been cuttin' capers in Wyomin' right along. It looks like he'd cut his last one, this time!"

Chapter XXVI

GONE TO GLORY

I CAN'T see him!" Billy Farragoh groaned. "Ronda, nothing ever made me feel so rotten in my life. To think that Reb should come to such an end! . . . I would have sworn there was nothing but the best in him. He was so straight and good, so gay! Mother loved him—and I think I worshipped him. *You* were so proud of him, Ronda! And now I fear he has let us down. . . . What can I say to him?" He was imploring, asking in vain for assurance that this thing was not so.

"Why, Billy!" Ronda Cameron's tone sounded shocked. "Of course you'll see him! He has been calling your name steadily—does anything else matter?" Her courageous eyes plumbed the last subterfuge of his pain.

"It matters terribly," Billy managed huskily. "I would have staked my life that he would keep his word. Governor Hamer—"

"Governor Hamer, and you, and the rest, should be ashamed of yourselves," said Ronda, but she said it gently. "You haven't even got Reb's word as to what happened, yet you are all convinced that he has broken his solemn promise. I am not so sure." She laid a steadying hand on her companion's arm.

Billy looked up hopefully. His clean young face was marked with lines of suffering, of striving to keep the faith. "If I could believe otherwise, nothing would keep me from him," he burst out impulsively. Then his eyes dulled again, dropped. "But I could never bear to hear the truth from his lips," he went on bleakly. "As it is now, there's always the hope of some mistake. But if he were to confess . . ."

They were standing in a reception room of the hospital at Lander. Reb Santee had been brought here, delirious, fighting for his life. He had called brokenly for Billy since his arrival; and now that the young man was almost face to face with his friend he had lost all his stoic fortitude.

News of the abortive train robbery at Rock Creek had spread like wildfire. The newspapers set up a howl of indignation. Reb Santee, notorious leader of the Wild Bunch, they said, was robbing trains at precisely the same time when he was supposed to be serving out his sentence for another crime at Laramie Penitentiary. It was too much.

It was a bitter blow to Billy: the finding of Reb at the scene of the robbery—the logical conclusion, so quickly pounced on by all, that Santee had betrayed the trust imposed in him. Billy had suffered many disillusionments during his swift rise to a position of power, but never one so cruel, so bewilderingly against all probability, as this. He was stunned and wretched, his thoughts scattered. He did not know what to think.

Ronda, on the other hand, did not share his dejection. Since hearing the unwelcome news she had refused stoutly to believe the worst of Reb until it was proven beyond doubt.

"Billy, what will you think of yourself, deep in your heart, when this is over?" she pleaded persuasively. "There will be no need then to remind you of what Reb has meant to us. He was our shining model of all that was fine and true. And if there was the faintest chance that you had failed him in the end—would you ever forgive yourself?"

It was a telling argument. Billy's hand came down from his corrugated brow. He bucked up, his shoulders squaring.

"I am ready to see him now," he said steadily. Ronda squeezed his arm gently, her fine gray eyes softening with compassion, with brave hope.

A moment later a nurse entered the room.

"He is awake now," she told them.

They followed her to a little room whose window overlooked the shining sage of the plain beyond the edge of town. Reb lay outstretched on his bed, his face flushed, his flaxen hair tousled against the pillow. His eyes lit with a strange light as they fell on Billy's and clung.

"Reb, old man—" Billy stopped at the edge of the bed. "I'm sorry it had to come to this," he broke off lamely, with extreme difficulty fighting a wave of deep feeling.

"I knew yuh'd come, Billy," Reb whispered. He made an effort to smile. "Yo're all I been waitin' fer —all I can expect—you an' Ronda." His words were slow and labored, but they were gratified, too.

Ronda was at Billy's side. She saw the dangerous luster of Reb's eyes, the grayness of his lips. It was she who reached forth for his hand.

"Reb, don't try to say too much," she told him. "You must save your strength. Nothing else matters to—any of us." Her voice was bravely cheerful. "We shall have you out of here in good time, and in a better place."

In her sweet and gentle regard there seemed all that Reb had ever hoped for. He shook his head, however, his mouth relaxing. "Not me, Ronda. No need to fool ourselves. I've got my—finish, this time." It did not seem to bother him so much as the blight that rested on Billy's features. "Billy, look at me," he urged huskily. "Is it—do yuh—" He broke off, finding his question harder to put than he had dreamed. He knew only too well what gnawed in Billy's mind.

It was Ronda who broke the spell.

"Reb," she said in her clear voice, "Billy wants you to tell him that your word to him is unbroken. He wants to believe it of you. Nothing else means half so much to him. . . . Can you?"

The electric moment stretched out. Billy Farragoh felt his muscles tense to aching. Energy crept into Reb's voice, vitality—yes, and pleasure—into his crinkling eyes. "Why, shore I can," he drawled. "There was nothing in me tryin' to stick up that train. I said to myself you two'd be the only ones to understand."

Billy manfully concealed a measure of his leaping gratification, his boundless relief. "Tell us, Reb," he said, and his words trembled.

Ronda forebore to halt Reb as he told his story—how he had become involved with Doc Lantry, and then with the Wild Bunch; and his efforts to resist—how circumstance had driven him on until his word to Billy and Governor Hamer had stood in the way—how the Sundance Kid had defied him, and he had determined to stop the Kid's raid, with the tragic results. He was perspiring, not alone with the effort of talking, before he was done and his voice sunk low, but there was a triumph in his look as impossible to resist as his old smile had been.

"I made up my mind Logan would listen to me," he wound up; "either he'd stop his work, or we'd all go to glory in a ball of fire." He trailed off. "That's what happened," he ended, with a pathetic grin.

There was more that concerned them all, which the nurse attempted to halt; but Reb wouldn't have it. It put more life into him, he declared, than all the doctors in Wyoming could do.

"There's jest one thing more that weighs heavy on me," he murmured, when the nurse had been sent packing. His eyes held those of the girl and the man before him bravely. "When are you two gettin' married? I want to see it done an' over with."

Ronda and Billy looked at each other.

"Ronda came to Lander to marry me next week," said Billy slowly. "But now—" His reluctance suggested that they could not think of such things, for the present at least.

"Not a bit of it!" Reb protested, lifting his head in alarm. "Yuh got to go right ahead before I'll consent to—to—" His gaze became frightened at the temerity of what he was about to say. "I'd like to see it come off," he got out; "—be a witness, like."

Ronda dropped by his side with a little cry. There were tears on her lashes—tears of pride, of gladness. "Reb, you shall," she promised in rich tones.

Billy was troubled to be thinking of his own happiness in the face of death—there was no further refuge for any of them in the pretense that Reb was not dying —but he readily assented. This flaxen-haired man on the bed had taken a weight off his heart this morning for which he would be grateful all his days.

"That's—fine," Reb breathed, turning his head toward Ronda. "Ronda, I always—" but his resolve broke down; he could not tell her of his love—"I always thought the very best of yuh. An' if I know you an' Billy are fixed right, I'll rest easy."

Ronda knew what he was trying to say. Her heart was full. She could only look her thanks, and her sorrow that life had treated him so shabbily.

It was a strange ceremony, that wedding beside a hospital bed, which a dying man watched with his heart in his eyes and a smile curving his lips. It was not delayed, for Reb weakened hourly as his time drew rapidly nearer. Some there were among the chosen guests who cried unashamed—Mother Farragoh was one—and the tears were bitter. . . . A strange honeymoon as well, at its commencement, with the bride watching over another man while the sands of his life ran out.

They would not have had it otherwise. There was an expression on Reb Santee's homely, freckled countenance as he breathed his last that said this was for the best. They would not have dreamed of denying him that.

"It's the end," said Billy gently, leading his wife from the bed when it was over. "Reb lost nearly everything in life for which he played, but at the close we were able to give him one thing he wanted, and he was content. . . . He was a man."

"Gone to glory," Ronda murmured through her tears. She caught herself then, and with a womanly grace lifted her arms and lips and kissed her husband. "Nothing went out of him, ever, but the memory of it will make our lives better and more full, dear."

Billy's agreement was fervent. In his heart there was only honor for the one who had passed. Reb Santee had faltered, he had made mistakes. But whatever else he was, he had proven that there was a streak of nobility in him that men would not forget.

The End